KEVIN DOYLE

A River of Bodies

·THE·
BLACK
·STAFF·
PRESS

First published in 2019 by Blackstaff Press
an imprint of Colourpoint Creative Ltd, Colourpoint House,
Jubilee Business Park, 21 Jubilee Road,
Newtownards, BT23 4YH

With the assistance of The Arts Council of Northern Ireland

LOTTERY FUNDED

Cover image: 'Industrial School, Letterfrack, Co. Galway' by Robert French. This image reproduced courtesy of the National Library of Ireland – L_ROY_05373, www.catalogue.nli.ie

Printed in Berwick-upon-Tweed by Martins the Printers

A CIP catalogue for this book is available from the British Library

ISBN 978-1-78073-233-6

www.blackstaffpress.com
Follow Kevin on Twitter @kevidoyle

To the memory of
Alan MacSimóin

Kevin Doyle was born and brought up in Cork. He holds a Master's in Chemistry from NUI (Cork), and worked for a number of years in the chemical industrial sector in Ireland and the United States. He has been published in many literary journals and shortlisted for a number of awards, including the Ian St. James Award, the Hennessy Literary Awards and the Seán Ó Faoláin Prize. He won the Michael McLaverty Short Story Award in 2016. He has written extensively about Irish and radical politics and, with Spark Deeley, he wrote the award-winning children's picture book, *The Worms that Saved the World*. His first novel, *To Keep a Bird Singing* was published in 2018. *A River of Bodies* is his second novel.

Prologue

The photos were poor quality. Taken in low light, in a hurry, and not even properly framed. That annoyed Albert Donnelly. He would like to complain, but that wouldn't achieve anything. The main picture showed some type of display board, leaned against a wall. It was large, made from sheets of industrial plywood braced together with clips. Pinned to the display were several photographs and sheets of paper.

He had been provided with enlargements of those photos, and these were of better quality. One showed Albert's closest friend, the late Father Brian Boran, when he was a young man. What interested Albert, though, was not the image – he had better ones elsewhere – but the pretty Napoleon hat clock visible on the mantelpiece to Father Brian's left. Albert recognised the clock – it was from the drawing room in his old family home beyond Ballyvolane in Cork. He understood then that the photos on the display were actually still frames, taken from the missing film, one of Albert's old home movies. From 1962 or '63 or thereabouts.

The next still was of Leslie Walsh, but Albert hardly looked at that. Instead he moved immediately to the third, which showed another young man's face. Albert was struck by the individual's expression – sure and confident. Under this photo the words 'third man' had been written. Albert found a marker and, on the printout he had before him, wrote, *Is that you?*

The final close-up he'd been given was a shot of three white pages. These had been arranged in a semi-circle on the display board and Albert was unsure at first what they represented. He fetched his magnifying glass and was soon able to make out some of the detail. Large faces had been drawn on two of the pages, with 'fourth man' and 'fifth man' written under each, respectively. The final page was marked too. It contained a collection of smaller stick faces – four in all – and the word 'More?'.

He sat back in his chair. His beard itched. He had been advised to grow one, but he hated it. It was irritating and the heat didn't help. Bucharest was way too hot for a beard and too dry as well. Was he the only one to notice this? Why was it that nobody else minded the horrible heat? Or that the air-conditioning never worked. Or that most of the window panes were cracked. No, it didn't suit him at all.

Albert had once imagined moving here permanently and had gone about getting a place of his own – one that was near the school and comfortable – but he realised now that he missed Llanes a lot. He missed Cork too. It is one thing to leave your home by choice, another entirely to be forced to stay away.

His thoughts were interrupted by the sound of playing children. From outside, from the far yard. Was it that time already? He needed to get to the Italian Church by mid-afternoon.

Returning his attention to the remaining photo, he took up the magnifying glass again. It was a close-up of a different part of the makeshift display. Substandard too; underexposed as well. The magnifying glass had a light on it, and he switched it on. It didn't help. He cleaned the glass thoroughly and tried again. There were two faces in the picture. Single, capitalised letters had been placed at the side of each – an 'A' and a 'B'. He lingered on 'B' – a boy's face, a closely shaved head. There was little else distinguishing about 'B' and yet Albert recognised him. Paul Corrigan, from nearly fifty years ago, the one who started it all.

Albert leaned away for a moment, holding the magnifying

2

glass to one side, thinking about that time. Corrigan had run away from the farm. He was missing a few days and Albert had feared the worst; that the boy had escaped. Eventually he had found him hiding in a thicket of brambles. The boy had fought back and Albert had had huge difficulty extracting him. He'd succeeded, finally, and couldn't forget what had happened then.

Sweating, he took out a handkerchief and slowly wiped his forehead, ears and neck. Using the magnifying glass again, he tried to make out what had been written on the slip of paper pinned beside 'A' and 'B'. *Y-A-U-O-H-A-I*? Or *Y-O-U-O-H-A-I* maybe? He changed the final letter to L and that gave him *Y-O-U-O-H-A-L*. He had it then. Of course. It was *Y-O-U-G-H-A-L*. So they knew that too.

A Name
Is Everything

1

Noelie Sullivan arrived at Court 4 as the coroner was being seated. There was a large crowd present and the main aisle, leading to the front of the courtroom, was congested. He made his way slowly and with difficulty to the front. His sister Ellen was already there, in the seating area reserved for witnesses, her arm slightly raised to draw his attention. Noelie made it over but there was no room beside her. He sat in the row behind, alongside a woman he didn't recognise. After a moment he looked again, as discreetly as he was able, and wondered did he know her.

The coroner called the court to order. He was a soft spoken man, about sixty, with fair lank hair. He announced that there were two cases to be heard that day and that the case of Shane Twomey was scheduled to run first. He advised anyone not directly connected to that case to leave – and quite a few did. In the interlude, as seats were vacated and re-occupied by those standing, a jury of five was sworn in; four women and one man.

Noelie looked around. A few years earlier the city's courthouse had been extensively renovated. Court 4, in particular, had changed. The dark wood furnishings and the old-fashioned judge's throne had been dispensed with in favour of bright modern furniture; there was a surfeit of audio-visual terminals and even the windows looked clean. It was quite the makeover.

He recognised a few faces. His sister's neighbours were present – people who had helped search for Shane in the days after he went missing. Bunched together in seats near the door were some of Shane's mates. A few cousins and two of Shane's uncles on his father's side were also in the public gallery.

Noelie was glad to see the support. He was glad for his sister. It mattered that people had taken the time and that there would be familiar supportive faces in the public gallery when the evidence was being heard. It was expected to be a formality: the court would hear from a handful of witnesses who had seen Shane on the day he disappeared. Noelie would give evidence; the investigating detective, Byrne, would testify. Perhaps, most important of all, the pathologist's report into the cause of death would be read into the record. It was not going to be easy – Noelie was certain of that – and he steeled himself for what was ahead.

The coroner explained to the courtroom that the terms of reference of the inquest were strictly confined to the examination of the when, where and how of Mr Twomey's death.

'I will not be indulging any questions pertaining to any other matters,' he added emphatically. 'I further remind all concerned that it is their duty to respect proceedings here and to maintain decorum and civility at all stages, to the court, to the jurors, to the family of the bereaved and to the witnesses.' After a short pause he added, 'Unless there are objections, we will follow, in the initial stage, the timeline of events leading up to Mr Twomey being reported missing. May I enquire, are there any objections?'

Bernard Taylor, the solicitor engaged to represent the Twomey family, stood briefly. 'None, coroner.'

'In that case I call the first witness, Ms Ellen Sullivan-Twomey.'

2

Leaving the courthouse area, Noelie walked down Washington Street towards the city centre. On Grand Parade, a series of abandoned shop fronts were decorated with posters decrying the IMF and their austerity measures. In Amsterdam, where Noelie had been for the previous month, there had been little evidence of the momentous financial meltdown that Ireland and most of the world was going through. Noelie had even been able to pick up some part-time work there – with a moving company linked to the furniture restoring business Meabh Sugrue worked for. In Cork now, it all looked quite different. Noelie could feel the pinch of financial ruin just walking along the street. Parts of the city appeared to be closed for business and there weren't even that many people around.

South Mall was in better shape – of course. Cork's financial thoroughfare was a broad, long, tree-lined street. Even now it looked calmly prosperous, and who was to say it wasn't benefiting from the slew of vulture funds that, it was rumoured, had already moved in on the city's prime property offerings. Wasn't there a saying that one man's recession was another's opportunity? Noelie paused opposite Butler House, the building where Albert Donnelly had his brief foray into law practice. It was an elegant four-storey Georgian town house, now home to an auctioneering firm.

Noelie often thought about Albert Donnelly. Since the night of the fire at Church Bay six weeks ago, there hadn't been any further sightings. The latest rumour conveniently claimed that Albert had drowned that night trying to escape, and that his body was subsequently carried out to sea. Noelie gave the

9

version short shrift even though it was, apparently, supported by a witness who had observed Albert hurrying along the cliff face at Church Bay on the night he vanished. Whatever the truth, he was nowhere to be found for now.

Crossing over to Parliament Street, Noelie approached the bridge and stopped on the apex of the hump. The south channel of the Lee rushed underneath. The sound of the river was pleasant. Upstream he could see South Gate Bridge, and beyond that Elizabeth Fort and St Fin Barre's Cathedral. Looking downriver, he carefully scanned the rooftops along the quays on the south bank and then on the north bank. Finally he saw a mast, on a building near the corner of Father Mathew Quay. He wondered for a moment why it was so tall and then realised that it was the mast for RTÉ Cork, the local studio of the national TV and radio station.

That mast, he decided, had to be the one. It was certainly prominent enough and, from what he could see, there were three mobile phone receivers attached to it. They were actually easy to spot, even from where Noelie stood. Two were square and one was round; all three were white in colour.

An hour earlier, the inquest had unexpectedly and suddenly adjourned – a development that took everyone, including Noelie, by surprise. His sister, Ellen, gave her testimony in a hesitant, careful voice. She explained about owning a business, a clothes shop. Normally she opened at 10 a.m. on weekdays. Usually this meant that she left home around 9.30 a.m. and that had been the case on the day her son went missing.

As Shane was on holidays from school, he had taken to sleeping late. More often than not she didn't call into his room before she left for work – 'Coroner, there was no point as I wouldn't even get a grunt of acknowledgement out of him.' – but on this particular morning she had. She looked into his room and told him that his Uncle Noelie was downstairs – in case he heard noises and was wondering. She checked that he had heard what she had said and she received a muffled reply: 'I did, Ma.' Those were the last words she heard him speak.

His sister's evidence concluded, it was Noelie's turn. He took the stand and swore an oath. He began with his visit to his sister's house on the day Shane went missing. Ellen had been surprised to see Noelie so early in the morning. They spent a short time chatting – he didn't mention that they had had an argument – and then Ellen left for work. A while after that Noelie called up to Shane's room to tell him his news. He had an ulterior motive, he informed the inquest. He wanted to use the Internet at his sister's but had forgotten to ask her to log him in before she'd left. So he'd knocked on Shane's bedroom door and regaled him with the story of how, a couple of days earlier, he had found his entire missing collection of punk records in a charity shop on Castle Street in Cork.

Noticing the perplexed expression on the coroner's face, Noelie clarified why this was significant. The record collection had gone missing twenty-six years earlier, in 1984, in a robbery at Noelie's flat. Noelie had abandoned all hope of ever seeing the collection or any part of it again. Then suddenly, in a stroke of unbelievable luck, he'd found the entire collection on sale at a giveaway price in the charity shop.

Noelie had given Shane the names of some of the LPs that he had recovered, and had invited him to come over to his flat at some stage to listen to them. He'd also asked his nephew to log him on to the house computer, which Shane duly did.

As Noelie remembered it, Shane didn't return to bed. Instead he went to the kitchen to make himself breakfast. Uncle and nephew had bantered back and forth about this and that. Some fifteen or twenty minutes passed. When Noelie was finally done on the computer, he decided to leave. He couldn't remember if he had repeated his invitation to Shane to call over to his flat to listen to the records, but he guessed that he may well have. He left his sister's house at around 10.30 a.m. He never saw his nephew alive again.

Giving evidence hadn't been easy. Those days in June and that whole awful time came back to Noelie in full force – in particular the fear he'd felt when he'd heard that Shane was missing. He'd vanished just as Noelie made the discovery that Special Branch had probably been involved in the murder of missing Corkman, Jim Dalton. Noelie thought that there could be some connection between the two events. Nothing was ever proven, nor had anything ever come to light to suggest that there was any link – all the same, Noelie remained convinced that there was one.

Cian Nason, one of Shane's friends and classmates, gave evidence next – he was the last known person to speak to Shane. The two boys met briefly around noon. Shane called to Cian's house to ask him about going into town to hang out. Cian couldn't go as his uncle's family were home from Australia and a barbeque was planned. He chatted to Shane for a short while then Shane left, saying that he would probably head into town anyway.

The solicitor, Taylor, asked Cian about Shane's mood that day and Cian had replied, 'He was in good form. I didn't notice anything different about him. I've been asked a lot of times about this and I can't remember anything unusual. He was normal, he was fine.'

The inquest then moved on to Shane's subsequent movements, in as much as they could be discerned from his mobile phone records. It was at the end of this interrogation of the record that the upset had occurred.

On the afternoon he vanished, Shane had sent and received a series of text messages. These enabled the gardaí to track his journey from his home on the inner north-side of the city into Cork's city centre shopping area. After spending some time near Paul Street, a short distance from the main street, Patrick Street, Shane had moved southwards and crossed the River Lee's south channel. His final text message had been triangulated to an area around Summerhill South, about a kilometre south of the Lee. Thirty minutes after that, his phone disconnected from the mobile phone network; the time was 3.04 p.m. and Shane's location was triangulated to an area farther south again, close to Cork City FC's soccer grounds at Turner's Cross. When Shane's body was found three days later it was in an entirely different area of the city, at low tide in the Lee's upper north channel; his mobile phone was never recovered.

During cross-examination of the investigating police officer, Detective Byrne, Taylor had requested further details on the missing boy's trail of text messages. He'd asked Byrne to read into the record all of the phone messages and the detective had complied. However, Taylor had then asked her to provide all the corresponding beacon identifiers for all the phone masts connected to the teenager's final communications trail.

Up until that moment Detective Byrne had been reading from her own notes. She asked for a moment to find a different document and, after shuffling through a selection of files, had read this information to the silent courtroom – a series of alphanumeric descriptors. Each message and location that was identified was defined by a triangulation that was set from the three closest phone masts to the phone at the time the message was sent into the network.

There hadn't been any problem until the detective called out the final, and possibly the most significant, set of identifiers relating to the position of the phone when it permanently signed off the mobile network. The triangulated area reported for this final signal indicated an area around Turner's Cross in Cork. However, Taylor disputed this. He told the inquest that he had been provided with a record of Shane's mobile phone trail and that this suggested he had been in an area much closer to the city centre when his phone left the network. Instead of Turner's Cross, Taylor's record denoted the beacon at Father Mathew Quay – the one Noelie was now looking at from Parliament Bridge. Although Taylor was only disputing one cardinal point in the triangulation of the boy's location, that one position made a considerable difference to where Shane may have been located when his phone left the grid: Father Mathew Quay and Turner's Cross were almost two kilometres apart. Establishing the correct record was quite significant.

An unseemly disagreement had ensued, which led to the coroner's intervention. He asked to see the data from the detective and from Taylor. Presenting his document, the family solicitor admitted that his record was not an official communication from the mobile phone operators, Dream. He had acquired it unofficially and he was not attempting to mislead anyone regarding this fact. At that point, and following Taylor's admission, it had looked to Noelie that the coroner was about to rule in favour of the detective. But the coroner hesitated. For a moment it wasn't clear what the problem was. Then, somewhat meanly, Noelie felt, he had held up the detective's document and stated, 'This does not appear to be an original either, Detective, this is a photocopy. Assure me that somewhere there is a proper record of communication between you and the mobile phone operator for this investigation?'

Detective Byrne had looked surprised and uncomfortable at the same time. After examining her file again, she'd asked for a moment to check her briefcase. Eventually, embarrassingly, she'd announced that she didn't have Dream's original document with her. She'd then requested an adjournment so she could return to Anglesea Street Station to locate it.

The coroner, with the merest shake of his head, admitted that he had no option but to agree. The inquest would resume the following day at 2 p.m.

It was not clear yet what the correct situation was – if the detective or Taylor was right. Byrne was now required to produce the official communication that the gardaí had had with Dream. Until that was read into the record, a question mark hung over Shane's final movements.

Talking to his sister immediately after the adjournment, Noelie learned that Taylor had sought further information on Shane's mobile phone trail after talking to Ellen about the inquest and what she expected from it. Ellen had told the solicitor that she couldn't accept that her son had ended his life – one of the explanations being offered to the Twomey family to account for the sudden and unexpected death of their son. Taylor had followed up on this and had gone over every aspect of Shane's case one more time. He wouldn't reveal his source but Noelie gathered that an employee in Dream had parted with the details of Shane's final communications by mobile phone for a small sum of money.

There was no doubt that if the error was confirmed it would be significant. The focus of the search for Shane following his disappearance had been informed by the phone record related to the family by the gardaí. Noelie recalled searching for Shane in the Turner's Cross area of Cork, even though there had been no actual sightings of the teenager in that locality. Now he wondered if they had they been looking in the wrong place the entire time.

He had one other job to do. He walked down George's Quay, crossed to Mary Street and on to Douglas Street – where he had lived for many years. The long narrow street was quiet for the late morning. At Solidarity Books he stopped. There was a display of photos in the window of US troops passing through Shannon Airport on their way to and from war. The photos were good, the title of the display revealing. It read 'Neutral?' in big bold letters that looked as though they dripped with blood.

Noelie went in. There was a woman at the till and a couple of customers browsing. He'd been hoping to speak to Ciarán, one of the activists who worked at the shop, but when he asked the woman at the till about him, she shook her head.

'Do you want to leave a message?' she asked. 'He'll be in later for sure.'

One thing Noelie had learned over the summer was not to make unnecessary arrangements with anyone, particularly ones that might involve talking about important matters on the phone. He shook his head.

'Look, I'll be in another day anyway. Once I know my schedule I'm hoping to sign up to the volunteer rota for the shop. I'll see him then hopefully.'

He picked up a leaflet about the property tax and a copy of the new edition of *Workers Solidarity*. He dropped 5 in the donation box for the shop as he left.

Outside, he looked over at his old flat, just across the road. He had spent many happy years there. He missed having his own place and living on Douglas Street. He wasn't sure how long he could last at Hannah's: there was little room and his life's belongings were scattered in boxes and crates.

Farther along, on the same side of the street as Solidarity Books, he noticed a workman emerging from a house and hauling a length of rolled-up carpet. The outside of the house was scorched and burned from a fire, particularly around the windows, upstairs and downstairs. He went over. He knew the house: it was Sheila Carroll's home. He was friendly with Sheila and had visited her many times, for tea and a chat. He went to help the man lift the carpet into the skip.

'What happened?' he enquired.

'Bad fire. Late Saturday night, Sunday morning.'

Noelie explained that he used to live on the street and knew Sheila well. 'Is she okay?'

'Quite badly burned, I believe. She's in hospital, in CUH. I'm just clearing the worst of the stuff away for now. To be honest the fire brigade did more damage than anyone.'

The man returned inside. Noelie followed him a short distance down the hall. He was right about the fire brigade. The house looked and felt sodden. There were puddles of water everywhere and it smelled foul. Noelie looked up the stairwell and was able to see the sky.

He wondered what to do. He didn't really have time to call to the hospital today. Tomorrow would be better, even though the inquest was scheduled for the afternoon. Still, he'd make time. Sheila was a sweet woman and a real character on the street. She had been very helpful to Noelie a few times too. He hoped she was okay.

3

At the entrance to Hannah's apartment block, Noelie paused. Some students passed. Across the road, a man in a boxy jeep was looking at his mobile phone. Farther along the street a traffic warden issued a ticket.

He climbed the stairs to the second floor. Pausing at the apartment door, he heard Katrina's voice and then a loud laugh. He guessed she was on Skype.

She gave him a half-wave as he came in and, as he nodded in response, he saw that she was indeed on the computer – a woman's face was clearly visible on the screen behind her. He left his jacket on the armchair and went to the spare bedroom where he was billeted again. It was the smallest room in the apartment and had functioned as a spare room when Hannah was alive. Noelie had moved in following his eviction from Douglas Street in the summer. To make it some way more comfortable he had moved a lot of his boxed belongings out into the hall – cluttering that area. He still needed a proper bed, not just a mattress on the floor. Looking at the space now he wasn't sure how much longer he could live like this, running his life out of suitcases.

He returned to the kitchen/sitting area and put on coffee. Hannah's apartment was really nice – open-plan and modern. The kitchen melded into a spacious lounge-dining area that, at one end, looked out over the south channel of the Lee; at the other there was a view on to busy Washington Street. The riverside end had big windows and was south facing; it was Noelie's favourite part of the apartment and he always gravitated to it. It looked out on to a particularly pretty quayside area of the River Lee.

The apartment had been Hannah's home for nearly eight years and for Noelie its association with her was total. Although, he realised, probably not for much longer. Katrina Flynn was Hannah's other best friend and she had been staying there for most of the past month while Noelie was in Amsterdam. Katrina had rearranged the furniture in the sitting area, moving the dining table nearer to the window with the river view and placing the sofas closer to the Washington Street side. It wasn't an arrangement that Noelie liked but he wasn't going to object either. At least Katrina hadn't re-arranged the collection of artwork and pictures – for now they remained where Hannah had placed them.

He knew a little about Katrina from conversations he had had with Hannah. The two women had met in Dublin in the mid-nineties when Katrina had done a work experience stint in a newspaper Hannah was with. Katrina had later moved to Australia and, as far as Noelie knew, she was now settled there for good. She was a trained researcher of some sort. Hannah had told Noelie once that Katrina was working on some long-term project to do with land rights but he didn't know much more than that, or if that was still what she was working on.

He had met her for the first time at Hannah's funeral. She had been the proverbial lifesaver, arriving with the wherewithal and time to take on an organising role. Noelie hadn't functioned well during those days and in the end it was Katrina who delivered the eulogy. She had done a great job. The funeral was a bit over four weeks ago now and Noelie had travelled to Amsterdam the following day. He thought it would help, but he still felt a terrible emptiness.

Although Katrina had said she would only be staying on for a while in Ireland, on his return Noelie had found her ensconced in Hannah's old bedroom. Apparently she had gone to Dublin for a while and then across to Galway where she hailed from. What she was still doing in Cork, he didn't know.

When her Skype call ended she joined him near the riverside window where he had gone to enjoy his coffee.

'You look as if you have the weight of the world on your shoulders,' she said.

'Apparently I look like that even when I don't.' He nodded to the view. 'Thinking about old times here really and how good they were. It would be nice to have them again.'

'It's bad,' said Katrina, shaking her head. 'It must be even harder for you, Noelie. You know this apartment from when Hannah lived in it. It must hold a lot of memories.'

'It's shit,' he stated. 'I don't mean exactly here now, it's not that … it's just, sometimes it really gets to me.' He sighed heavily. 'I can't bear thinking about it actually. I don't know if I'll ever be able to come to terms with Hannah's death.'

'I had one of those moments this morning. You know all that lavender Hannah had in the bathroom? It's dried out to a powder now nearly. Well, I knocked against it and it all fell on the floor. I was on my knees instantly trying to gather it back up. It was like it was a part of her and I didn't want to lose it too.'

Noelie pulled his seat nearer to the window and stared at the river. He could look at it forever. When he was lonely, like now, it was particularly soothing to watch the water rush by, ever-changing.

'How did the inquest go?'

'Not well.'

'Wrong verdict?'

'No, nothing like that. It didn't even get that far.'

He told Katrina the details. 'No one's quite sure what the story is now. It has to be re-checked. In the meantime, it was adjourned.'

'Incompetence?'

Noelie thought about it. He knew Detective Byrne and liked her. She had been kind to him after Hannah's death and had passed information to him that he would otherwise not have had. In particular, information about one of her killers, Andrew Teland – a defrocked priest from the States with a nasty past. Noelie had some confidence in Byrne and hoped she hadn't messed up.

'Too early to say,' he answered.

'How did your sister take the news?'

'I think she had been forewarned by her solicitor to expect that an issue might arise. But this error, if it's upheld, is upsetting too.'

Noelie had chatted briefly to Ellen before leaving the courthouse – she had been understandably subdued. If errors had been made during the search for Shane then there would be recriminations. The problem was, it wouldn't change the outcome.

Katrina sat down on an edge of the windowsill and stared out at the river too. There was silence for a while. Noelie figured she was in her mid-thirties. She was an outdoorsy woman – Hannah's description – and it showed. Her hair was cut short and she looked like she was ready to run a marathon.

She opened the window. Fresh air and the sound of the river and the city traffic rushed in. 'Better?'

Noelie nodded. Katrina pointed to something but it took Noelie a moment to see what it was. A heron was perched on a rock, revealed by the falling tide. The bird was the colour of the dark water. She was watching for food.

'Perfectly camouflaged,' he commented.

Katrina nodded. 'I'm thinking of staying around, Noelie.'

'Why?'

'No "That's great news, Katrina" or "I'm so pleased to hear that, Katrina" or anything like that?'

He shook his head. 'It's nothing personal, Katrina.'

'No?'

'Of course it isn't. You and Hannah were very good friends, I've always known that. Any friend of hers will always matter to me.'

'You're misunderstanding me, Noelie. I'm staying around because I want to help.'

'With?'

'With what you're doing. Look, when you were in the Netherlands I went down to see Black Gary in Sherkin. I wanted to find out more about what had happened. I only got some of the details at Hannah's funeral. You know what it was like, during those days. It was hard to focus on anything other than what we had all lost.'

Noelie remembered well. 'You were great, Katrina. I really mean that. At least you were able to function.'

'Look, I functioned because I needed to. But it's hit me since. I've found this all very hard too. I need to get back to my job in Melbourne eventually, but they'll give me time. I loved Hannah, Noelie. She meant a huge amount to me. She was special.'

Noelie didn't look at Katrina even though he knew she was staring at him. He was doing his best to play down what had nearly been between Hannah and him. He no longer wanted to go there; it was just too sad.

'Black Gary thinks it's a good idea that I get involved.'

'It isn't, Katrina. It's a terrible idea. None of us involved in this are safe, do you realise that? I don't feel safe. Since I stepped off the fuckin' plane in Cork last night, I haven't felt safe. I'm already looking over my shoulder every other minute.'

'I know danger just as much as you.'

Noelie shook his head disparagingly, finally meeting her eye. 'I doubt that very much.'

Katrina looked annoyed and Noelie knew he was crossing a

line. Still, if falling out with her would keep her safe then so be it. 'You haven't a clue actually. Not an idea.'

He got up and went to the kitchen counter to get Hannah's old transistor radio – the thing practically ate batteries and emitted an incredible amount of static, but it also had sentimental value. Hannah had loved it because it was given to her by a favourite uncle; it had all the old radio station names written across the tuning band.

He set it down near the window, switched it on and turned up the volume. He spoke quietly. 'Special Branch killed a man here in Cork, Jim Dalton, to protect the identity of a mole they were running inside Sinn Féin. Not exactly upstanding behaviour, right? Now, if I thought that that was all there was to this, that we were just dealing with Special Branch, I might say, "Fine, come along and help." But Branch isn't half the problem we face. Some sort of an abuse ring operated here in Cork in the sixties. They've murdered to protect their cover. Six times. Three men were butchered in 1970; in 1998, a former Branch officer who opposed them also went under – that was Meabh Sugrue's dad; and last month, another ex-Branchman, Don Cronin, was taken out. A murder that I very nearly got done for, by the way. And finally, of course, they murdered Hannah. That's what we're dealing with. These people aren't just dangerous, they're lethal.'

'I said I want to be involved.'

'No,' Noelie said, shaking his head.

'Except it's not up to you. Black Gary said that you have an arrangement, that you all decide together. That that's how it is with you. I like that, it's a good arrangement. So let's ask the others. Let me put my case to them and if they still say no I'll consider returning to Australia. Consider, mind you, is what I'm saying. I'm not saying I will.'

Noelie eyed Katrina again. 'It's true we've agreed to joint decision-making but every one of us has a veto too. I'll use mine.'

23

'Fuck you,' said Katrina under her breath, standing up.

He watched her walk away. Hannah's old bedroom was just beyond the kitchen area at the other end of the apartment. Katrina went in and slammed the door behind her.

Not long after Hannah's funeral, Katrina had gone to Church Bay to see where the abuser turned Sinn Féin informer, Father Brian Boran, had lived under the pseudonym Tommy Keogh. It was also where he was believed to have murdered Hannah. With relative ease she had been able to access the burned-out remains of Keogh's home. Part of the house was stone and brick and had survived the fire; the remaining wooden section had been totally destroyed. In all, the ruins didn't look like much any more.

Walking around the small garden, it was the view out over the Celtic sea that she found herself drawn to. It was a beautiful vista and it reminded her of a time during Hannah's last visit out to see her. It was 2008 and they had flown to Alice Springs, hired a four-wheel drive, and travelled towards the Western Australian border. Katrina was already familiar with the area due, in part, to an assignment she had been involved with, helping to map the territory of the Ngaanyatjarra for a land rights claim.

It was as remote a place as you could find, and one night Hannah and Katrina had talked about whether two women alone would be in danger in such an isolated location. Katrina pointed out that anyone was vulnerable in an area as remote as the one they were in. If you came across the wrong person with violent intent there was probably little you could do.

Only half-joking, Hannah had said in reply, 'Well, just so as you know, if anything ever does happen to you I'll come looking. Never doubt that.'

Strange then that it had worked out the other way round.

Katrina had never anticipated anything ever happening to Hannah, but now that it had, she knew she had to do something about it.

Noelie was counting SIM cards when Katrina returned. One of the things he had learned over the summer was how easy it was for the intelligence services – in particular Special Branch – to listen in on their conversations and track their movements through their phones. With their work now about to recommence, Noelie wanted everyone involved to use burner phones and to regularly change their numbers using a ready supply of SIMs. James Irwin, the ex-industrial schoolboy who had helped with their investigation over the summer, had stumped up the money for the luxury. Although now back in Australia, where he had lived since 1971, Jamesy was in regular contact with Noelie about the direction of the investigation into the whereabouts of Albert Donnelly, a man they knew for certain had had a hand in Hannah's death.

Katrina turned off the radio, then went to Hannah's portable CD player, which was still sitting on the kitchen counter. 'If we must have noise interference, let's have something decent.' The Jam's 'A Town Called Malice' began to play. 'Appropriate?'

Noelie was sorry now and nodded grudgingly. He really didn't want Katrina involved but he didn't want to fall out with her either. He liked her. He knew she had moved to Australia in part to escape the conservatism of everyday Ireland. They had a lot in common.

She handed him an A4 page, and he was surprised by what he saw. On it was the emblem used by the Christian charity, Let There Be Light: a Tree of Life, a Celtic triquetra and a starry-eyed Jesus looking toward the heavens. It had been enlarged to fill the whole page.

'Where did you get this?'

'Hannah sent it to me. About a week before she was killed. She wondered if there was anything special about it. I took a module on Celtic symbolism in university and I know a bit about that kind of thing, so she asked me to look into it.'

The emblem had been on the back of an invitation for the month's mind memorial Mass for Leslie Walsh who, as a young man, had been involved in the 1960s Cork abuse ring. When proof of that involvement had emerged – Noelie had inadvertently stumbled upon a home movie made at the time – Walsh, then a prosperous developer, had killed himself. But the invitation, and the reference to Let There Be Light, had led Noelie to Albert Donnelly, a man they now knew to have been involved in organising the abuse.

'And?' Noelie prompted.

She pulled over a chair and positioned it beside him. She spoke quietly, 'In Christian lore, the three interlocking rings of the triquetra most often refer to the Holy Trinity. There isn't anything particularly unique about that, so discard. The figure of Jesus is also standard issue and, on first appearance, so is the Tree of Life, which often refers to the tree in the Garden of Eden and our state of innocence before Adam and Eve were corrupted by Lucifer. However, on closer examination it isn't that type of an emblem.' She pointed at the Tree of Life on the page in front of them. 'Notice anything?'

He looked at it for a while and shook his head.

'What about these severed branches?'

'Stumps. Pruning?'

'Close. Removing rot, imperfections or unwanted growth. Why? The trees used in the Tree of Life are all usually perfect. But in this example, there are seven main living branches and six severed branches. Seven and six are biblically significant of course.'

Noelie glanced at Katrina. He was well out of his depth. 'Okay …'

'In symbolism very little is insignificant and that proves to be the case here too. After a bit of research, I located where I believe this emblem originated. I had to go back to the thirties, to Spain to be precise. A Christian sect with links to Franco were promoting eugenics in the thirties, forties and fifties. That's where the severing of these branches comes from.'

Noelie shook his head slowly. 'Jesus. We already had something of a connection to Spain – Albert Donnelly was born there, brought to Ireland and granted in some way to Old Donnelly who was his adoptive father. Old Donnelly had gone to fight in the Civil War for Franco, so the story goes, and he was injured there and lost his leg. It was implied that the gifting of Albert to Old Donnelly was some sort of a compensation but it's not exactly clear.'

Katrina nodded. 'I looked into this sect. The people associated with this particular Tree of Life believed in eugenics. They were a small but powerful group of Catholics who held that certain traits should be 'bred out' of the population for the betterment of society. A psychiatrist by the name of Vallejo-Nájera was their intellectual heavyweight. He had links to proponents of eugenics in Austria, individuals who later went on to have a role in the Nazi's extermination programme. Although the Nazis and their style of thinking was completely discredited by the end of the Second World War, Vallejo-Nájera and his group remained afloat in Spain and continued promoting his views well into the fifties.

'The thing is, they were not quite the same as the people who populated the Nazi programmes. One branch of eugenics proposes that, for want of a better term, "bad blood" should literally be exterminated. But the Spanish faction seems to maintain that "bad blood" should be forcibly exposed to Catholicisation to cleanse it. Hence their involvement with the theft and sale of orphans after the Civil War. Quite a number of Catholic orphanages were involved in that.'

Noelie knew a little about this, too – a similar programme involving the sale of babies had occurred in Ireland and a Mother and Baby home in Cork had recently been under the microscope. 'Down the road, in an area known as Blackrock, there's a place called the Bessborough,' he told Katrina. 'They've been implicated in baby selling to the States. All sorts of other irregularities have been uncovered. Huge numbers of babies and infants died there due to ill-treatment and neglect. No one appears to know where any of these babies are buried or what even became of them.'

'This fucking country,' said Katrina shaking her head.

'Tell me about it.'

'Do you know much about Let There Be Light?'

'Not much. It's one of the things we're looking into.' Noelie thought for a moment. 'Albert Donnelly is very religious, and we know he was in it. On the night we discovered that Hannah had been murdered, he was present. He was one of the ones that got away. We've heard that he drowned down in Crosshaven, but I think he was spirited away. There's some link between these heavy-duty Catholics and some places in Eastern Europe. Romania is one that has been mentioned.'

They didn't speak for a while, but The Jam continued loudly in the background. Noelie examined the emblem again. Could he really stop Katrina getting involved? He didn't even know if he wanted to any more.

'I'm going down to Sherkin later, to Black Gary's,' he said. 'Martin Aherne is already down there. After Hannah's funeral we made a pact, all of us, to meet again on the day Shane's inquest resumed. Meabh can't be there, but she knows about the meeting. She's coming to Cork at the weekend. The idea is that we push on from here, try to get to the bottom of this. We want to identify the men involved in the abuse of those boys back in the early sixties. Secondly, we want to find the victims, find out who they are. We've a lot of work ahead of us. But different people have been following up different aspects of the investigation, including about Let There Be Light.'

'Why Sherkin?'

'Black Gary knows the place and knows who is about down there.' Noelie nodded towards the CD player and lowered his voice even more. 'It's a safer place to meet and talk, we think.'

Katrina nodded.

'Maybe you should come along? Put your case to the others. If they agree to you getting involved, I won't stand in your way.'

'A change of heart, Noelie?' asked Katrina dryly.

'More a change of mind. My heart still tells me that I should try to stop you getting involved. My head says the opposite. My head tells me that we need all the help we can get.'

4

They reached Baltimore in the late afternoon. The sky was clearing after a heavy shower. Sherkin lay ahead on the other side of the harbour with hilly Cape Clear in the far distance.

Noelie picked up milk and bread at the shop and they continued down to the car park. Katrina found a parking space beside the closed fish and chip stand and reversed in. They walked with their backpacks over to the protected inner harbour. A ferry had arrived and passengers were disembarking – the pier was busy.

Noelie had visited Sherkin with Hannah in July, just as she had been getting into her stride with their enquiries. Without realising it, that visit to Sherkin had been a turning point. It was there that they learned about Albert Donnelly and his links to Danesfort, an industrial school outside Cork with a history of brutality. It was also Noelie's first time meeting Black Gary, who had since become a good friend.

'What ferry are we taking?' asked Katrina.

'We're being collected. Black Gary has the loan of a boat apparently.'

'Interesting. I thought this was one of those low-budget investigations.'

'I wouldn't get my hopes up, now.'

They waited, enjoying the fresh sea air and harbour bustle. Eventually Noelie saw a boat coming towards the inner harbour, its prow high in the water. The man on it waved.

'There he is.'

They went down the slipway. Black Gary nosed alongside. He was wearing waterproofs. His scraggly wild hair looked even wilder than usual. He threw the bowline to Katrina who caught it easily.

'We've come up in the world, I see,' said Noelie.

'Not quite my ship,' Black Gary admitted, winking. 'Sleeping arrangements rather confined too as you can see, but I can usually get it whenever I want. Works out cheaper than the ferry in the long-run and more convenient too.'

He passed them life jackets and they climbed on board. Reversing immediately, he took them in a tight circle and they left the harbour again. The water was choppier here but Noelie felt himself relax. He had been on edge since his return. There was no exact reason for this other than the feeling they were being watched. Here, on a boat with Black Gary and Katrina, he could believe that they were alone.

Martin had arrived earlier, and had offered to make dinner for them all. As they neared Sherkin pier, Noelie saw the younger man standing on the concrete promontory waving frantically. As they drew nearer, he shouted, 'Welcome to my exclusive island restaurant, victims.'

Noelie nearly fell into the water climbing out of the boat. On terra firma again he hurried up the steps to greet Martin. He hadn't seen his ex-neighbour in more than a month and they hugged. They had grown close these past few months, and Noelie was concerned for his friend. He was the youngest of them and had got involved in the investigation mainly because he was Noelie's downstairs neighbour. With Hannah's death and the general danger they were in, Noelie had suggested to Martin several times that he should consider dropping out.

Martin wouldn't hear of it. 'I'm IT support. Where would you be without me?'

Noelie knew he wasn't exaggerating. At twenty-four, Martin knew his way around the Internet, including security and staying somewhat anonymous online. Noelie hadn't embraced the Web but that was changing. Over the summer he had seen its potential as well as the dangers it presented.

Martin smiled at Katrina the moment he saw her. 'So are you in?'

'Apparently that will be down to a vote,' she answered.

Martin eyed Noelie suspiciously, adding, 'Well, you have mine.'

Arriving up the pier steps with their bags Black Gary said, 'The more help we have the better.'

Noelie heard the worried tone. 'Has something happened?'

'Unfortunately, yes.'

Black Gary's place was a short distance away, on the left at the top of the hill. One of the neighbours joined them on the walk there, so instead of hearing Black Gary's news, Noelie had to listen to an exchange about the weather and the news that the environmental station, a small employer on the island, was letting more people go. Austerity again. Although it involved only a small number of jobs, it would have a big impact on Sherkin's tiny economy.

Reaching Black Gary's, they stood at the gate for a moment admiring his place. He had repainted his window frames pale blue and this had sharpened up the look of the cottage. The garden had also been mowed; there had been lots of lupins and foxgloves but these had long gone to seed.

'You must be important visitors,' observed the neighbour. 'Himself didn't do a tap to this place for years, now it's fit for kings.'

Inside the house it felt cool after the walk. Black Gary got water for everyone and closed the door. Martin checked that the dinner was okay and returned with a printed-off page from an online magazine, *Unwire*. He put it on the table for the others to read.

'Phones,' said Black Gary. He passed around a plastic lunch

box for their mobiles. Noelie opened his backpack and took out a ziplock pouch with three phones and three batteries in it.

'Three?' enquired Katrina.

'A burner, my ordinary phone and one for Jamesy Irwin in Australia.'

Black Gary took the mobiles to the utility room and left them there. Martin nodded to the print-off. 'It's Wikileaks. Seems that the organisation has only ever been a few people. Just a few activists a couple of steps ahead of the CIA and Russia's FSB. They've been handed some dangerous information in the last few years and that's what's now causing them trouble.' Martin paused. 'In July, they published the Afghan war documents – basically a series of logs maintained by the US military on the war in Afghanistan. To date it's been the biggest single release of classified documents ever and the response from the US has been, not surprisingly, of the fire and brimstone kind. Assange and others are being threatened with the Espionage Act, which is very serious. All sorts of allegations are being thrown at them, including that they have put lives at risk. '

The print-off was titled 'The War Inside Wikileaks'. Martin had highlighted a section.

A cache of highly sensitive documents and files held by the Wikileaks organisation may have been permanently lost, it has been confirmed. The news comes as rumours circulate concerning a major rift inside the organisation. Daniel Domscheit-Berg is reported to have left the organisation however this is, as yet, unconfirmed. The tranche of missing files lodged with Wikileaks for safekeeping include information from the USA's NSA surveillance operation, as well as information about a number of leading right-wing organisations in Europe. However, an unknown amount of other data may also have been compromised. Wikileaks, already under scrutiny following the release of a cache of Afghan war documents in July, is currently making contact with all those parties whose information may have been compromised in the security breach.

'That appeared five days ago,' Martin told them. 'It's been followed by other reports from other security watchers confirming the situation. Yesterday, we got formal notification from Wikileaks confirming that our files are no longer securely held.' Martin shook his head. 'Not good.'

Katrina knew about the home movie that Noelie and Meabh had discovered in August. It was proof that a network of abusers had existed in the Cork area in the early sixties. She hadn't seen it, but the others had told her generally about it and the shock waves it had caused.

Noelie swore loudly.

Turning to Katrina, Martin said, 'The film was our protection too. If one of us was harmed, Wikileaks was under instruction to release it instantly on to the Internet. It's called an "Armageddon Defence". Those threatened by the film would bring about their own downfall if they ever tried to harm us in anyway. It's certainly kept us safe so far.'

Noelie nodded at the article. 'Who else knows about this?'

'Everyone, Noelie,' answered Martin. 'Okay, I pay attention to these things so I know. But don't forget that Assange and Wikileaks are enemy number one in some quarters. Like with the security organisations of several superpowers. There's no way they don't know what we now know.' 'Special Branch?' asked Noelie.

Black Gary nodded. 'Sure, why not?'

There was silence apart from the occasional faraway screeching of seagulls. Martin spoke again. 'Look, I still control the other digital copy. It's hidden safely online. For now, everything I'm doing on the Internet is being tracked, so

34

I can't really check on it without exposing its whereabouts. But there's no reason to think there's any problem. Let's give this a few days. Wikileaks might be in trouble but it's not finished. As early as the weekend we might well be in a position to renew our arrangement with them.'

Noelie was reassured. Black Gary asked if they wanted tea or coffee and Martin offered to get these. While he did, Black Gary arranged some chairs in a neat semicircle facing the rear wall. He then got two large sheets of plywood, bracing them together with orange clamps. Noelie wondered what he was doing.

'It's an ideas board. Sometimes it's easier to solve a problem if you can put all the different parts to it in one place together.' Black Gary winked. 'Professional, no?'

Noelie nodded. He recalled Hannah suggesting something similar in the summer when they were trying to work out the mystery around Jim Dalton's disappearance. He took a coffee from Martin and went over to one of the windows, where Black Gary had positioned a brass telescope on a stand. It was a seafaring antique, although still in working order. Looking through the eye piece, he could see a part of Horseshoe Bay. The sky beyond was mostly blue, criss-crossed with contrails.

They took seats. Black Gary pinned two A4-size photos to the plywood display. Both were head and shoulder shots; snowy black and whites.

'These are the boys from the home movie. Last month, before Noelie's departure for Amsterdam, we agreed to work on different aspects of this case. I offered to look into the identities of these boys due to my connections with the network of industrial school survivors.' Black Gary gestured to the face on the left. 'This one is between eight and ten years of age. We don't have a name for him. From now on we'll refer to him as "Boy A". Sorry for being so unimaginative.'

The expression on A's face was neutral. He had close-set eyes, a mild squint and dark, wavy hair. His overall dark

35

complexion contrasted with that of the second boy who looked like a child skinhead and had a pale complexion; he looked gaunt as well as afraid.

'"Boy B" could be even younger. He's possibly in the seven to nine bracket but it's difficult to tell. If our age estimates are correct, then these individuals would be around sixty today.'

Black Gary had spent time optimising the photos of the two victims; a friend on the mainland had helped him. In the interim he had contacted nearly a hundred and fifty former attendees at a variety of industrial schools in the Munster area, making a particular effort with contacts who had been at Danesfort between 1956 and 1962. 'And, for your information, I've decided to embrace email. I'm half plugged into the World Wide Web now too. I do have to front up to the Jolly Roger pub to get my emails but so far so good. I've been pleasantly surprised to find that lots of people in my age bracket are on email.' He paused. 'Anyway, to get to the point, right now these may as well not exist.'

'Meaning?' asked Noelie.

'No one recognises them. I can't find anything on them.'

'It's been a long while of course,' pointed out Martin. 'I hardly remember people I was in national school with and that's not so long ago.'

Black Gary shook his head. 'Industrial schools are different. Something I've noticed over the years, maybe because the experience was so scarring, but faces and memories are etched in people's minds. It's particularly advantageous to have photos of individuals when they were at school. Much more difficult if you only have photos of the person in question as an adult.'

'Could these kids be from another industrial school, one other than Danesfort?' asked Martin.

'I'm looking at Greenmount in Cork city too and there was an industrial school here in Baltimore as well. A horrendous place, one of the worst actually. There are other candidates, a couple of schools in Kerry. But from the outset we have worked off the premise that it was Albert Donnelly's access to children from Danesfort that was key. I still think Danesfort should be the focus.'

Noelie turned to Katrina. 'The Donnelly farm availed of an arrangement whereby youngsters from the industrial school worked for free on their farm. Quite a lot of farms did this back then but the Donnellys had more influence than usual in who was loaned to them. The oldest Donnelly brother, Tony, was a senior figure in the religious order running Danesfort, the Rosminians, and Albert, the one who we believe recorded the films, actually managed the farm that belonged to the industrial school at Danesfort for a while. Another thing worth keeping in mind is that the Donnelly farm was located quite a distance from Danesfort Industrial School, so when boys were loaned to the Donnellys to work on their farm they were often sent to them for longer periods than would've been the norm. Which of course made them even more vulnerable.'

'Jesus,' said Katrina.

'I think it is reasonable to assume that these unidentified boys were from Danesfort,' continued Black Gary. 'Although, I agree, it is worth looking elsewhere too. I still have a few more people to get to. The problem is that if we have to widen the number of schools that we are looking into, it will mean devoting a lot more time to the search.'

'Time we may not necessarily have,' pointed out Noelie.

'Precisely.'

'I could give you a hand,' offered Katrina. 'Maybe that's where I should slot in?'

Black Gary thought that was a good idea, but he wasn't finished. 'There is one angle that shows promise. It's a case we know a little bit more about, involving a boy from Youghal who went missing from Danesfort in the early sixties – I've been calling him "Youghal Boy" for want of a better name.

Apparently, he's another of these youngsters who was loaned to the Donnellys to perform farm work. What we know is that at some stage Youghal Boy vanished. Much later on, his sister went looking for him and that's where this gets interesting.'

Noelie spoke. 'Our source here is James Irwin. You might remember him from Hannah's funeral, Katrina? His grandson Garret was there with him too.'

'Sure. I was talking to him a few times. He was really cut up over Hannah.'

'He feels responsible for what happened to her, I think. It was Hannah who established the link with him in the first place. That eventually encouraged him to come out of hiding. A brilliant bit of work really by Hannah. But when he heard she had been murdered, he was sorry he hadn't come forward sooner. He's a Danesfort survivor too. He moved to London in the late sixties for work and made friends there with three other men, also Danesfort survivors. The group of four – Jamesy, Michael Egan, Peter Spitere and Alan Copley – went on to constitute the group that tried and failed to blackmail Albert Donnelly.'

Black Gary spoke again. 'Copley is the important name here. He was also from Youghal and there's the link. The missing boy's sister found out about Copley, that he was from Youghal and that he had been to Danesfort, and approached him for information on her brother. There was something else though. Copley knew of a boy who had gone missing from the Donnelly farm – the story was that the boy ran away from the farm and never returned, going about his life and never looking back. However, there was another rumour that Albert Donnelly went after the missing boy, found him and beat him so badly he died.'

Black Gary paused. 'The reason that Youghal Boy is more promising is that we have a name for the missing boy's sister. Irwin recalls from conversations that he had with Copley that her surname was Kearny although sometimes that's spelled Carney. Assuming that this sister wasn't married when she was in contact with Copley – I'm thinking probably not as she was just a young woman then – we might be able to go to the Rosminians in Clonmel and find the file on him. Believe you me, in this game, a name is everything.'

They agreed that the lead was promising. Black Gary added a blank page to the display board and wrote 'Youghal Boy' across it. 'Mind you,' he continued, 'getting the Rosminians to play ball is another matter entirely. The moment they find out you're not a blood relative, they'll shut the door in your face. Been there many times with them on that. Frankly, I'll be up for assault and battery one day over the matter.'

Black Gary sat down. 'Gets to me sometimes. I find myself thinking, why did these people have to be so horrible? We were just children and we had so little. I had nothing. I was just myself and they were terrible to me.'

Martin stood. As he passed Black Gary he squeezed his shoulder. 'So, I volunteered to look into the organisation, Let There Be Light,' he said. 'It's an international charity with an Irish chapter. I have no idea who is in it. There is no published membership list. In a general sense, though, there's a fair bit in the public domain about them. They are not hiding themselves away in that sense. Founded in 1972 by a Swiss priest based in Madrid, Father Ranier. Up front it's a standard Catholic charity with a mission to help the poor wherever they are to be found, which as you know is just about everywhere. In its early years, it was predominantly active in Africa, Asia, the Philippines and Latin America – mainly in Chile and Peru. If you Google the organisation you won't find much about them, other than its own promotional material, of which there is a lot. El Salvador is the one exception. I didn't know much about this, I'm sure you might, Noelie, but the one bit of scandal I found on them is linked to the assassination of

Archbishop Óscar Romero in 1980. The chapter of Let There Be Light in El Salvador was involved in a public spat with elements loyal to Romero, suggesting that the cleric was a fig leaf for communist insurgency. An allegation was made later on again that someone in Let There Be Light in San Salvador, the capital, had close links to the death squads in the city. That's the one piece of controversy about them in the public domain that I could find.'

'Who made the allegation?' asked Katrina.

'A local priest. I have his name. Today Let There Be Light has substantial memberships in Spain, Italy, Germany, France, Switzerland and Ireland. I'll deal with Ireland shortly. Membership worldwide is estimated to be in the region of eighty thousand. Officially the group is endorsed by the Vatican. In recent times, the last decade or so, it has also developed a presence in a number of the former Eastern Bloc countries and now has bases in Romania, Ukraine, Moldova, Bulgaria, Poland and Belarus.'

'Doing?' asked Noelie.

'All sorts of things: programmes in schools with a Catholic Christian emphasis; general charity work; orphanages; combating prostitution and sex trafficking and so on. Their main competition comes from the Protestant evangelical orders. It's a busy organisation from what I can see.'

Noelie turned to Katrina. 'The first time we heard about Let There Be Light was in relation to Meabh's father, Sean. He was quite religious. After he left the gardaí, he was due to go to Romania to take up a post as lay missionary. According to Meabh it was with Let There Be Light. It's never been confirmed whether he was going there as a genuine missionary or if he was following up on something more sinister that he knew about regarding that organisation.'

'Which takes me neatly on to membership,' said Martin. 'Technically it is open in that you can download an application form, fill it in and apply. However, you must be endorsed by two members in the "Superior" category. I found that in the small print. It's clearly stated, too, that eligibility is based on past spiritual commitment and a willingness to work for the organisation's aims. I think you must make a financial contribution as well. A branch was formed in Ireland in 1976.'

'And this Superior category is?' asked Noelie.

'I'm guessing a seniority thing or a more committed level. But the oldest Donnelly brother, Tony, is mentioned at one point as being a Superior. He is also mentioned prominently as being one of the founders of the Irish branch. By the way, Father Tony Donnelly is also Dr Tony Donnelly. He wrote quite a lot and his papers are openly available on the Let There Be Light site. He seems to be something of an authority on penitence and original sin.'

Black Gary grimaced. 'The Donnellys had original sin on the brain.'

Katrina looked at Black Gary. 'Why do you say that?'

'You know that I was in Danesfort and that I worked on the farm there?'

Katrina nodded.

'Well it was through that farm that I came to know Albert. He was like the overseer. I don't know if he knew anything about farming, but he pretended he did anyway. He was down on me in particular. I often thought it because I didn't have a dad and he loved to rub that in my face. He told me once I was original sin. Me, personally I mean.' Black Gary was upset again. 'Look, let's move on.'

Noelie glanced at Katrina. 'Maybe you should tell them what you found out?'

Katrina told them the meaning of the Tree of Life image in the Let There Be Light logo, and how it was linked to a sect in the Catholic Church in Spain who were supported by, and supporters of, Franco.

'That's great work,' said Black Gary in a more optimistic tone.

'These people in Spain are committed Catholics,' Katrina went on. 'But Let There Be Light isn't the heart of them. It was created in the seventies, as Martin said. However, preceding that there was Deum Fidem, which has its own seminary in Salamanca, a city sometimes described as the beating heart of Spanish Catholicism. There's very, very little known about Deum Fidem. Extremely secretive.'

Noelie stood for a moment, to stretch his legs. He reminded the others of the month's mind Mass in Glenville that he had attended with Meabh in July. 'Obviously I'm not an authority here but it didn't feel like a standard Irish Catholic event at all. At the end six men in gowns, replete with pointy hats that reminded me of the Ku Klux Klan, delivered a series of gifts to the Walsh family. It was different, it really was.'

'So, is there more to this connection?' asked Black Gary. 'To this Spanish angle, I mean?'

'Whether there is or not,' answered Katrina, 'it's going to be very hard to find out more. When an organisation has layered membership – as Let There Be Light seems to – it's usually very difficult to penetrate. It's designed to stop casual inspection: vetting to join in the first place, then a Superior category inside that. There's more than likely another category closer to central leadership, and inside again is the core which could be Deum Fidem.'

Martin smiled. 'Want to know something interesting though, about them? Their Irish headquarters is here in Cork, near Blackrock to be precise.'

Noelie was surprised by this. It was unusual, rare even, for anything to be headquartered outside of Dublin. 'Perhaps that is due to Tony Donnelly's role?' he said.

Martin agreed. 'Yes, quite possibly.'

'We could take a peek at some point,' suggested Noelie.

'Just tell someone before you go,' warned Black Gary. 'We don't want anyone else disappearing on us.'

Noelie didn't mention it right then, but Meabh was working on a related angle in Amsterdam. It was partly why she hadn't returned to Ireland with him. After numerous attempts she had finally made contact with an organisation based in the Netherlands that rescued people from trafficking. She was looking for specific information on Romania. A lot of the trafficking in the region involved criminal entities but other, nominally legitimate fronts, including religious operations, were also involved and had attracted scrutiny. Meabh was intending to come to Cork at the end of the week after she had met the anti-trafficking activists.

Martin had the address for Let There Be Light. Castle Road, Blackrock. Noelie thought he knew where it was. 'Blackrock is downriver, past the old docklands area. First there's Blackrock Village and then Blackrock Castle. I think Castle Road links the two. It's exclusive enough around there.'

Black Gary rolled his eyes. 'If I told you once, I told you a thousand times Noelie, that lot are never short of coin until it comes to compensating their victims. Then it's *béal bocht* like you've never heard it before.'

5

They took a break and went outside to the back garden. It was grassy and bordered by a low ditch wall. Near the vegetable patch a small gate gave access to a path. Katrina followed it as far as the brow of the hill and then called to them all to join her. Noelie went. The sky was now entirely clear of clouds and the sun felt warm. There was lots of scrub and heather around; the heather looked like it was thriving.

From where she stood, there was a view of Horseshoe Bay. The headlands, forming the jaws of the inlet, sloped down to a narrow gap at the mouth. Beyond, the open sea looked choppy.

Martin and Black Gary joined them. Martin announced he was going to have a swim and Katrina decided to go too. They went across spongy ground, along rocks to a pebbly inlet that allowed easy access to the water. Noelie watched them strip and wade in.

Katrina swam out. 'It's beautiful,' she called.

'Liar,' shouted Noelie.

'Really it is,' said Martin waving. 'Come on in.'

Black Gary watched Noelie. 'I'm thinking the water isn't what it used to be for you.'

'It was never my first love but you're right, recent events haven't helped the relationship.'

Noelie had nearly drowned in the summer. He had gone with Meabh to visit Albert Donnelly at his home, Llanes, on Sunday's Well Road in Cork. Albert had drugged him, and when Noelie woke up he'd found that he and Meabh had been imprisoned in an underground cavern, which was beginning to fill with water. Noelie had nearly died. Meabh had rescued him. Later on they had worked out that the cavern was hidden under the garden at Llanes. It was positioned close to the Lee river so that when the tide rose and fell, the cavern filled and emptied of water. Noelie knew he was very lucky to be still alive. He regularly had nightmares about what had happened in the cavern.

He shivered. To escape the memory he said, 'It is beautiful here, it really is.'

'I love it. It's good having you all here of course, but I like when I'm on my own here too.' He put an arm around Noelie's shoulder. 'Don't worry. We'll be okay.'

Noelie smiled. 'Okay, I'll try a paddle. Face my fears. Isn't that what they say you should do?' He removed his shoes and socks, rolled up his trouser legs and waded in to his knees. 'They'll slag me unmercifully. Paddling at my age.'

'It is a bit sad,' agreed Black Gary.

Noelie heard a cry from the swimmers. It was Katrina. 'Get in, you wuss.'

On the far side of the bay, close to the eastern headland, a yacht was anchored. People were jumping from the boat into the sea, having fun. Laughter travelled across the water to where Noelie and Black Gary were standing. Noelie went over to a large flat rock and sat down. Black Gary joined him. They watched Martin and Katrina, who were chatting as they treaded water, about twenty metres out.

'I took a look at Llanes while you were away, Noelie. Borrowed Hannah's car and parked up on Sunday's Well, close by. No sign of Albert Donnelly, of course, but Robert came and went most days.'

Robert Donnelly was Albert's older brother. He was also a former head of the gardaí in Cork city; he had retired in the mid-nineties due to failing health. From what Noelie knew, Robert Donnelly was suffering from Parkinson's. Since

Albert's disappearance a full-time carer was staying with him in Llanes.

'Robert attends Mass each morning. They have a specially adapted car, a boxy thing, a Berlingo. Easy to spot. Leaves again most afternoons to take Robert over to the day centre in Bishopstown. A few other people came and went while I was there. No one I recognised. And a skip was delivered.'

'A skip? Building work?'

'Looks like it. There's something else too. New planting at the end of the garden along the riverbank. In the past you could see right into Llanes from the other side of the river. Not any more.'

Noelie thought about this. One idea they'd had was to break in to Llanes. Albert's stash of home movies was still in the house: multiple recordings made in the late fifties and sixties. Noelie knew better than to imagine that any of the abuse films would be left lying around but the regular home movies could be useful for a different reason. Albert might well have recorded some of the social events he had attended as a young man and these could help with building up a picture of his life and who his acquaintances were back in those times. That might help them uncover a link to the wider group involved in the abuse at the farm.

'Llanes is empty for about two hours each afternoon, weekdays. Two hours would be enough time for us to get in and out.'

'Two hours is plenty,' agreed Noelie.

Martin called to say he was coming out. Black Gary said he'd head back to the house to get towels for the swimmers. Martin tip-toed up the rocky shore.

'The worries of the world have gone for a few minutes, I hope?' he said.

'Forgotten.'

The younger man dripped water. Noelie noticed that he

was spectacularly pale and much too thin. 'You're only skin and bone, boy. You eating properly?'

'I am, mammy, I swear,' he said, shaking off the excess water.

'You realise you've ruined your hair-do.'

Martin laughed. 'Speaking of same, you got a right bazzer yourself. I'm not sure it suits.'

Just before he left Amsterdam Noelie had got his hair cut for his appearance at the inquest. He had asked for a shorter cut than usual. 'It suits me,' said Noelie. 'When it's short, it's manageable.'

Martin shook his head, hamming up a look of despair to go with the action. 'Hair, my dear man, should never be about manageability. That's the wrong state of mind. View it as your *pièce de résistance*. Are you listening to me?'

'I am, I am.'

'A change of mentality is required, Noelie. When all this is over, I shall personally oversee the transformation. I will be your stylist. Your days languishing on the shelf will be over.'

'You have my attention now. Is that a promise?'

'Absolutely.'

Martin sat close to Noelie facing the sun, which was now low in the sky. 'I was chatting to Meabh. She said you enjoyed Amsterdam.'

'I could stay there, I really could. I didn't want to come back. Nothing personal or anything. I'm thinking more and more in the long term I won't stay here.'

'You know I've been feeling the same. With what happened over the summer I've been thinking more about my life and what I want to do with it. I'm keen on Berlin. I'd get work there, in my line. I have the lingo too.'

They were silent then, looking out at the water. They watched as Katrina swam back to the shore. Noelie noticed how well she looked and stared for a moment.

'I'm glad Katrina's here,' said Martin.

47

Noelie nodded. 'Absolutely. I just want to be certain she understands the danger we're in. I'm not sure she does.'

Black Gary returned with the towels. He threw one to each of the swimmers.

'I like this hotel a lot,' said Martin.

They heard laughter coming from the yacht again. There were quite a few out on the boat going by the amount of noise that was being made.

'This is a wonderful place,' said Katrina.

'Well, you're all invited for a proper stay when we're done. In the meantime some food and then back to work.'

Noelie walked to the house with Martin. They talked about the inquest and the dispute over the mobile phone masts. Then Noelie remembered the fire on Douglas Street.

'Did you know?'

Martin was contrite. 'I've been in Kinsale a lot the last while. I was back to the flat briefly on Sunday and saw it then. Happened late Saturday apparently. I think Sheila got badly burned. I asked again yesterday and the word was that she's in an induced coma, which isn't as bad as it sounds. It helps reduce pain and shock. They'll keep her like that for a while and then bring her back to consciousness and see how she's feeling.'

'So, no visiting for now?'

'I don't think there's any point.'

Back at the house, Martin checked on the dinner – a large tray of pasta bake. While Noelie laid the table, Katrina brought over water and glasses.

As Martin served Noelie, he returned to their conversation. 'She was looking for you, Noelie. Sorry, I forgot to tell you. Last week. She asked about the inquest and when it was on. I told her that you were away in the Netherlands but that you'd be back for it. She said she might ring you.'

'I didn't hear from her, but my phone was off a lot. Battery out too.'

'I gave her your email as well.'

'The Eircom one? Ditched. You said they were simple to hack so I got a new one: Hushmail. If that's any better.'

'Better than Eircom anyway. Look, all you can do is make it a little bit less easy for them. The truth is if they really want to hack into your account, they can and will.'

Noelie wondered what Sheila wanted. She knew that he had moved to Hannah's but she wouldn't have known about him going to Amsterdam. Odd she would want to call him there. He realised he should've sent her a postcard, even for old times' sake. It was the kind of thing Sheila liked.

As they ate, Noelie told the others about a different development – the gardaí investigation arising from the discovery of human remains in Glen Park in the summer. 'A Cold Case unit, no less, has arrived in town to investigate some of the issues raised in James Irwin's statement to the gardaí. He'd spoken to them around the time of Hannah's funeral, setting out what he claims happened in Glen Park in 1970 when the blackmail attempt went wrong.'

Katrina had opened a bottle of red wine and was pouring Martin a glass. She noticed Black Gary looking at her. 'I'm listening, I can multi-task.'

'One of the things,' Black Gary said, 'that has become clear to us is that there are important links between the different strands of this story. The Youghal Boy mystery is a case in point. It was the search for more information on Youghal Boy that prompted Alan Copley, one of the London-based industrial school survivors, to return to Cork in, we think, the early summer of 1970. He'd heard that human remains had been found during site clearance work in the Glen, and of course he was suspicious. Whose remains were they? The missing boy from Youghal? From what we know he made no progress on that question and in frustration turned his attention to the Donnelly farm instead. Basically he broke into the farmhouse and stole some of Albert's home movies.'

'This again is information relayed to us by James Irwin,' clarified Noelie. 'According to Jamesy, the theft was a fuck-you directed at Albert. Copley knew Albert loved his home movies.'

'Risky,' said Katrina.

'He appears to have been a bit reckless on the whole – Irwin's words.'

'Anyway,' continued Black Gary, 'Copley netted a film recording the abuse of some boys at the farm. There had been other films as well but the content of those was innocent, just things going on around Cork.'

'The discovery of that abuse film,' said Noelie, 'led to the blackmail attempt on Albert, which as we know went disastrously wrong. Two of the blackmailers were lured to Glen Park, which was wilderness in those days, and murdered there. The survivors, James Irwin and Michael Egan, made their way back to London. However a few weeks later, in London, Egan disappeared. No one knew what had happened to him until his body turned up earlier this summer in Glen Park.'

'It's one of the issues we don't understand,' said Martin. 'Egan went missing in London, but why wasn't he just killed and left there? Instead he was brought back to Cork and his body dumped in a remote area of the Glen.'

'What about the other two men? Copley and Spitere?' asked Katrina.

'Reported missing too in 1970 and never seen again. Which is why the Cold Case unit is in town. It's following up on the issues raised in Irwin's statement, the murders and the whereabouts of the missing men. A detective named Oakes rang me twice in Amsterdam. I told him that I know nothing about what happened in 1970, obviously as I wasn't there, but he's insisting we meet anyway, at the Glen of all places. We've agreed on the day after tomorrow.'

'Why the Glen?' enquired Black Gary.

Noelie shook his head. 'Beats me. They've been searching there a week or more and found nothing. That's what I've heard anyway.'

Black Gary reminded them that they should be talking about something other than the investigation while they were eating, so the conversation turned to Katrina and her move to Australia. Noelie knew a little about her life there as the two of them had had plenty of time to talk on the drive to Baltimore. Since 2006, she had worked as a lead researcher on a mapping exercise in the remote Gibson Desert in Australia, which was a follow on from the Mabo legal case in Australia in the early nineties. As no one knew anything about the Mabo ruling, Katrina explained.

'Eddie and Connie Mabo are what's called Murray Islanders – it's an archipelago off the Queensland coast. They knew the customs of landownership on their island handed down to them over the generations. Apparently, one time, Eddie spoke about it at a public meeting and some legal eagle type in the audience heard him and realised the significance of what he was saying. A case followed that was ten years in the making. It went all the way to the High Court. Sadly Eddie died before a ruling was given but when it was it overturned *terra nullius* – the claim that Australia was uninhabited before Captain Cook arrived there and claimed the landmass for the British Empire. So in the end it was a huge win.'

'A heartening story,' said Martin, 'for a change.'

'All the same, how did they get away with that crap for so long?' asked Black Gary. 'No one there, like. Who were they trying to cod?'

They toasted Eddie and Connie Mabo.

'The Mabo ruling opened up a legal can of worms,' said Katrina. 'Various land and resource grabbers around Australia suddenly felt their rights and wealth were threatened by the decision. The small organisation that I work for provides assistance to those now taking cases to retrieve their lands. It's slow work but it takes me to places in Australia that are way off the beaten track. I'm quite happy at it actually. Never imagined it was what I would end up doing but it's different.'

The conversation, not surprisingly, veered on to the legacy of imperialism, courtesy of Black Gary. Noelie felt himself tune out. He was interested in what was being said but found himself thinking about how much his life had changed since the beginning of the summer when he had found his old record collection in the charity shop on Castle Street. It was a bizarre, unexpected discovery and it had put him on the trail of Jim Dalton's murderer and from there, to Albert Donnelly. There had been so many ups and downs. One of the ups was definitely the friends he had made. The down, well, it was pretty disastrous: losing Hannah.

After they had finished dinner and cleared away, they returned to their seats around the display board. Black Gary pinned up headshots of the three men from Albert's home movie. The photos he had generated were stills taken from the beginning of the film. The abusers were enjoying a glass of whiskey.

Black Gary pointed out Father Brian Boran and Leslie Walsh to Katrina, writing their names in neat print at the foot of each photo. 'The image for the third man, the one we haven't identified yet, is not the best. It will have to do, I guess.'

The unidentified man was in his twenties with dark hair, groomed and cut short. He had moderately pronounced cheek bones, deep-set eyes, protuberant lips and a squarish face.

Noelie spoke. 'I guess you'd say he's good-looking.'

'He has very regular features,' agreed Martin.

Katrina got up to have a closer look at the photo, then sat

again. 'Looks well-off,' she observed.

'Why do you say that?' asked Noelie, smiling.

'He looks healthy, I think that's what I'm noticing. I mean, he's not thin and his hair is cared for. There's something, I don't know … accomplished about him too. Now maybe I'm reading too much into it but there is a confidence about him. Certainly compared to the others, to Boran and Walsh. I'd say this man thinks he's better than them.'

'Interesting,' said Noelie.

'He's no working man anyway,' said Black Gary. 'None of them are, in fact. For now, we're calling him the third man.'

'Whoever he is, he's potentially another way for us to solve this,' said Noelie. 'Is he still alive is the question? He could be about seventy today, there or thereabouts. And what's his connection to these other two men? Finding that out could be key.'

'Do we know anything at all about him?' asked Katrina.

Noelie shook his head. 'Zilch.'

There was silence again. Katrina spoke. 'In the late fifties, early sixties, communicating wasn't as easy as it is now. People met face-to-face then, often through an activity they had in common. If we could find out more about these men, we might find out how they are connected.'

'By the way, there's no photo of Albert Donnelly here,' clarified Black Gary. 'We think he's the cameraman and we're figuring the location is the former Donnelly house in Ballyvolane. We know that Father Boran and Albert had Danesfort in common. Father Boran worked at the industrial school and Albert helped to manage the farm there for a while. We don't know how the two became friends or what the specific connection between them is.'

'Is Albert an abuser?' asked Katrina.

'We're not sure,' Noelie replied. 'When we confronted Father Boran the night Hannah was found dead, he described Albert as a sinner. That was the word he used, "sinner". He said that if you reminded Albert of it, that it would really upset him.'

'A sinner? What does that mean?' asked Katrina. ' A sinner could mean anything, although it does seem on the strong side, particularly when it's being used about a devout Catholic. Albert's supposedly a man of high standing in Let There Be Light, isn't he?'

Noelie nodded. 'We believe so. I'm inclined to agree with you, Katrina. When Father Boran called Albert a sinner I don't think he was talking about stealing apples. He meant something serious. So maybe Albert is an abuser and he enjoys documenting that too.'

'I think you've answered the question there, Noelie,' said Black Gary. 'Whether he personally likes boys or not, he has filmed the activity. Is anyone suggesting for a minute he doesn't look at those films at another time and get something from that?'

Martin nodded. 'Good point.' Noelie and Katrina nodded too.

'Going back to the connection between the men in the film, it could be as simple as class and social position,' suggested Katrina. 'You said Walsh was a public figure, one of the big developers here in the city, right?'

'At one time he was,' answered Noelie. 'A couple of big developments in the city are his. Meabh knows quite a bit more about him. I think the family were originally involved in imports and exports.'

'There should be something written about him so,' continued Katrina. 'Biog pieces, a profile or something like that. Even if he was uncooperative, someone will have done something on him. Business magazines are often the best for someone in the property line. I could take a look tomorrow.'

Black Gary added more pages to the display board. These

were blank white sheets with simple stick-style faces drawn in marker on each.

'So,' he continued, 'the film that Noelie and Meabh found in August was labelled "Gathering 3". It's reasonable to assume that there was a "Gathering 1" and a "Gathering 2" also. We don't know if there are actual home movie recordings of these so-called gatherings but it's quite possible that there are. In addition, we know about the film that Jamesy said he saw – the one they attempted to use to blackmail Albert. He said there were five to six men in that film. Most were in their twenties but there was one older man in his fifties, who was clearly identifiable as a priest. So let's assume for a moment that there is some overlap and that whoever was in our film is also in the film Jamesy viewed. If we leave out the fifty-year-old priest on the grounds that he is now probably dead, we are still left with a fourth and fifth abuser. These individuals could still be alive. And there could actually be more too.'

'The more there are, the more dangerous it is, right?' said Katrina, uneasily.

Noelie nodded. 'I did warn you.'

Black Gary produced another blank page and pinned that to the display as well. On it he wrote 'More?' He looked at the others then. 'So, how do we proceed here?'

'I suggest Black Gary and I do some research at the library tomorrow,' said Katrina. 'We'll try to find out as much as we can about Leslie Walsh. There just might be something in his history that will give us a clue. There are other things we have to do too, but we'll add that to our list.'

'Unfortunately I'll be tied up with work for a good bit of the day,' said Martin. 'Someone has to keep this economy limping along.'

Noelie raised the matter of a return visit to Llanes. 'The other home movies Albert recorded should be there.' He pointed at the third man. 'He could well feature in one of

55

them. If he is, it might give us the key to his identity.'

'I think it's worth a shot,' said Black Gary. The others agreed.

'I'll get on to Ciarán in Solidarity Books. He has a canoe, a decent one. He'll lend it to us. I'll have a word and see what the practicalities are.'

6

It was getting dark. Black Gary suggested they call up to the pub for a pint. He'd be able to check his emails at the same time. They walked together along the quiet boreen. It was a cool, cloudless night. Martin commented on how many more stars were visible in the sky once you were outside the city.

At the pub they got a seat near the window. The harbour below them looked peaceful. On the far shore, Baltimore was lit up and there were still plenty of yachts moored around the outer harbour. A pool table was free, so Katrina challenged Noelie to a game. Although he fancied himself, he was trounced. They agreed to the best of three but Noelie lost the second match too, although it was closer. He was about to suggest the best of five when a young woman with flowing black hair and a floral print skirt came over and put down her two euro; she was about Katrina's age. She indicated to a man who was with her. He was nursing a pint and smiled at Noelie.

'How about two against two,' he asked.

Katrina was game. The woman introduced herself as Virginia and the man as her husband, Luke. Katrina introduced herself and Noelie set up. The game that followed was close – mostly thanks to Katrina. It went down to the black but Virginia potted it.

Black Gary joined them. 'I see you've met my neighbours.' He received a warm hello from the husband and wife team. They joked about the game and Katrina complimented the opposition. She declined a rematch. Noelie could see that they were disappointed.

Back at their seats, Black Gary told them about the couple. They had moved in at the end of August to a house very near to him and planned to be there until Christmas. 'The place needed a lot of work done, and I helped them connect the water supply, but Luke seems handy enough.'

'What do they do?' Noelie asked.

'She's writing up her thesis. He's some sort of a coastal expert, doing a study on the islands or something. He's linked to the marine station.'

Noelie watched the couple. Another duo challenged them and lost as well. No one else was willing to take them on. He turned his attention back to the others. Katrina and Black Gary had got into a discussion about the industrial school that had been located at Baltimore at one time.

Noelie had his hand around his pint and noticed Martin looking at the missing fingernail on Noelie's little finger – the nail that had been ripped out by Albert Donnelly on the night Hannah died. A new nail was just starting to come in, but there was a while to go before it would look normal again.

'Do you ever think about that time?' Martin asked.

'Too often for my own good,' said Noelie. 'I think of Albert Donnelly too much as well. He shoved those pliers under my nail so hard I thought they would come out my elbow. Animal.'

Noelie shivered. In August, over a few days, his life had nearly ended twice. He just didn't sleep well any more.

Changing the subject, he asked Martin how life was going for him on Douglas Street. The trip to Solidarity Books earlier that day had made him realise how much he missed the area.

'It's not the same now that you're not there, Noelie. Really, I mean it. I miss not having you in the flat up above. And I just don't feel as comfortable there as I used to. Which is odd actually. I mean, it's been my first real place, you know.

But knowing that people were in there looking around and through my things. And how many times? I still feel I'm being watched. Do you ever feel like that?'

Noelie nodded his head vigorously. 'Definitely.'

He watched Martin. All the others had pints but Martin had a glass of wine. He was his own man for sure and quite the character when he was out on the town. Noelie had tagged along once or twice. He wondered again if there was any chance he could convince him to drop out of the investigation. Or even take a back seat. He had tried to enlist Meabh to help him dissuade Martin, but she had dismissed the prospect out of hand. She thought it was good for Martin, that his generation needed to sharpen up their game anyway. That comment had led to an argument between them. It wasn't so much that Meabh was calculating with other people's lives, more that she was often prepared to drive on at what she wanted regardless. Whereas when Noelie looked at Martin all he could see was a young man with a life still to live. He sometimes felt that this wasn't even Martin's fight.

'I've spent a lot of time in Kinsale these last few weeks. Just kept away from the flat a bit. What's your take on Kinsale, Noelie?'

'It's all right, I guess. Not really my cup of tea.'

'Ollie has a gorgeous spot there. A friend of a friend has let him have this place virtually rent-free until Christmas. It's nice.'

'So it's going well with Ollie?'

'He hasn't kicked me out yet anyway.'

'I thought it might be the other way around?'

Martin thought about his answer. 'Probably will be in the end. He's more settled than I am. He actually talks about staying in Kinsale long term.'

'Not for you?'

'What do you think?'

'I'd say not for you.'

Martin raised his glass. The others noticed and joined the toast. 'To the future,' he said.

On the way back from the pub, Noelie walked with Martin while Katrina and Black Gary followed a short distance behind them. Noelie found himself thinking about the Wikileaks issue and what it could mean. It had been an absolute failsafe protection for them since August but now it was gone. He asked Martin again how long it would take to get a new arrangement in place.

'Not long, I hope. We have to be ready to move quickly once we decide to retrieve the digital copy of the film I've hidden. The arrangement with Wikileaks will need to be reset and, in an ideal scenario, they will be waiting for us to deliver the new digital copy to them. The last time, I must've hit the sweet spot because Wikileaks were ready and available immediately. Communications don't seem as good now.'

An ancient car came up behind them and they stepped in to let it pass. Black Gary got a big hello. After it passed, Martin asked Noelie about the original hard copy version of the abuse film.

'It's safely hidden too,' confirmed Noelie.

The security of the Bell & Howell double-8 film reel was something that they had worried about from the minute they had found it. Although they had made digital copies, they decided they needed to retain the original film reel too. In the end, they passed it to James Irwin to take to Australia. He had left Cork a few weeks ago and had sent word to say that he and the film had arrived safely.

'I think we're okay, Noelie, really,' Martin concluded. 'We'll just be extra careful for the next few days.'

Black Gary and Katrina caught up with them. Martin used

the opportunity to remind the older man that using the pub's public computer was not very secure. 'Don't put anything sensitive in any correspondence up there.' He added, 'That goes for you too, Noelie. And you as well, Katrina.'

'You're talking to the converted with me, Martin,' Katrina replied. 'We've had to deal with security issues constantly around this work that I'm doing on land rights and so on. Mostly it's company-hired spies, but honestly they're sometimes worse than anyone.'

'Told you she's a know-it-all,' said Noelie.

He was pushed into the ditch for his comment.

Martin was returning early the next morning for work. Noelie was intending to leave early too to get signing on out of the way. Apparently the queues at the dole office were still a mile long so he was bracing himself for a wait. Afterwards he planned to see Ted Toner, the elderly historian who had helped Noelie over the summer. Toner had left word to say he had some new information. That left the afternoon conveniently free for the inquest, which was set to resume at 2 p.m.

Black Gary had beds made up for them all. Katrina had her own room, while Noelie shared floor space with Martin. Although the airbed was comfortable he couldn't sleep. Earlier, Black Gary had moved the plywood display of their investigation nearer to the door leading out into the hall. From where Noelie was lying he could see the grainy pictures of young Father Boran, Leslie Walsh and the third man in the dim light. Who would this third individual turn out to be? And what about the other figures involved? Would they be nobodies or much more high profile? It was true that the Donnellys were a propertied, well-to-do family, so they wouldn't have been hanging around with any old muck. But as Hannah used to remind him, it is easy to be led astray by your own preconceptions. Right now, it was difficult to know.

He eventually gave up on sleep and went outside for some air. Standing at the front door, he took in Black Gary's pretty front garden, complete with picnic table and bench.

The September chill was difficult to ignore and it had him thinking about the coming winter and, inevitably, Christmas. He had spent the last two with Hannah. She'd often had others along so it was a nice festive indulgence. What would he do this year?

The lights were on in the next house down from Black Gary's. Was that where the two pool players were staying? If so, they were close neighbours indeed.

'Can't sleep?'

Noelie turned to find Katrina standing beside him. She was wrapped in a bright yellow dressing gown.

'I know, I look a sight,' she said.

'You get away with it.'

She smiled then went to sit on the picnic table, wrapping the dressing gown tightly around herself.

'How did I get to this place?' he asked.

'What do you mean?'

'I'm suspicious of those pool players now, from earlier.' He shook his head in dismay. 'There was something about them I didn't like.'

'Would they really have got in our face like that if they were spying on us?'

'Who knows?'

'You think the other side know we're all here and up to no good?'

Noelie nodded. 'There's no doubt about it. They're watching us.'

The night's silence was suddenly broken by an animal shrieking in the distance. They both looked in the direction of the noise, then, feeling slightly spooked, Noelie went to sit beside her on the table.

'Something I should've said earlier. You remember that Jamesy is the source of our information on Youghal Boy? Well, one of the things I remember him telling us in August was how Alan Copley got quite excited when he heard that human remains had been discovered during site clearing work in or close to the Glen. This was in 1970, I think. It was that news that provoked Copley to return to Cork.' Noelie paused. 'There should be a record of that discovery of those human remains somewhere in the public domain. In the papers, like?'

Katrina nodded. 'I would think so. Finding remains is nearly always serious and dramatic enough to get into the papers. Great, that's another item for me to look into tomorrow.'

'Sorry, I didn't mean to be dumping work on you.'

'I didn't mean it, like that. I prefer to have a few things to look up when I'm going to spend the day in a library. Better for the concentration. Variety and all of that.'

After a further silence she said, 'I was thinking about something too, also from around then. Irwin and his friends, the group that tried to blackmail Albert Donnelly, well, they totally misread the situation, didn't they?'

Noelie wasn't sure. 'With the benefit of hindsight, I guess you could say that. But … look, the thing about Albert is that he's a slick operator. On first appearances I'm not sure you'd guess what he's capable of. That's how he struck me anyway. I was totally disarmed by him when we first met.'

'But these ex-industrial schoolboys are different, Noelie. They would have known about Albert by reputation, wouldn't they? Didn't one of them really dislike him?'

'Yeah, you're right, Copley did. Irwin said that he really hated Albert.'

'Why I'm saying this is that something's just not adding up here. Why, for example, weren't Albert and his associates just happy to retrieve the film that was being used to blackmail them? They could have taken the film back while giving Irwin and the others a good hiding. Threaten them with worse if they ever returned. Wouldn't that have sufficed? Why murder them?'

Noelie thought about this. 'Yes, and in those days who would've listened to the words of a few ex-industrial school malcontents anyway? Now maybe someone would, but not then. Especially not over the word of Albert and his well-connected brothers. It's a very good question.'

'So, was there more at stake, is what I am wondering? Just say, for example, those remains discovered in Glen Park that you were just talking about. Did their discovery cause more trouble than we know about? Was there a real threat that the abuse circle was going to be exposed? Did that make them even more ruthless than usual, more unwilling to leave any loose ends?'

Martin appeared at the front door then.

'Can't sleep either?' Katrina asked him as he sat down beside her.

'Kind of. It's so nice here.'

'If you are wrapped up well, as you two are,' said Noelie. 'I'm perished.'

'What were you talking about?' asked Martin.

'We were plotting some more,' said Katrina, 'but you're too late now: we've shut up shop. Excuse me one moment.' She darted inside the house, then returned with a spliff all rolled and ready. 'Had this for the right occasion. Which I feel is now.'

Noelie smiled. She lit up.

Martin complained about having to work the next day. 'I'd much prefer to move here permanently.'

'It was Berlin and the high life earlier. Jesus, Martin.'

'I'm fickle.'

Katrina took a few drags and passed it to Noelie. 'It's good to be fickle when you're young,' she said.

'I'll drink and smoke to that,' said Noelie. He offered Martin the spliff.

'Can't risk it,' said Martin. 'Had to sign up to drug monitoring at work. Frightful imposition, it is.'

Noelie felt good after a few puffs. He looked at the night sky and listened. Far away he could hear the sea pounding on to the rocks.

Déjà Vu

7

Ted Toner rose with an arthritic sigh. 'Don't ever get old, Noelie' he said.

'I feel old.'

Toner stopped and put a hand on Noelie's shoulder. 'Believe me when I tell you you're not. You're a young lad still. Make the most of it.'

He walked over to a rectangular table that was nearly the width of the room. The window behind it overlooked a small tidy backyard. Folders, books and stacks of documents were arranged neatly on the table alongside a small computer that Noelie hadn't noticed the last time he'd visited.

'How are you finding that computer?' he asked.

'The daughter got it for me,' Toner said, returning. 'I've been asked to write two articles, one for the local newsletter and the other for the folklore project, based up there in Knocknaheeny. They want me to send the material to them all typed up. I'm giving it a try but I love writing with a pen.'

Noelie had a cup of tea in front of him. He sipped it.

'At your friend Hannah's funeral, I got chatting to the Sherkin man.'

'Gary Maguire's his name. Everyone calls him Black Gary. A nickname he got in Danesfort, I gather, that stuck.'

Toner nodded. 'That's the one. He told me that you and Hannah were close. I didn't realise. I'm very, very sorry.'

'Yeah, we were, a lot closer than I realised, I have to confess. I just did nothing about it. I've got slow.'

'I was married to the same woman for forty-five years. We met when we were seventeen. I didn't think I'd survive after

69

she went but here I am. We had our time together and I always try to think about that when I feel lonely. Someone else will turn up, Noelie.'

'Letting me in on a secret, are you?'

Toner winked. 'I have my admirers, yes. But promise me this.'

'What?'

'You won't be slow the next time.'

Noelie smiled. 'You have my word.' He nodded at the page in Toner's hand. 'What have you got for me?'

'Something that I hope makes this visit worthwhile.'

It was a photo, a black and white that had turned yellow with age. A corner was missing. 'One of my cronies in our local historical group had this. We have it on loan. You can copy it if you like.'

There was no one in the photo. It was a simple straight shot of a house, taken from a distance of perhaps forty or fifty metres. The building itself was a square construction, with four windows upstairs and two on the ground level: one on either side of an expansive front door entrance. Seeing the weathered white eagles perched on the two front corners of the portico, Noelie realised what he was looking at.

'That's the house in the home movie we found.'

'Well, that's the Donnelly house.'

Noelie beamed. 'Brilliant.'

The older man had something else for Noelie: an article cut from an old *Cork Examiner* with the headline, 'Professor warns about the threat to our heritage'. Noelie read the piece, which described a meeting held at the Arbutus Hotel in Montenotte in which a professor from University College, Cork was lamenting the lack of protection for historically important buildings in the area. The Donnelly family abode was mentioned. It had been an intelligence centre used by the local IRA during independence and, later, in the Irish Civil War.

'There are reports that people were tortured there,' added Toner. 'During the Civil War, I mean.'

Noelie checked the date on the cutting. He was surprised. 'February 1971. Which means that the house had been demolished by then.'

'Anyway, the interesting part of this, my friend was telling me, is that some part of the house is still there. He told me where it was. Ruins, I suppose.'

'Far away?'

'From here, no. Fifteen, twenty minutes' drive.'

Ted went to get his coat. While Noelie waited he examined the photo again. Sometimes it took weeks to find anything useful and other times the information just dropped in his lap. The picture of the house was only a small piece of the puzzle, but it was confirmation that the film had been shot in the Donnelly's old homestead. It was a substantial dwelling too, Noelie noted. An estate house rather than a large farmhouse. He wondered how the Donnellys had come by it.

They crammed into Toner's Punto – Noelie had come by bus – and set off.

'I haven't been out this direction for a while,' said Toner. 'The roads were favourites of mine at one time, but you can't walk around here any more for fear of being mowed down.'

They left the edge of the city and joined a narrow road wide enough for one car. On one side was a sloping field containing large rolls of cut hay. They passed a copse of trees, then Toner slowed to show Noelie a partially-constructed derelict building site. 'Our local ghost estate.'

'Every parish should have one.'

'Every one does.' Toner added, 'You'd laugh if it wasn't such a tragedy.' He told Noelie how the local hurling teams had been gutted in less than a year by the latest round of emigration.

After a while, Noelie noticed the road that they were on was bordered on one side by a granite stone wall. He mentioned this.

'I think this is their area now,' Toner suggested. 'Most of what's on the other side was once the Donnellys.'

The family was clearly a lot better off than Noelie had imagined. He'd been thinking they were prosperous farmers, but this was a proper estate. Of course, it made some sense. During the fight for independence, rich and poor alike fought in the ranks of the IRA. However with the formation of the Irish Free State, the better-off elements were the first to be selected for the new Irish police force. Old Donnelly, Albert's father, had been a high-ranking officer during much of the twenties.

They arrived at a gateless entrance. The pillars on each side were covered in moss. Toner slowed to a stop and rolled down his window. Beyond the entrance, Noelie saw a rutted weed-infested lane. It hadn't seen traffic in years.

'Up there, I'd say,' said Toner. 'I'm not sure the Punto is up to it though.'

'Let's walk.'

'Fine for you, boy. I'll go a bit of the way. We'll see what we can see. I'm guessing the house is a good bit in.' There was a small wood farther on. The remnants of the drive went through it. It was pleasant, although the damp smell reminded Noelie of his march though the Galtee Mountains in August to see the site where Jim Dalton's remains had been found, buried in a remote area in the mountain's foothills. Finding the remains had been a breakthrough – one of the positive things that had happened in the summer. Ethel Dalton, the missing man's widow, was often in contact with Noelie. If he didn't answer the phone to her, she would leave a long message on his voice mail sending him her family's well wishes and thanking him again. She was sweet. He'd call to see her one day soon, once matters had settled down a bit. If that would ever happen.

'Were you ever around here as a boy?' Noelie asked.

Toner shook his head. 'Not this far out. Also, at one time the Donnellys were like aristocracy around here. I mean, maybe a lot of it was airs and graces, but they had the land and in those times, as long as you didn't squander money, that meant you got to be fairly rich.'

Noelie remembered the story about Old Donnelly losing a leg during his stint out in Spain fighting for Franco. For a farmer, losing a leg like that would've been a blow. But it was clear that Donnelly must've had farm labourers who did the work for him. He asked Toner about that.

'They had staff for sure. They had a farm manager, I think, which in those days was something. They also had a nanny for the boys at one time. This was after the war.'

'The Second World War?'

'Exactly.'

'What about house staff? I'd be very interested to talk to anyone who worked there.'

'I'll ask about for you, no problem.' Toner stopped then, his expression serious. 'You know, I heard about that film you found, showing boys being interfered with …'

Noelie nodded. 'They were just kids and they looked so frightened. Two boys stripped to their underwear in the company of grown men.'

Toner had a long face lined by age. He shook his head sadly. 'Terrible. You know, Noelie, there were things that went on years ago … people knew about them but it was very hard to say anything or to speak up. All that abuse in the industrial schools and the Laundries, I think a lot more people knew about all of that than are letting on now. In fairness, it was in some of the left-wing press but then they were dismissed as agents of "Godless Russia" and all the rest of it.'

They continued on. After passing through a small screen of woodland they arrived at a large rampart of earth shoved across the roadway to emphasise that the road was no longer in use.

'Would you remember the Cork 800 event at all?' Toner asked him.

'Vaguely.'

'Bit of a tourist gimmick, I suppose, to celebrate when Cork got its city charter. But it got local historians like me excited. Anyway, a few of us did a big history of this entire area, after getting a grant as part of that event. We discovered that Cromwell once stayed around here. Needless to say those who helped him were rewarded and those who didn't, weren't.'

'Which side were the Donnellys on?'

Toner didn't know. 'I'm not thinking the family got on with Cromwell. They've been known as staunch Catholics for as long as anyone can remember.'

Noelie climbed the earthen rampart and described what he could see for Toner.

'Those trees on the far side are where the house is. You go on if you like and I'll wait here.'

Noelie couldn't see anything resembling a wall or ruins in the distance but he said he'd have a look.

He made his way across a large field. In one corner was a bunch of sycamores. As he got closer, he saw a fence inside the tree line. He tried to recall the double-8mm film scene to work out the location of the house against the landscape he was seeing but he couldn't. He remembered there being a low hill in the film, but he couldn't see it now. He wondered if the sycamores were new and if they were now obscuring the vista of farmland and hills evident in the film. He couldn't be sure without seeing the film again – and that was no longer easy to do.

The farmer who now owned the land had allowed the weeds and grass to grow high around the sycamores. Noelie negotiated nettles and some brambles, finally reaching the fence. To his surprise he saw that it was in good condition. It was not new, but it was not more than five or so years old either. He walked along the perimeter and eventually reached a gate wide enough for vehicular access. It was locked with a chain and a heavy-duty lock. A sign read 'Secured by Moroney Fences'. Nearby, a much larger sign declared 'Danger. No Trespassing'.

Inside the fence was an area of about an acre. In parts it was wild and overgrown with bushes but in other places there was little growth. There was no actual evidence that a house had once existed on the site he was looking in on, let alone a sizable estate house. So much for the 'ruins' Noelie had been thinking he would see. Except at one place he saw a mound. He moved closer, but with the heavy shade from the trees around it wasn't clear what he was looking at. He thought he could see stone and wondered if the heap was the remnants of the house's sturdy block walls.

There was little else to see so he headed back. He found Toner near his car. The older man gestured to Noelie to be quiet. In the undergrowth, near one of the pillars, was a red squirrel.

'A rarity these days,' Toner whispered, narrowing his eyes conspiratorially. 'Those foreign greys are taking over.'

'Taking all of our jobs too no doubt.'

'Exactly.'

They both laughed. Noelie told the older man what he had seen. 'No ruins, just a protected section of ground.' He added, 'Like why?'

Toner didn't answer, instead he offered Noelie some of the blackberries he'd been picking while he'd waited. The two stood beside the Punto eating the haul.

'Really you can't beat a Cork blackberry, can you?' said Toner.

Noelie asked him again about the fenced-off site. 'Why would they hang on to that, do you think?'

'Sentimental reasons perhaps. Maybe Old Donnelly's ghost is still up there.'

Noelie laughed. He asked if Toner knew which farmer had acquired the land around the old house.

'O'Neills, according to my friend. Out White's Cross direction. One of them lads was the finest hurler that has ever come out of this place. You'd like to visit, I'm guessing?'

It took them about ten minutes to reach the area that held the O'Neill farm and another twenty to find the farm itself. It was a warren of narrow roads and boreens, down which cars and tractors drove at speed. Noelie was glad he wasn't at the wheel.

They were able to drive all the way into the farmyard. Some sort of cattle inspection was going on. A modern dormer-style house was visible from the roadway beyond the yard and sheds.

A young man came over. Toner did the talking.

'My dad's inside. He'll come out, I'm sure.'

They waited beside the car. It was a fairly mucky place all around. Noelie thought of Hannah. She would've said, 'It's the country, Noelie. What do you expect?'

'They're pig farmers here,' Toner said. 'Get the smell.'

'I didn't like to say.'

'Apparently Old Donnelly kept pigs too'

'This crowd are no relation though?'

Toner shook his head. 'No.'

Patrick O'Neill came out. He wore a green quilted jacket that was fashionable with farmers. He was quite overweight – a burly man with white hair. He had been eating something and was still chewing it as he approached. He nodded to them.

Noelie explained about his work on Old Donnelly. 'I'm researching a history of the area and he seems a particularly notable figure, having made it out to Spain and all to fight for Franco.'

O'Neill nodded warily. 'Notable is not how I'd describe him.'

'Did you know him personally?'

'I met him a few times when I was dragging after my father. My dad knew him well and had to deal with him on occasion. Difficult. That said, I don't know much about him. They were private people. My father knew him as a neighbour only.'

'The family home – do they still have ownership of the house site?'

'Oh yes. The Domain, that's what we call it. Old Donnelly called it that too. Keeping that was a condition of the land sale way back in the early seventies. But about ten years ago we had a plan to consolidate our farm in the town direction, so we were keen to buy out the Donnelly plot and be done with them once and for all. But they wouldn't budge.'

'Who did you deal with? Albert?'

'Well, it had to be. Robert wasn't well. He would've been better to deal with actually but, yes, it was Albert we talked to. Frankly we're all a bit shocked about what we've heard about Albert.'

Noelie was interested. 'What have you heard?'

'About him and that IRA informer. It seems to me they murdered that young woman too.'

Toner looked at Noelie. Although Noelie was interested to hear what rumours were circulating about Albert, he didn't want his precise connection with the events and with Hannah to be noted in O'Neill's company. It would complicate matters, and he might want to talk to O'Neill again.

Toner said nothing, taking his cue from Noelie.

'Do you have any theory on why Albert wanted to hang on to that foundation site back there?' Noelie asked.

O'Neill shook his head. 'Oddness? Look, he was straight about it. We asked him to sell up for good but he said no. But he was polite. He gave us the driveway up to site, which is why there's a big field all around there now. He still has a right of way in there. But, look, I don't think he's been up there in years. And I didn't get the impression he was going to visit any time soon either. But he was adamant, so we left it.'

'The fence is maintained.'

O'Neill frowned. 'You took a look?'

'Just a quick sconce.'

'My dad did the original transaction with him and the idea was that the house was going to be built on again one day but, as I say, it never happened. Which we're all glad of. The current arrangement, while not ideal, is tolerable. Why look a gift horse in the mouth, right?'

'Definitely. Well, thanks for talking to us, I appreciate your time.'

The men shook hands, and O'Neill went back inside.

On the way out, Toner said, 'I'll look into it a bit more for you if you like.'

Noelie smiled at the older man. 'I was hoping you might. I'd be particularly interested to talk to anyone who ever worked there.'

8

There was no one else at Hannah's when Noelie returned. He went through the CD rack and found a baroque recording Hannah had brought back from one of her trips to Prague. She played the CD only occasionally but Noelie had fallen in love with the organ-style music. He had gone to Prague with Hannah in 2006 on a city break. She loved the city and knew quite a lot about its history and about the various writers from there who had made their names during the Soviet years – Kundera, Škvorecký and the like. It had been a memorable trip.

He made coffee and went into Hannah's old room. It was hard to miss that Katrina had moved in but he didn't mind that. The bedroom was still the way Hannah had kept it. He went to the old wardrobe. Her coats were still inside. One in particular, an amber and black flecked jacket, had been a favourite. She looked wonderful in it.

Closing the wardrobe door again, he left the room and went over to the riverside window. The heron was still on duty. The tide was out too and the rocky sides of the river, up against the quay walls, were visible. For some reason, people loved to throw shopping trolleys into the Lee. From where he stood, he could see three.

His thoughts returned to the old Donnelly homestead – where the so-called 'gatherings' were held. But why there? Was it just convenience? Or was there more to it? And why were these different men there? Was there a reason for them being present at the Donnelly abode for reasons other than their proclivity for boys? There had to be, he felt.

After a frustrating and near fruitless search of his boxed

belongings he eventually found the file he'd been looking for. It contained information that he had gathered in July and August during the investigation into Jim Dalton's death – notes, photos, names and various questions that had come into his mind at the time. At the kitchen table, he sifted through the contents. Sunlight streamed over his workspace. He remembered when he'd first read about Danesfort Industrial School and realised its significance. When he and Hannah went looking into Jim Dalton's disappearance in July, it was making the connection between Dalton and Danesfort that had been the key breakthrough. While the school was still important, Noelie no longer felt that it was at the centre of what was going on. Instead the focus had shifted to the Donnelly family itself – a family with links to Danesfort but with its own secrets too.

He removed two pages from a notepad and taped them together end-to-end. He marked out a timeline using decades as milestones. He wanted to get a sense of what he knew and didn't know about the family. Two things in particular were on his mind. Firstly, what was significance of the Donnelly homestead that he and Toner had visited? Secondly, was Katrina on to something important when she'd remarked on Albert's murderous assault on his blackmailers back in 1970? Had there been more at stake, and if so, what was that?

He began filling in what he knew.

1900s	Old Donnelly born: Year?
1910s	Old Donnelly active in the Old IRA: c.1919–21
1920s	Old Donnelly joins new Irish police following Independence: c.1922/23
	Marries Clara Riordan: c.1928/29
1930s	Old Donnelly forced to leave the police force: c.?
	Employment? Farming?
	Birth of first son, Tony (Father Tony): Year?
	Birth of second son, Robert: Year?

Death of Old Donnelly's wife, Clara, in childbirth:
    c.1934?
Old Donnelly goes to Spain: 1936
Old Donnelly returns from Spain: c.?
Birth of Albert Donnelly in Spain: c.1938?
Albert Donnelly arrives at Ballyvolane farm. Year?

1940s   ?

1950s   Tony Donnelly joins the Rosminian Order: c.mid-50s
Robert Donnelly joins the gardaí: c.late 50s
Tony Donnelly posted to Danesfort Industrial
    School: Year?
Danesfort boys loaned to Donnelly farm as
    labourers: c.late 50s

1960s   'Gathering 3' double-8 home movie recorded
    (features Father Boran, Leslie Walsh and a
    third unidentified man; recorded by Albert
    Donnelly): 1962.
Other gatherings? Other films?
Disappearance of Youghal Boy: Year?
Father Boran moved from Danesfort to Newry,
    N. Ireland: 1965
Danesfort closes: 1966

1970s   Human remains found in Glen during site
    clearance work: When?
Ex-Danesfort boy, Alan Copley, returns to Cork:
    Spring 1970
Copley breaks in to Old Donnelly house at
    Ballyvolane: Spring 1970
Blackmail attempt on Albert Donnelly: August 1970
Peter Spitere and Copley murdered in Glen Park:
    August/September 1970
Third member of Danesfort blackmail group,
    Michael Egan, abducted in London:
    September 1970

Destruction of Ballyvolane house: c. late-1970
Father Boran's death faked in Belfast: 1970/71?
Fate of Old Donnelly?
Albert moves to Llanes, Sunday's Well Road: c.1971
Special Branch informer known as 'Brian Boru'
    becomes active inside Sinn Féin
       – handler, Robert Donnelly
Let There Be Light, Irish branch founded: c.1978
Future whistle-blower Sean Sugrue transferred to
    Cork from Tralee: 1979

1980s   Ex-Danesfort schoolboy Jim Dalton recognises
    Father Boran in Cork: 1989
Dalton makes a complaint to the gardaí
Dalton ensnared in Special Branch operation
    against Sinn Féin–IRA in Cork area: 1989/90

1990s   Dalton murdered by Special Branch: 1990
Meabh Sugrue tells her father about being abused
    at Llanes: 1993
Robert Donnelly retires from gardaí due to failing
    health: c.1995/96
Sean Sugrue approaches Garda HQ as a whistle-
    blower: 1997
Sean Sugrue dies in a car crash with Father Tony
    Donnelly: 1998
Sugrue's file about Dalton (and other criminality
    in the Cork gardaí linked to the Donnellys)
    goes missing: 1998
Defrocked US priest Andrew Teland arrives in
    Ireland and stays at Llanes with Albert: 1999

2000s ?

2010   Sugrue's file re-discovered at Dillon's Cross, Cork.
Contains documents alleging murder of Jim
    Dalton and one of Albert Donnelly's double-8mm
    home movies

> Egan's body found at Glen Park.
> Don Cronin, colleague of Sugrue's, murdered
>   (probably by Albert Donnelly)
> Father Boran exposed as Tommy Keogh, acting as
>   a deep mole inside Sinn Féin
> Dalton remains recovered
> James Irwin, fourth and only survivor of the Glen
>   Park blackmail attempt comes forward,
>   alleging three murders in Cork in 1970
> Hannah Hegarty murdered

Noelie stopped. *Hannah Hegarty murdered.* The words were stark.

It was much easier to see, with the timeline set out, that Katrina was possibly on to something significant about the time period around 1970. A lot had happened and, although it wasn't clear if or how the different events were linked, big changes had occurred. The Donnelly family homestead and farm had been abandoned for a new urban dwelling in Cork on Sunday's Well Road. Also, significantly, 1970 marked the beginning of Brian Boru's tenure as a mole inside Sinn Féin.

So why had Albert's men murdered the two blackmailers in Glen Park and followed a third to London, kidnapping him there and murdering him also? Only one of the four blackmailers escaped alive – Jamesy Irwin – and he was so traumatised by what had happened he hadn't spoken out about Albert Donnelly again for nearly forty years.

What else had been going on at that time? Or had it more to do with who was involved? Was one of the abusers someone particularly important? The abuse had taken place in the early sixties so by the time of the 1970 blackmail attempt, nearly ten years had passed. Was that enough time for someone to rise from obscurity to a position of importance? Possibly, but Noelie didn't think so. Was this person of significance someone with a prominent future in government? Did protecting that person's identity warrant the violent response?

If it wasn't that, what else could it be? Had something even more macabre or ugly taken place at these so-called 'gatherings' than child abuse? Had those involved, or a number of them anyway, become embarrassed and ashamed of what had taken place? Noelie didn't know, but the entire business was murky and getting murkier with each passing day. He went to get a glass of water, bringing his timeline with him. Periods of inactivity, long silences, and then bursts of action, which almost always involved a number of deaths: in particular, 1970. Copley, Spitere and Egan were murdered; Irwin disappeared to Australia to avoid the same fate.

In the aftermath of that violent interlude, the secret about what had happened at the Donnelly farm had been safe once more.

Another long silence then followed. The seventies were largely quiet. The eighties, too, for the most part. In 1989/90, Jim Dalton went to a garda station in Cork claiming that a notorious abuser from Danesfort Industrial School, a Father Boran, was alive and living openly in Cork. Dalton's claim touched on events going right back to the early sixties. But Dalton clearly had no idea what he was sleep-walking into.

By 1990, Father Boran had evolved into a valuable mole inside Sinn Féin – code-name 'Brian Boru'. The first stirrings of the future Northern Ireland peace process were taking shape. Jim Dalton's allegations that Father Boran was still alive posed an existential threat to the mole Brian Boru. So, the decision was taken to kill Jim Dalton, who as a victim of child abuse, was unlikely to go away quietly. How far up the chain of command in the Irish state did knowledge of that killing go? Who could authorise an execution like that? Enter Special Branch officer Denis Lynch, whose career prospects improve and improve after Dalton's death.

The next big ruction came in 1997/98. Sean Sugrue approached Garda Headquarters with concrete evidence of criminal wrongdoing inside the gardaí in Cork, linked to the Dalton execution and more. Sugrue had a reputation for being diligent and honest. Winner of a Scott Medal for bravery, he was not easily dismissed. Furthermore, on hearing that his daughter was abused at a religious event linked to Albert Donnelly, he started to look into matters he really didn't want to investigate. Now a new front opened up. The problem was that Sean Sugrue wasn't going to be put off easily, nor was it possible to buy him off. Sugrue eventually found proof that one or more of the abusers were being protected by elements in the gardaí. He told Garda Headquarters about this suspicion. Nothing happened and then Sugrue conveniently died in a car crash. There was silence once more. Until 2010. Then all hell broke loose again.

Noelie and Hannah had realised one important thing in summer: they were facing not one but two sources of danger. One was represented by Albert Donnelly and those involved in the murders in 1970. The other derived from a cabal inside the Cork gardaí who, over the years, had clearly made a few deals with the devil in order to progress the war on Sinn Féin.

9

Noelie climbed the steps that led into the courthouse. He passed through the rotating doors and entered the main foyer where he saw a few disparate groups – families, teens, adults – milling about amongst the barristers and solicitors. He knew a few people who had studied law back at university and occasionally he saw them around the city. He nodded to a barrister with ginger hair, who had also been on the fringes of the punk scene in her day.

He scanned the crowd, looking for Ellen. Figuring that the inquest would be in the same courtroom as the day before, he made his way to the back area, passing through a new glass-covered atrium that linked the building's two wings. He finally saw Ellen and her husband, Arthur, speaking with Taylor, the family's solicitor. They were standing in a corner beside a potted palm tree.

He went over. Ellen said hello and squeezed his hand. Taylor did a quick re-cap for Noelie's sake. He had been hoping that the gardaí would have had some insight into the mobile phone discrepancy, and its possible repercussions, but so far nothing had been forthcoming – he felt that the situation was worse than the gardaí were admitting. 'For now, the coroner will, most likely, want to hear as much of the remaining evidence as possible. Though, obviously, any final verdict will be deferred until we receive a definitive explanation regarding the mobile phone trail. So a further adjournment seems likely.'

Noelie liked Taylor. He was measured and calm; instilling confidence when he spoke. He was also 110 per cent committed to the inquest. Although he dressed well for court, there was nothing smart or sharp about his appearance. Taylor was someone you could easily underestimate.

Ellen was nervous. Shane's death made no sense to anyone but now there was the added complication of a mistake having been made. The question remained though: where had the teenager been during the last hours of his life?

Taylor was cautious about what lay ahead. 'Let's take this one step at a time and see what happens. Remember, we're not in any hurry. It's far more important that we're satisfied that we have asked every question we want to ask.'

When Taylor left for the courtroom, Noelie hugged Ellen and she reminded him that the inquest had moved to Court 1 on the ground floor. 'The dreariest place, I'm afraid. Like something from Dickens.'

It was only around the corner from where they were standing. Ellen hung back to go in with her husband and Noelie went on. In the busy corridor outside the courtroom he almost collided with Denis Lynch. The retired garda inspector was talking to someone but as Noelie squeezed by, he turned and looked. Their eyes met and Noelie was instantly on guard. If Lynch was surprised to see Noelie he didn't let on. Noelie was certainly surprised to see him. What was Lynch doing at the inquest? He wasn't a witness as far as Noelie knew. Didn't people do other things when they retired? It was a strange moment too because it was Noelie's first time seeing him since the night of the fire and the confrontation at Church Bay when Hannah had been found murdered. Lynch looked well – he seemed relaxed and had lost some weight – but his face brought back a lot of bad memories.

Noelie fought a desire to pick an argument with him. He was sure Lynch knew a lot more about Hannah's death than he had ever admitted. Lynch looked away finally and Noelie entered Court 1. A bitterness about the injustice of it all – Lynch sidling off into comfortable retirement while Hannah was dead – welled up in him. Crossing the court floor, he took a seat right at the back on the elevated tier of the main public gallery; this would allow him a clear view of the courtroom and entrance area. Lynch came in a moment later and took a seat in one of the overflow side galleries and Noelie wondered again why he was attending the inquest.

Court 1, although refurbished and refitted with new audio-visuals had, furnishing-wise, been left largely as it had always been. The witness stand was up a flight of stairs; the coroner's seat was also raised on an elevation above the main floor. All the benches and the tables and galleries were made of dark wood. It was a dreary place, as Ellen had said.

The coroner appeared punctually at 2 p.m. He clarified that there was only one item scheduled for business and thanked the jurors for their patience and for returning to their duty.

'Detective Byrne, you were to update us on the log pertaining to Mr Twomey's mobile phone usage on the day he went missing?'

Byrne climbed the steps to the witness stand and placed a thin green folder on the lectern. She was immaculately dressed in a navy-blue trouser suit and an open-necked white blouse. When she finally spoke, she couldn't be heard.

'Speak louder please', said the coroner. 'Adjust the position of the microphone if you must.'

Byrne fixed the gooseneck microphone into a horizontal position and cleared her throat. The sound reverberated around the large courtroom. She seemed hesitant and clearly did not have good news to report.

'Unfortunately, coroner, I have been unable to locate the original correspondence log which was forwarded by Dream after Shane Twomey was reported missing. I apologise unreservedly to the court and the Twomey family for this. I will continue to search at the station but in the interim I have applied for a new copy from the provider. However, Dream was not in a position to deliver this to me as of 1 p.m. today.'

The coroner stared for a long moment at the detective and then cocked his head to one side. Byrne briefly consulted her folder before looking at the coroner once more. Noelie felt sorry for the detective. He was actually surprised too. Byrne's admission didn't confirm yet if the garda record was inaccurate, but the question mark over what was going on in Anglesea Street Garda Station was getting bigger with each passing day.

Taylor sought permission to speak but the coroner directed him to sit down.

'What do you think has happened to this document, Detective?'

'It appears that I have mislaid it.'

'That's stating the obvious.'

'Yes, Coroner.'

After a further difficult silence, it became clear that Byrne wasn't going to elaborate on the nature of the misplacement. Noelie noticed his sister down in the front row leaning over to speak to her husband.

'What have Dream indicated regarding a replacement, and when will they be able to provide it to this inquest?'

'We expect to have the document by the end of business hours today.'

'Can you guarantee this?'

'They understand the urgency of the matter.'

A deep, frustrated sigh emanated from the coroner. 'That's a no, I take it.' He dismissed Byrne, advising her that he didn't want to hear from her again until she had Dream's documentation to hand.

The detective descended the steps of the stand and left directly. The courtroom door crashed shut behind her.

'We will continue with the remaining witnesses,' announced the coroner calmly. 'Dr Canning, if you are ready, we will hear your evidence next.'

Noelie watched the pathologist climb the steps to the stand. It was the same woman he had found himself sitting beside the previous day – the one he had recognised but hadn't been able to identify. He had since remembered her name, Andrea Canning. She had been studying biochemistry when Noelie was at college – and had obviously changed disciplines in the interim – although the reason he remembered her had nothing at all to do with her academic interests.

Around 1985, the South African ambassador was invited to Cork to defend apartheid at a debate at the university. Although a protest at the college had been planned, a small reception committee headed out to Cork airport to greet the diplomat. It was one of the better-organised ambushes that Noelie had ever been involved in. Blissfully unaware, the ambassador had strolled out of Arrivals only to be set upon by a boisterous group of protesters. Andrea Canning had distinguished herself on the day by landing an egg on the side of the diplomat's head. Noelie could still see the eggshell and yolk dripping from his ear and cheek. A bullseye. Afterwards the ambassador never even got to speak at the debate.

She was still on the slight side, had light brown hair cut to medium length that was clipped behind one ear. She wore a nicely-cut suit over a silk blouse. After swearing an oath on the Bible, she put on her glasses and began.

At the same moment, the courtroom door flew open again and a young man entered. He was thin with black hair and was dressed in a dark Adidas tracksuit. It was Jim Dalton's son, Colin. He stood in the middle of the floor looking around; the coroner eyed him warily. Eventually the young man spotted Noelie, came up the stairs and sat beside him.

'How are they hanging?' he whispered.

Noelie put a finger to his mouth, nodding towards the pathologist who was now reading her testimony.

'Not such a big man out of uniform, is he?'

Noelie frowned. 'Who?'

Colin pointed across the courtroom at Lynch. He didn't actually agree, but he wasn't going to argue the point there and then. He put his finger to his mouth again. 'Ssssh,' he said gently.

Watching and listening to Canning's evidence, Noelie was drawn back once more to those days in late June.

'... the former Irish Distiller's warehouse along the north channel of the Lee, at approximately 6.10 p.m., a fully clothed young male was lying partially submerged in river water.'

Canning explained how initially the body had been left in situ until the area around was checked and examined. Once it was determined that the location had not been the point of entry into the river, the body was removed to University Hospital for a post-mortem examination.

'The cause of death I have determined to be consistent with drowning. The reliable signs to indicate this manner of death were present and visible at autopsy. First, the presence of fine froth in the lungs and air passages. Secondly, voluminous water-logged lungs. Thirdly, the presence of water in the stomach and intestines. There was evidence of some damage to the fingertips that was more pronounced than was normal. This could possibly be explained by attempts by the victim to maintain a grip on a concrete or walled surface.'

Hearing this piece of evidence, Noelie remembered his own near-death experience in Albert Donnelly's cavern at Llanes. If he had died that night, he imagined that this is what his own inquest would sound like.

A detailed explanation of the different injuries found on his nephew's body followed next. Evidence of rodent attack on the soft tissue of the face consistent with the body's discovery close to the river shore. Post-mortem marks on the back and buttocks consistent with being dragged on or along the riverbed floor.

'There was no evidence of any bruising or marking on the body or neck region consistent with attempts to restrain or restrict the breathing of the victim. There were no injuries consistent with the victim falling into the water from a height and suffering concussion.'

Canning paused, turned a page in her report and continued again. Noelie wondered how many times she had done this.

'There was no evidence of any alcohol being present in the victim's bloodstream. The victim also tested negative for a range of narcotic drugs. Analysis of the water found in the lungs is consistent with a fresh and salt water mix of approximately nine to one. This would be not be unusual for the Lee. In respect to the time of approximate death, I looked at this matter a number of times in view of its importance to the victim's family. The time is difficult to calculate with certainty due to a combination of factors. These are: the body's prolonged immersion in water and the inconsistency in water temperature and water constitution in respect of the repeated falling and rising of the tide level on the Lee. My best assessment is as follows. The time of last known contact with Shane was 3 p.m. on the afternoon of 23 June. The body was found at 5.12 p.m. on the afternoon 26 June, approximately a little over three days later. The optimum time the body could have been in the water was 74 hours. My own calculations suggest that the body was immersed in water for at least 48 hours and possibly as many as 72 hours. That completes the summary of my evidence, Coroner.'

Canning remained standing and the courtroom was quiet. If there were any doubts or lingering suspicions with respect to the cause of Shane's death, Canning had closed those down resolutely. Notwithstanding the confusion caused by the phone log and Detective Byrne's error, Noelie felt that evidential certainty had been re-established.

'Mr Taylor?' the coroner prompted.

The solicitor stood. He sifted through some pages on the table in front of him.

'Look at that fucker,' said Colin Dalton nodding over at Lynch.

'Jesus, Colin, leave it,' said Noelie. 'This is not the place.'

Colin Dalton gestured at the retired garda anyway. Others in the courtroom noticed, including the coroner. Either Lynch hadn't noticed, or he was pretending not to.

'You're in a courtroom,' repeated Noelie. 'Please.'

'As if I give a fuck. I want him to know I'm here. Have you ever seen his house? It's fucking huge. He didn't get a house like that on an inspector's salary. I'm telling you, that man's bent in two.'

Noelie put a hand on Colin's wrist and squeezed it. 'This is my nephew's inquest, Colin. Please, show some respect.'

Thankfully, Taylor began his cross-examination. He reviewed the marks on the body – where they were located and what might have caused them. The interrogation provided no surprises and Canning dealt authoritatively with each of the questions put to her. Noelie could feel the tension in the courtroom ebbing further. Canning was not in any doubt as to how Shane had died and she repeated this determination with considerable authority. She looked imperturbable ... until the very final line of questioning.

'What drugs were tested for?'

Canning opened her file. 'We screen for amphetamines, barbiturates, benzodiazepines, cannabinoids, metabolites and cocaine, methadone, the opiates, phencyclidine, propoxyphene and salicylates.'

'Did you test for gamma hydroxybutyrate and if so, what level was found in Shane's bloodstream?'

Canning's hesitation was a form of reply. She addressed the coroner. 'It would not be normal to test for gamma hydroxybutyrate, or GHB as it is colloquially known, in a case such as this. If some suspicion of foul play existed, then certainly the test could have been done but in this case that didn't arise. Normally we only screen for the range of drugs as outlined earlier.'

'I understand,' said the coroner. 'Mr. Taylor?'

'So, you did not determine if GHB was present, is that correct?'

'That is right.'

Taylor studied his folder again. Eventually he addressed the coroner. 'The question of what drug residues are tested for as a matter of routine here in the city is a matter of considerable importance. The Twomey family are understandably concerned that something may be missed. I wonder myself if economic considerations are at play ...'

The coroner frowned. 'Economic considerations, Mr Taylor?'

'The cost of testing. Budgets, et cetera.'

The coroner looked over at the pathologist. 'Is that a factor, Dr Canning?'

'Absolutely not, Coroner. A line needs to be drawn somewhere regarding any drug-testing regime. Otherwise we wouldn't be able to get through our workload. We take careful advice, in particular from An Garda Síochána, and we would certainly not cut corners. If a test is required, it would be done. It simply didn't seem required in this case.'

Taylor cut in immediately. 'All the same, Coroner, the family remains concerned that something is being missed. As an adjournment is planned, I request permission to return to this matter at the next sitting.'

'To what end though, Mr Taylor? It is clear that Dr Canning is following best practice. Are you suggesting that this is deficient?'

'Coroner, the family are at a total loss as to why their son drowned in the River Lee. With respect to all concerned, this is their very last opportunity to have their questions answered in any meaningful way. This is hardly an onerous request given the circumstances.'

The coroner glanced at the pathologist. He looked unhappy. 'I am loath to request that Dr Canning return for a third time, however I accept it is more important that this inquest addresses the questions that the Twomey family have in as much as that is possible. So be it, Mr Taylor.'

Dr Canning returned to her seat. Thanking the jurors, the coroner adjourned the inquest until the following morning at 10 a.m., pending news from Detective Byrne.

Noelie stood. Colin Dalton got up too. He put a hand on Noelie's shoulder to stop him leaving immediately.

'What?' asked Noelie.

'Lynch is hiding something. How many people do you know drive out to the car park at Tescos in Douglas, leave their car there and then get in another car and drive off in that? And he returns home by the exact same route. Now, don't tell me that's normal.'

Noelie nodded. 'That is odd. Any idea where he goes?'

Colin shook his head. 'No, but we could follow him sometime. We could meet up?'

Noelie thought about the suggestion. 'Okay,' he said, 'I'm interested. Just not right now. Another time?'

Colin looked satisfied with that. He nodded.

Noelie was about to leave but then held back again. He liked Colin Dalton but he also knew that he had a short fuse. Perhaps it was understandable given the appalling treatment the Dalton family had endured at the hands of the gardaí.

'Look, Colin,' he said, 'Lynch is an ex-cop. You know the saying, once a cop, always a cop, right? If you start running around after him, he'll do the same back to you. Just be careful.'

'I'm not afraid of him.'

'It's not about being afraid. Just don't have a bust up with him. You'll only be giving him what he wants.'

'He killed my dad. I won't be forgetting that any time soon.'

'No one's forgetting it, don't worry.'

Noelie finally excused himself, went down the stairs and over to Ellen. She was standing with Taylor and looked dazed. He gave her a hug. Arthur was nearby, talking to someone Noelie didn't recognise.

'Where are you going after this?' Noelie asked her.

'I think I'll go to work. I'm better off in the shop. It takes my mind off all of this.'

They hugged again. This time Ellen held him close and tightly.

Outside, he hurried down the steps and along the side of the courthouse building. Andrea Canning was on her phone, standing beside a silver Volvo station wagon. He went over. The boot was open and inside it was a set of perfectly folded yellow rain wear – the kind a fisherman might use – Wellington boots and boxes full of folders.

Recognising Noelie she smiled. A garda approached and positioned himself near Canning.

Covering the phone's mouthpiece, the pathologist said, 'Not necessary, John.' Noelie received a warning look anyway. Canning finished the call and placed her briefcase in the boot, closing it.

'Well, well,' she said.

Noelie smiled, nodding at the cop. 'Times have changed.'

Canning looked at the garda. 'Do you mean John? Oh, he's okay. He doesn't have much to do, I think. Anyway, I'm not surprised he thought my life was in danger given the way you were bearing down there. Still cultivating a dangerous look, I see.'

'No way,' said Noelie, feigning indignation. 'Anyway, how are you? I thought that was you beside me in the witness area yesterday.'

'I was surprised to see you too. Not pleasant circumstances though. I'm very sorry, Noelie. I'm sure it's been awful.'

'It's been bad,' he admitted. 'We don't know where we stand really. Maybe we will get some answers now. Look we must meet up though, sometime, have a coffee perhaps?'

Inconveniently for Noelie, Canning's phone began playing the opening to 'The Blue Danube'. She checked the number and said, 'Just a minute, I need to take this.' She opened the driver's side door, but didn't get in. When the call ended, she said, 'I'd like that. But I think it would be better to meet after this is over. Right now, with things in flux, it's not a wise idea.'

'Of course.'

Canning got into her car. She looked at him again, 'I'm very sorry, Noelie.'

10

At the library, a book launch was underway. A crowd had gathered close to the lending desk around where the author was sitting signing copies of her book. A promotional poster described the work as a 'solo travelogue through Russia's Arctic'; it looked interesting.

A computer eventually came available. Noelie searched for more information on the Wikileaks schism. Although it wasn't hot headlines, he found plenty of links to informative articles that all confirmed the bad news. Wikileaks was under unprecedented pressure since the release of the Afghan war documents in late July. The leak of classified documents was huge, in the region of 75,000 individual items with more to come. The USA was out to get Wikileaks, which was itself straining to function under its new-found notoriety. Named and unnamed sources also accused Assange of being difficult to work with and of making too many unilateral decisions.

They had miscalculated, Noelie realised. They hadn't looked beyond the headlines on the organisation and now it was quite possible that there could be a price to pay. Leaving the computer and the main lending area, he climbed the stairs to the reference section, then up again to local history. Katrina and one other person sat at the reading tables. Katrina looked engrossed, surrounded by stacks of broadsheet-sized folios. He received a quick smile and sat down beside her. He had forgotten that the Cork afternoon daily, the *Evening Echo*, had been a broadsheet back in the seventies. It was a format he liked, he decided; much more stylish.

He read a headline in an *Echo* edition that was open near

him. 'Catholics Satisfied With Army Protection' – it was a report on the deployment of the British Army to Catholic areas of west Belfast back in 1970 as the Troubles were getting started. He began to read the report but Katrina passed him a sheet of paper, adding, 'That's the good news there.'

It was a photocopy from an edition of the *Echo* from October 1969. She had highlighted the short paragraph of interest.

Clearing work was halted at the site of the new house-building programme planned for the Glen Heights yesterday after workmen discovered bones later determined to be human. Gardaí were called. It is believed that the remains were those of a child and they were later taken to the Cork city morgue.

Noelie read it again, hardly able to believe what he was seeing. 'Well done.'

'Found it after about an hour of searching, but there's nothing else anywhere at all. No follow up, nothing, nada. I've been back and forth through every paper six months on from that report. There has to be something more, but I can't find it. Been through your *Cork Examiner* too. That's what's taken up all of my time. I'm goggle-eyed from staring at column inches.'

Noelie was delighted by what Katrina had found. It was confirmation, plain and simple, of one important part of Irwin's account. There had to be more, somewhere. It stood to reason. If there was a record, then there might be a name. He told her this but she reminded him they were in the library and to keep his voice down.

She whispered, 'I rang the coroner's office, wondering if they could help. But they only get involved when a death cert is issued, which requires identification.' Katrina pointed to the photocopy. 'Right now, we don't know who that is.'

'The timing is right though,' persisted Noelie. He was not going to be put off. 'This is quite possibly the report that

Copley heard about, that spurred him to return to Cork in 1970. In fact, it has to be. Unless there were others?'

Katrina shook her head. 'That's the only find like it, of human remains I mean. I've looked over an entire three-year period and there's nothing else. They found other things during the works excavation, including a buried John Deere tractor from the 1930s.' Katrina rubbed her eyes. 'When I hadn't found anything after an hour of searching, I started to wonder. But then I had a lucky break. I found a photo that set me on the right track: a picture on its own, no article, of the site work at the Glen taken in the summer of 1970. In the photo I noticed that some of the house units were actually already constructed. I mean, that was a huge site of its time, right?

'For sure. It was one of the biggest building projects for its time. Certainly the biggest ever in Cork.'

'Anyway, I realised from the photo that the site clearance work had to have taken place much earlier than we had been thinking: back in 1969, if not 1968 even. So I started to look at earlier newspapers, and that was when I found that small report.'

'Any point looking again? One more time?'

Katrina nodded unenthusiastically. 'Maybe fresh eyes will do it.' She passed Noelie a folio. 'They come in three-month batches. Let's try one more time before closing.'

Noelie began looking. The *Echo* had been much more international in its coverage back then. There were in-depth pieces on the Vietnam war. He began reading an article about the My Lai massacre, only to be called to order by Katrina.

'Stay focused. Otherwise you're a waste to me here.'

Noelie found it difficult to maintain concentration. Column after column, page after page, paper after paper. It was tough work. Katrina used a ruler to guide her as she ran down page after page. In the end, they were forced to wrap up before completing their review as the library was closing.

Downstairs, Katrina asked if they could sit for a while in the fresh air before returning to the flat and they walked over to the boardwalk by the river. There, Katrina passed Noelie another photocopy: a profile of Leslie Walsh from *Business Ireland*, written in 1992.

'It's all in there about him. Might make more sense to you. A lot of the places mentioned in it don't register with me. He was in a seminary for a time. Farranferris. Maybe that's important?'

'That's an institution here in Cork. I nearly ended up there myself. Supposedly you got a fine education from them. It was a seminary college first and foremost and at the entrance exams they always asked you if you wanted to become a priest. You were supposed to answer yes, irrespective of whether you wanted to be or not. My dad warned me to say yes but when my turn came, I said no. Frankly the place gave me the creeps.'

'From what I read it's closed now.'

'In the late eighties, I think, it shut up shop. They were hit by the collapse in vocations.' Noelie looked at the article. 'Says here that Walsh made a big profit on land he purchased around the hospital and at the Link Road area closest to the hospital. Apparently these developers are often tipped off years in advance as to the city's development strategy. So they know where to buy, they buy cheap and all they have to do then is sit tight. Eventually *ker-ching*, *ker-ching*.'

Katrina nodded. 'Same the world over, Noelie.'

Where they were sitting, near the river, was breezy. It was nice though. There was evening sun and lots of people around too, many heading home from work.

Noelie watched Katrina. 'Tired?'

'A bit. But I'm fine.' She looked at Noelie. 'It all takes time. I know it of old, sometimes you have to do the long graft in the library to get anywhere.' She nodded to the article in Noelie's hand. 'No mention in there about Walsh having any connection with Danesfort. I guess there wouldn't be anyway. The thing with business magazine articles in general is that they usually soft-soap their subject matter. They don't often want to stoke any controversy. To find what we're after we're going to have to look deeper.'

They decided to return to the apartment. On the way, Noelie told her all about the Donnellys – now that their history was fresh in his mind having done the timeline. He remembered to tell her too about the demolition of the Donnelly home out past Ballyvolane in 1970.

'Seems to have been some year, 1970.'

'So maybe those remains found in the Glen in 1969 will turn out to be important. We just don't know yet, do we?' Katrina added.

As they approached the entrance of Hannah's apartment block, Noelie reassembled his main phone. A car passed slowly as he waited for the phone to go live and he noticed it pulling in close by. It was an unmarked cop car. He wandered nearer while pretending to check his phone. The car flashed him. Going over cautiously, he saw that it was Detective Byrne.

'Got a moment?' she asked.

'Sure.'

He called to Katrina that he would follow her up to the apartment, then he got into the car. Byrne didn't look happy and stared ahead. Noelie remembered her appearance at the inquest.

'Bad day?' he asked.

'That's an understatement.'

'Certainly didn't look good.' Noelie nearly added 'for you' but stopped himself in time. Ahead, up the street, a large crowd of pedestrians were crossing the road. They were nearly all young. Noelie guessed they were connected to the college; some sort of an orientation tour of Cork city centre was taking place.

'There's something up,' said Byrne.

'That much I know.'

Byrne didn't appreciate Noelie's attempt at wit. She looked annoyed. The only other time he had ever seen her look that way was following the discovery of Shane's body. The first time he met her, he hadn't liked her at all, but his relationship with her had improved with time.

'Leave aside what happened at the inquest earlier. Since August I've been frozen out at the station. It was small stuff initially and I didn't take much notice. But I haven't got any new work of substance in quite a while. It doesn't matter to me in one way as I hope to transfer out of Cork next year, but this latest issue with your nephew's inquest is different. I am as certain as I can be that I checked the mobile phone data the very first day I was put on the matter. I'm certain it was Turner's Cross.'

Noelie's phone rang – the one he had just put the battery back into. He glanced at it quickly and saw that it was an unknown number. He looked at Byrne again. He didn't really want to ask her if the document she had checked had been an original – it just seemed too obvious. It would be like asking a chemist if he used his finger or a thermometer to tell the temperature of a solvent in an experiment.

'It just looks terrible,' she added.

Noelie nodded; it certainly did. He decided against saying any more though. The question of who was right – Taylor or Byrne – would be resolved once Dream produced their data. For now he didn't want to be making Byrne feel any worse than she was.

She looked over at Noelie again, her expression softening somewhat. 'Anyway, the reason I'm here is that I want to say that if you need a hand or want something looked into, you can ask me. It can only be low level, anything on the q.t., but I'm starting to worry about that fucking station too. As I say, it's not just this inquest, it's the way I've been kept out of things in the last while there.'

It was a surprise offer and a tempting one too, and Noelie nearly said yes there and then. There were a lot of things that Byrne could help them with: the human remains found in the Glen in 1969, for one. It would be tricky for an ordinary citizen to find out more about that.

But he decided it was best not to let his guard down. 'I'm not sure what you mean, a hand?'

Byrne frowned. 'Oh come on, Noelie. I know you're looking into things. In fact, everyone does. That film? You think people aren't wondering. Don't be under any illusions that the crowd over in Anglesea Street don't know what you're up to. They're watching closely.'

Noelie shrugged slightly. It wasn't like what Byrne was telling him was news, but it was another thing entirely to fess up and admit to it. Byrne raised her eyebrows but Noelie's expression remained unchanged.

'Okay, but at least now you know the offer is there. Think about it. Use me if you wish, is all I'm saying.' She handed him her card. 'My private number is written on the back. And use your burner too.'

Noelie took the card. 'How'd you know I have a burner?'

'If you have any sense you have.'

As he got out of Byrne's car his phone rang again – the same unidentified number. He waved goodbye to the detective, then answered the call.

It was Martin's boyfriend, Ollie. He was wondering if Noelie knew where Martin was. Noelie told him he hadn't seen Martin since very early that morning as they left Baltimore. Martin had taken his own car and said he was driving directly to work. Noelie added that they were expecting to see him later, but not until 9 p.m. or so.

'He mentioned that to me,' agreed Ollie. 'But he was coming

to me here for a few hours, for tea, and then heading away again. He should have been here ages ago. His phone's not answering either.'

Noelie was making his way up the stairs. 'Hang on a minute, Ollie.'The apartment door was ajar and he pushed it open. He called to Katrina. 'Have you heard from Martin?'

She shook her head and then checked her phone. 'No missed calls either.'

The two looked at each other then – Ollie was still on hold. Noelie felt the first inkling of unease.

Ground Zero

11

The cafe at University Hospital was full. Noelie waited by a table he figured would be coming free and when it finally did, he cleared and cleaned it, moving it away from its neighbours so that he had a bit of privacy. Although he had caught some sleep during the night he was exhausted.

The previous evening felt like Groundhog Day. First the feeling of mild concern when he'd heard that Martin had been on his way to Kinsale in the late afternoon but hadn't arrived. Then calling Martin's phones – his ordinary phone and burner – and hearing both ring out. When they still hadn't heard from him after checking at his flat on Douglas Street, they drove out to where he worked – an IT outfit located in a business park on the western edge of the city.

The receptionist there told them that Martin had left work around 4.30 p.m. They asked if someone could check in case he had changed his mind and returned, but one of his colleagues confirmed that he'd definitely left. Noelie knew there were two main routes used to get to Kinsale from Cork and that the one via Hallway was by far the easier one to get to from Martin's work. They checked again with Ollie for news – there was none – and eventually decided to drive out towards Kinsale. They were both very quiet and Noelie knew something had happened. He was right.

The crash had occurred just before 5 p.m., about six kilometres out from Kinsale, where a long stretch of straight road gave way to a series of moderately sharp bends. There were no witnesses to the accident but it was suggested that Martin had lost control as he took the bend, crashing through a low ditch into a hollow formed by a small river stream.

A local woman, whose house was located a short distance from the main road, had found Martin. She had heard a loud noise and had gone to investigate. She hadn't noticed anything unusual at first – traffic on the main road was passing normally – but as she returned to her house, she saw smoke and steam coming from the hollow. She called an ambulance but there was a delay getting to Martin as petrol had leaked around the crash site. Luckily it hadn't caught fire. Martin was unconscious and had to be cut out of the wreckage by the fire brigade.

Noelie and Katrina reached the accident site around 7 p.m. Leaving Martin's workplace they had made good progress until they hit a traffic jam a short distance past Hallway. After enduring a long and torturous traffic diversion put in place to deal with the crash, they abandoned their car on a country lane and returned on foot to where they had seen the gardaí diverting traffic. From there they walked to the crash site, where Katrina liaised with a garda and gave them their details. When they were told the make and model of the car involved in the crash, their worst fears were confirmed. Noelie threw up on the side of the road.

There was nothing for them to do there; it was bleak. Eventually they contacted Ollie but he was unable to get to them, so they arranged instead to meet him at the hospital. They all waited together for Martin's arrival. He was brought in just before 8 p.m. and taken directly for emergency surgery. His parents and his sisters arrived from Limerick around 11 p.m. and his brother just after midnight. Noelie and Katrina had stayed at the hospital for a good bit, left again to catch some sleep and then returned first thing in the morning.

Meabh had flown in on an early flight from Amsterdam and Noelie and Katrina went to the airport to collect her. They told her more about what had happened and what they knew

– which wasn't much. Arriving at the hospital Meabh went directly to Intensive Care with Katrina to check on Martin's condition. Noelie didn't go with them: he already knew that it was looking quite bad.

Eventually the two women came in to the large café area. He stood and waved, and they made their way over. Meabh still wore her hair in a long French plait streaked through with different bright colours. She was wearing a tight leather jacket and jeans. As usual, Katrina was dressed almost entirely in black. Katrina looked drained.

Collecting a chair from another table, Meabh sat down opposite Noelie: she looked upset and pale.

'Couldn't get to see him,' she said. 'There's no change though, if that means anything.'

Noelie looked up at Katrina who had remained standing. 'I need another coffee,' she said. 'Anyone else?'

Meabh nodded.

'If they do anything like an extra shot, I'll have one of those too,' added Noelie.

After Katrina left, Meabh and Noelie stared at each other for a long time. 'I'm really glad you're here,' he said finally.

Meabh looked like she would explode. The previous evening when he had called her in Amsterdam to tell her about Martin's accident, she had let fly at him. Was it too much to ask that they should stay together and protect one another? How had Noelie let this happen to Martin? He should've known better – he was older, more experienced.

It was a broadside with expletives, the like of which Noelie hadn't been on the receiving end for a long time. However, before he could muster a reply, she apologised. It was wrong of her to blame Noelie and she was sorry. She was just angry; she didn't mean what she had said.

Her reaction didn't really bother Noelie. He found it hard to get offside with Meabh even when he felt she was wrong about something. Maybe it was to do with the fact that she had saved his life. And anyway, there was a grain of truth in what she was saying. Those proverbial warning bells had been sounding and red lights had been flashing but he had ignored them all. He didn't quite understand it himself.

'How did we let this happen?' she asked now.

He shook his head. On the way in from the airport earlier, he had told her the other bad news – to do with Wikileaks. It was very worrying, they had all agreed on that – not least because of the speed at which things had happened. Of course it might turn out that Martin's car crash been a very unfortunate accident. On the other hand, it was very possible that someone had forced him off the road at a particularly dangerous place. If it was the latter, they were all in imminent danger.

Noelie lowered his voice. 'Martin is the only one who knows where the other digital copy of the film is hidden. So now we've lost access to both copies. And Martin was the one who was in communication with Wikileaks. Apparently that's all password protected and not straightforward either.'

Meabh put her head in her hands. After a while she asked, 'Do we have a leak?'

'I think it's more that we haven't taken enough care. For example, Black Gary has new neighbours down Sherkin. Look, I don't know if it was them. They're young, not the sort you'd associate with Albert Donnelly, more cop types. They could easily have been watching and listening in. And we only found out that they were close at hand after we had spent the day talking about everything to do with our investigation. They could even have Black Gary's place bugged. It's wide open down there and he's away a lot too.'

'Where is Black Gary?'

'He's with a friend on the mainland for now and coming up later.'

'Does he know about Martin?'

'He knows. But not about how bad it is.'

Martin had received a serious head injury in the crash and, although there were other injuries that had not yet been assessed, it was the cause of most concern. If he survived, it was quite possible that he would have brain damage. The situation looked so bad Noelie had stopped thinking about it. In Sherkin the prospects for their investigation had looked decent. It was never going to be easy but there were grounds for optimism. Everything had now changed.

Meabh got up and went to the water fountain. She came back with a cup of water for each of them. They were both quiet for a while.

'We've really fucked up here,' she said, eventually.

He nodded. 'I know.'

He decided to tell her more about Sherkin and the meeting they'd had there. He had hoped to be reporting more progress, especially on boys A and B, but they still had a long way to go. He finished with the news about Katrina's discovery at the library. 'Human remains were found during site clearance work in the Glen in October 1969, not 1970. Which ties in with Jamesy Irwin's statement. It's possibly the same discovery that brought Copley back to Cork in 1970, which in turn led to the blackmail attempt. It's an important find.'

Meabh didn't look impressed and Noelie noticed. 'You don't agree?'

'Forty years, Noelie, that's what I think. That's a long time. It'll be very hard for us to do anything about something that happened so far back. I'm not saying it's not important, it's just that I can't see how it's going to help us find Albert Donnelly ... and that's what I feel we should be doing.'

Noelie shook his head in dismay. 'The past is important. It can help shine a light on what we are up against. Your very own situation is all caught up with the past, Meabh. Don't suddenly tell me the past isn't important.'

Meabh leaned towards him, her tone hard. 'I'm not the past, Noelie. What happened to me isn't the past.'

'I didn't mean that. It came out wrong. I'm sorry. What I mean is the past and present both matter.'

Meabh wasn't appeased and Noelie apologised again. He often forgot what she had gone through. She had told him only once about the abuse she had endured and they hadn't spoken about it again. He should have asked her more about it in Amsterdam, but he had bottled it. He wasn't sure how to talk about something so personal and so traumatic, but that excuse just wasn't good enough any more.

Meabh rubbed the back of her neck and kept her eyes on what was going on around them in the cafe. Noelie knew she was still upset, much more than she was letting on. Over at the cafe dock Katrina had actually made some progress. Noelie had already worked out that the cafe wasn't large enough by a long stretch for a hospital as big as this one. There were people milling about constantly looking for non-existent free tables.

'What do you think?' he asked nodding at the queue.

'About?'

'Katrina.'

'I like her,' said Meabh. 'She was great at Hannah's funeral. She took on a lot. I'm really glad she wants to help out. In case you haven't noticed, we need help.' After a pause she added, 'You're not so sure?'

Noelie shook his head. 'No, it's nothing like that. It's more what just happened.' He hesitated. 'Look I told her how dangerous this might be and I think she got it. I think she knows the risks. It's just when I was telling her, I was talking more in the hypothetical sense. I hadn't seen this happening the way it has.'

'Maybe Martin's crash was an accident, Noelie. Maybe we shouldn't jump to conclusions.'

'And you believe that, do you?'

Meabh didn't answer.

Noelie looked over again at where Katrina was standing in line. She was about to be served. 'No, I like her. I'm glad she wants in. And she was great in the library yesterday. Stuck with it. Meticulous.'

'A quality you admire in women of course, Noelie. Isn't that right?'

'Ah, fuck off,' he said.

'Just so as you know, she's spoken for.'

'Never crossed my mind.'

Meabh smiled. 'It crossed mine.' After another silence she said, 'I know the Glen stuff is at the centre of all this, I'm not disputing that, but what's happening now, what's current, might be the better way to go.'

'Romania?'

'Yes, Romania.'

Meabh's particular interest in Romania stemmed from her late father's connection to the country. A short while before he died, Sean Sugrue had signed up for a lay missionary assignment in Romania. Meabh hadn't been able to find out where exactly he was going but she had come to believe that this assignment hadn't been as innocent as it had first appeared.

In the year before his sudden resignation from the gardaí, Sean Sugrue had worked secretly on gathering information about various criminal activities inside the Cork gardaí. He had gone to the garda commissioner to outline his suspicions and had been stonewalled. Meabh's take on it now was that her dad wasn't going to Romania to fulfil a life-long ambition to serve the Catholic Church. She figured he was going there to find out more about Albert Donnelly's activities in the country. She hadn't any proof of this, but Noelie agreed it was a reasonable supposition. She had taken to calling her suggested strategy the Route 1 Approach.

They had talked quite a bit about the Romanian angle while in Amsterdam. It wasn't that it was a mad idea – far from it. For Noelie it was more about logistics and safety. Through a contact in the Netherlands, Meabh had acquired the name of an activist involved in rescuing women and children who were being trafficked, but they knew no one in the country who could help them. He felt it would be insane to head to Romania without there being something solid there, support-wise, that they could rely on. As well as that, a number of notorious criminal gangs were supposedly active there. They could easily end up in a confrontation with people with more resources and no compunction when it came to killing their entire group. On top of that, they didn't know if Albert Donnelly even had a connection to trafficking. Noelie personally doubted it. He didn't know for sure, but he believed that Albert's interests had more to do with the Catholic Church than anything else: his past undoubtedly held the key. But Noelie knew better than to go on about that to Meabh – Albert's story began even further back in time, in the late thirties and forties. If he went on about something that far back, she might let fly again.

'My mother's been in contact by the way,' Meabh said, suddenly.

'Wonders will never cease.'

'Exactly. She wants something, let's not be in any doubt there. I don't know what it is but it does present me with an opportunity. I'm certain she knows where my dad was going in Romania before he was killed. I'm going to squeeze that information out of her. And I bet Albert Donnelly isn't very far away from wherever it was my dad was going. Now that would be something solid to focus on, wouldn't it? Albert's lair.'

Noelie couldn't disagree with the logic, but he wasn't going to change his mind any time soon, and Meabh knew that. Coldly she added, 'Look, Noelie, abusers don't just pack it in because people get wise to their operations. They move elsewhere. Wherever Albert is, children are being harmed. Of that I have no doubt. That's what I want to stop.'

Katrina finally arrived with their food. 'I feel for the staff up there. That's one long queue. Non-stop service.' She passed out the coffees and Danishes. Looking from Noelie to Meabh and back again, she said, 'Something up?'

'Apart from everything you mean?' Noelie replied. 'Meabh, you explain.' Meabh quickly went over the conversation she'd had with Noelie.

'So,' said Katrina taking a sip of her milky coffee, 'you're asking for my view on whether we should focus on the past or the present?'

'Exactly,' said Meabh.

'It's a false choice, no? Both …'

Noelie rolled his eyes. 'A diplomat. Just our luck.'

Meabh spoke. 'You know, I've noticed something about you, Noelie. I noticed it in Amsterdam actually. When a man speaks you always listen. When I speak or Katrina here opens her mouth, you're jumping in right away before we are even halfway into what we have to say. Hear her out.'

'That's not true,' he protested.

'It is true.'

'I agree it's true, too,' said Katrina, 'so you're outvoted, Noelie.' In an overly patient voice, she continued, 'As I was about to say before I was interrupted, to the best of our ability we should keep all options open. Look, we cannot stop for a moment now. Particularly if what happened to Martin wasn't an accident. I think we should expedite everything. A couple of hours in Youghal might give us the name of the missing boy we are looking for. Kearny or Carney is a good start. With that we might have something solid to move forward with.

Noelie said nothing. He was still licking his wounds.

Meabh half-shrugged. 'Okay, I'll go to Youghal. I'll do the library work, but you're all on notice. You in particular, Noelie.'

12

Despite the coffee, Noelie fell asleep on the drive to Youghal. When he woke up, Meabh and Katrina were talking about Dublin as they had both lived in the city at one time.

The road to Youghal was familiar to Noelie. On his return from the States in '98, he had initially accepted a job with a pharmaceutical company in Dungarvan, the next main town east of Youghal from Cork. It was okay work, but the commute had eventually proved impossible – ninety minutes each way even when there wasn't congestion. In the States no one would think twice about that length of a journey to work, but in Ireland at that time it seemed daft. Eventually he found a different job in Little Island, not as good, but closer to Cork.

He tried to focus on that time of his life, to think about anything other than what had happened to Martin, but he failed. The scene of the accident came to mind again: coming along the road and seeing the multiple flashing emergency lights in and around the crash site from fire trucks, ambulances and garda cars. From the moment they had learned that there had been a crash on the road, Noelie had feared the worst. Yet, when the worst was confirmed, he just couldn't believe it or accept it.

He sighed heavily and caught Katrina's eye in the rear-view mirror.

'Feeling better?' she asked.

'Yes,' he lied, 'thanks for indulging me.'

Out the window he saw the flat grasslands and high dunes that indicated they were nearing Youghal.

'A question for you both,' said Katrina. 'These men involved in the abuse all those years ago … Just say we were to identify one of them tomorrow morning, what exactly could we do about it? Without proof we couldn't accuse him of dot. It's not like any of these men are going to put their hands up and say "I admit to everything".'

Noelie thought about the question and knew Katrina had a very good point. 'I guess it's why we need to keep our focus on this third man,' he answered. 'At least we have something solid on him. Although we haven't a clue who he is.'

'Let's look at what we know,' said Meabh. 'Father Brian Boran and Albert more than likely found each other through the Danesfort–Donnelly farm connection? The next person who we know for definite was an abuser was Leslie Walsh. I've been thinking about this as well and I feel that he could be the key person to focus on. Why? Because as far as we can tell, he had no link to Danesfort. Whatever his connection is to the Donnellys could be the key to us discovering how the other men got involved too. So, for example, was he a friend of Robert's or of the oldest brother, Tony? Had he been in school with one of them? Could it be as simple as that?'

Noelie addressed Katrina. 'Did you tell Meabh about the biog piece you found on Walsh yesterday? It said Leslie Walsh went to Farranferris. Meabh, do you know Farranferris?'

'I've heard the name but I don't know anything about it. I know this, though, that wasn't where he went to school. It was someplace else.'

Katrina asked how Meabh would know this.

Meabh gave a cynical smile. 'You forget I grew up with a lot of these people in one way or another. You know about my dad, right? He was quite religious. Both my parents were. After my dad's death, we were taken under Leslie Walsh's wing, in a manner of speaking. He paid for me to go to college in Dublin. Apparently, he was very fond of my father … It was a generous thing for him to do, as my dear mother has reminded me a hundred and one times. Anyway, Walsh came to my graduation and on a few other occasions when I was in Dublin he took me out to lunch too.'

Katrina was intrigued. 'What was he like?'

'He was fine. Very polite. Proper in a way. He used to actually ask me if I went to Mass every week. He wasn't over the top or anything, but he was serious. He had no idea that I was more in the mind to burn down a church than enter one. But I could tell he had that really cast-iron belief that by going to Mass you were helping yourself to stay on the right path.'

'Hilarious, isn't it,' said Noelie, 'given what we know about him.'

'I'll look into it more,' added Meabh. 'But I'm almost certain it's not Farranferris.'

'Odd it would be in that article then,' commented Katrina.

They were entering Youghal, passing the site of the old railway station. Youghal had been a seaside destination for Corkonians for many a year, particularly when the trains still ran from the city, and Noelie had been a couple of times. He had happy memories of the town.

They found parking close to the District Court. Noelie wandered over to the quay wall. The Blackwater estuary was wide; the sea grey and unappealing as far as he could see. Farther along, several trawlers were tied up. Youghal had once had a thriving fishing industry. Noelie reckoned it had lasted up until the seventies. He guessed there was only inshore fishing now.

Meabh joined him by the water. She put her arm around his shoulder and gave him a gentle squeeze. Then she whispered, 'Are your phones dead?'

'They are.'

'You know in August when we first saw the abuse film? At the hotel. I made a copy of the film with my camera that afternoon, remember?'

121

Noelie nodded.

'I still have it. I actually forgot about it. It's low quality as you know but it's not useless. It's in Amsterdam. For now only you and I know about it. Let's keep it like that, okay?'

'Okay.'

Noelie needed to talk to James Irwin soon anyway. The older man was now sitting on the only other good copy of the double-8mm film – the original hard copy. Now it was over in Australia, on the wrong side of the world.

They walked the short distance to the courthouse. It was an unusual structure, built from cut sandstone. The windows at the front were elegant, tall and round topped, perfectly positioned on each side of the entrance. Inside, it was thronged but eventually they located a court clerk, moving stacks of files from beside a desk to a room at the rear. He ignored them.

'Excuse me,' Katrina called out. 'Can we ask a quick question?'

'Everyone has a quick question.' The clerk indicated the paper chaos surrounding him. 'All this is just a quick question.'

'The court records for here from the fifties and early sixties. Where would they be?'

He pointed at the main doors. 'Dublin. That way. The National Archives.'

They looked at each another.

'What a grumpy fuck,' said Noelie loudly. The clerk glared and Noelie glared back.

Katrina wasn't surprised. 'Well it was a long shot. All court records are sent to the great metropolis after a set time, I understand. Probably not feasible to have them lying around here forever.'

'The library then?' said Meabh.

Katrina nodded. 'The library it is. If that gets us nowhere it'll be the Rosminians in Clonmel after that. Or to Dublin perhaps.'

'We'll all be dead long before that.' Noelie commented, but when he saw the unhappy expressions on Meabh and Katrina's faces, he added, 'Sorry, I shouldn't have said that.'

'Exactly, Noelie. We all need to stay positive here. What happened to Martin is terrible but we can't let it put us off either. We're going to catch these fuckers, right?'

Katrina consulted her notebook for the address of the local library. 'Church Lane.'

They walked in silence. Noelie was taken aback at the state of the town. Lots of the shop fronts were empty. Some looked as if they had been abandoned at a moment's notice. Whatever about Cork being on its knees from the financial crash, Youghal looked totally flattened.

Eventually, on a narrow side street, they found what they were looking for – a modest two-storey terraced townhouse. It was the old library building but it was closed. A notice pointed them to the River Gate Mall, which was back in the direction they had come, by the town's enigmatic Clock Gate Tower.

Most of the units inside the mall were empty too but the library looked bright and busy when they arrived. At the desk, Katrina enquired about the *Youghal Tribune*. She came back out.

'They don't have room here for the library's local history and newspaper deposits,' she explained. 'Most of it is back at Church Lane. We can go there and someone will be along shortly.'

They walked back to the old library to wait, and after about twenty minutes, a librarian arrived to let them in. They followed her inside. The downstairs area looked abandoned and had a musty smell but upstairs was different. Posters of Beckett, Joyce and Wilde dotted the walls and there were several tables in the middle of the room for laying out the newspaper folios for viewing and reading. The *Youghal Tribune* archive was arranged on a number of deep, tall shelves. It had been published between 1945 and 1957, when it merged with the larger regional weekly, the *Dungarvan Observer*. They were lucky. Another researcher would be along shortly. He was working on the town's Viking history. As he had permission to be in the building, they could stay as long as he was around. The librarian would check back with them later as well.

When they were alone Katrina sat and examined a folio. She cheered loudly. 'Bless the Lord, it's a weekly. That will cut down on our work hugely. And a weekly is often as good. It will probably still report on anything significant that happened in the area. Just with a lot less filler to wade through.'

Noelie and Meabh took their seats and discussed the search criteria. They were effectively working off second-hand information provided by James Irwin. Youghal Boy's family had apparently suffered some sort of a tragedy that brought them to the attention of the authorities and ultimately led to court involvement. The family was broken up and the children were dispatched to various industrial schools.

'It's not much to go on,' observed Meabh.

Noelie had brought his notes with him, and looked at these to see if there was anything he could add. 'Irwin believes that the family's name began with K and that it was Kearny or something like that – Keavney, Kelly even maybe. He thought that it could also be Carney with a C though. He's remembering a conversation he had over forty years ago.'

'Is his memory reliable?' asked Meabh. 'Sorry for being negative but it's worth keeping in mind.'

'We have to hope it is,' answered Noelie.

'A tragedy is what, a death?' asked Katrina. 'Would you use the word for anything less?'

'I don't think you would,' Meabh agreed, frowning. 'Have either of you read the Ryan Report, the survey on the Irish industrial school system? It's online now.'

Noelie nodded, but Katrina shook her head.

'Well,' Meabh continued, 'one of the things that struck me from reading that was that there were loads of ways to end up inside the industrial school system. Losing a parent to death or illness was an obvious way, but it could also happen if a child was caught stealing or playing truant from school.'

'That fits with what we know about Jim Dalton,' said Noelie. 'He was caught robbing from a shop. He didn't know his father, and his mother was considered a woman of ill-repute as she'd had Jim outside of marriage. He was taken from her and sent to Danesfort. To cap it all, she died when he was in there, making him an orphan.' He paused. 'I get what Meabh is saying though. Jim Dalton's case would not have warranted even a few lines in a local newspaper report. Maybe something would have been noted in the court reports section but perhaps not.'

'Worst-case scenario, we may have to go to Dublin and trawl through the court records there,' Katrina said. 'It's important to *believe* when you do research like this. The information is actually somewhere. It's about looking in the right place for it.' She added. 'What about when?'

'Irwin figured that the boy went missing in the early sixties,' said Noelie. 'Let's say between 1960 and 1964, okay? I think realistically this family tragedy will have happened before that – perhaps as early as 1950 but not much later than 1960. That said, we don't know if the boy was in Danesfort for long before he was sent to work at Albert's farm. Moreover, we don't know what age he was when he disappeared.'

'Can we, maybe, assume he was round about the same age as the two boys in the double-8mm film?' said Meabh. 'They looked to be about eight or nine.'

Noelie looked at Katrina for her view.

'It's a reasonable assumption,' she answered. 'At the same time, I think it's best to cast the net as wide as possible, initially.'

They took note of everything that resembled a tragedy: where the incident took place; who was involved; any children's names mentioned. Deaths from bicycle and car accidents featured strongly. Motor cars were new and appeared to have initially posed quite a hazard to cyclists and pedestrians. There were a number of house fires and a few farm accidents. They found just one incident involving a surname beginning with K, however it was a Kelly. It concerned a council worker who was caught stealing lead pipe from one of the supply stock yards and sentenced to three years in jail. In the short court report, the effect of the sentence on the man's family was raised. Leniency was appealed for and denied. The case was from 1951. They included it in their trawl, figuring that the jail term could easily have led to the family's impoverishment.

13

Beer cans, bottles and the remains of a bonfire were scattered around the car park overlooking Glen Park. Noelie could hear children shouting close by, having fun; further away, a dog barked.

'Odd place to have a meeting,' said Meabh.

'Not my idea, let me assure you of that,' answered Noelie. 'They've been searching over near where the Michael Egan remains were discovered in the summer. Maybe Oakes wants to show me something to do with that.'

They surveyed the wilderness that stretched below them. About half a kilometre in from where they were standing the park narrowed to a canyon before widening again on the far side. In the distance there was a duck pond and a playground, but these were hidden from view by a dense covering of tree tops. Despite the development all around – the noisy North Ring Road on one side, housing estates on the other – Glen Park retained an untamed, wild feel to it.

Katrina shook her head and looked at Noelie.

'What is it?' he asked.

'If I were blackmailing someone and I was trying to arrange the handover – the money or whatever it was for the blackmail merchandise – I'm not sure I'd agree to meet them down there. It looks bleak now. In 1970 it must have looked a whole lot worse.'

Noelie nodded. 'Definitely. It was off limits for a lot of people. I remember being warned by my ma not to go in there.' Noelie thought about Katrina's point. 'The blackmailers were certainly naive on some level and, as we know now, Albert was ruthless. Quite a bad combination.'

Meabh gave Noelie a quick hug. 'You better get going. We should too. We're heading out to my mother's next. Katrina's my bodyguard. What's your plan after meeting this Oakes fellow?'

'I'll probably go straight to the hospital to see Martin. Black Gary is there already, I think. Hopefully there will be good news.'

They parted and Noelie walked down the steep path into the park. When he reached the floor of the canyon, he heard the Glen River rushing unseen nearby. He continued in and met no one. The slopes drew in on both sides. Eventually he came to a security barrier and waited until a garda came over. He explained that he had an appointment with Oakes and was let through.

In July, when the search for Jim Dalton's remains was underway, there had been plenty of public interest in the Glen. The press, including a few TV crews, had taken up residence on the edge of the park. A small audience of onlookers kept vigil most days. From what Noelie could see now, there wasn't anyone else around other than for a few bored gardaí.

He reached a clearing in which a large white tent had been erected. A garda mobile unit was parked near it, a satellite disk protruding from its roof. A figure approached, wearing dark blue overalls, a heavy gardener's apron and Wellington boots. Noelie guessed it was Oakes going by the man's age: he looked about sixty. He had deep-set eyes and a bizarrely crooked face.

'I'm Detective Oakes.'

'Noelie Sullivan.'

They shook hands.

'Let's talk on the way.' Oakes went ahead quickly, turning just once to check that Noelie was following. They crossed the Glen River on a temporary footbridge and climbed through gorse. Not being as fit as the older man, Noelie felt the drag of the slope almost immediately. Oakes' pace didn't slow. Here and there, plastic steps had been put in place to make the going easier. Sections of the hillside were marked by white tape while other parts were cordoned off with yellow and red markings. Noelie had no idea what the different colours meant but he could see that a lot of work had been done.

Two thirds of the way up they emerged on to a promontory of ground nearly as narrow and small as a table tennis table. Four gardaí, gloved and in blue dungarees, were moving slowly up a marked rectangle of hillside about ten metres away. One struggled with an overhang of brambles, laden with blackberries. It looked like difficult work.

Pointing to a flagged depression higher up where there had been subsidence, Oakes said, 'That's interesting by the way. Take a look.'

Approaching, Noelie was assailed by a putrefying odour. In the hollow there was a decomposing animal carcass, now largely hide and skeleton, covered in maggots.

Oakes was pleased by Noelie's discomfort. 'We've netted some dead cats and dogs too.' He nodded up, smirking. 'My site office is above. Why don't we talk there?'

They passed through more gorse and arrived at another precarious clearing, a step higher on the hillside. Bizarrely, a red vinyl sofa had been positioned at the top so as to make the most of the view over the canyon below. Oakes sat on it immediately, patting the seat beside him.

'Sit here.'

Reluctantly Noelie did and found himself looking directly across at the Glen housing development, the area in which human remains had been discovered back in 1969.

'We found this sofa the day we arrived. Not in too bad a condition, is it?' said Oakes looking out at the view. 'I like to sit here occasionally and wonder why the fuck I'm doing this.'

His tone was as philosophical as it was bitter, and what struck Noelie, as he looked at Oakes, was how formidable the cop seemed to be. Noelie decided he definitely wouldn't like to meet him in an interrogation room.

'No luck then?' Noelie asked.

'What do you think?'

'Well, personally speaking, this hillside here wouldn't be my first port of call.'

Noelie received a sneering riposte. 'Oh fucking really?' said Oakes. 'Where would be your first port of call then?'

'Garda Headquarters.'

'Aah,' smiled Oakes. 'And how far do you think I'd get if I started poking around up there?'

'Wasn't it Margaret Thatcher who said, "Murder is murder is murder"? Shouldn't you be pursuing the investigation wherever it leads you? Even down the corridors of power?'

Oakes shook his head. 'That's never a good idea. Besides, I'm working off a statement made by James Irwin and, if memory serves me right, he didn't even mention the gardaí once as being involved in any of this.'

'The deaths of Irwin's three friends, Copley, Spitere and Egan, were directly connected to the existence of a film showing that boys were being abused out at the Donnelly farm. We know that one of those involved was Father Brian Boran who, as you well know, was forced into becoming an informer by Special Branch. He went on to become a high-level, highly valued mole inside Sinn Féin. So, do you really expect me to believe that there isn't a file or record of all this somewhere? Of course there is.'

'Look,' said Oakes, 'let's not waste time here. Anything like that will be protected by the Official Secrets Act so forget about ever seeing it.'

'Well, in that case, if there are matters that you are not going to delve into and there are questions that you're not going to ask, I don't see how you can give me grief about me wasting your time here.'

Oakes shook his head. He looked unhappy. 'I believe you've met Superintendent Kenny, Noelie?'

'I've had the pleasure.'

Noelie had met the newly promoted officer the same afternoon he was taken to view the body of Brian Boran. Apparently Kenny was one of a new cohort of garda commanders with experience in the army. He had practically threatened to have Noelie arrested when Noelie wouldn't hand over a copy of the abuse film. Noelie had not heard from him since.

'Well, Kenny is keen for me to bring you in for an interview. My feeling is he'd like to slap some sort of a charge on you – refusing to cooperate with a garda investigation or something like that. If I was after another stripe, that's probably what I'd do too. And there would be the added incentive of being able to give you a bit of kicking along the way as well.'

'You're strong on the old "hearts and minds" stuff, aren't you?'

Oakes didn't reply and Noelie glanced at him again. He wasn't sure what to make of the officer. While in Amsterdam, he had looked him up on the Internet. He had a reputation for success and the previous year had been involved in a long-running investigation into the murder of two sisters in Clare – the murderer had been tracked down to the Irish community in Chicago. More interesting was Oakes' involvement in the Nairac case in Louth, which involved the murder of a British intelligence officer who had been on a covert visit to the South during the Troubles. The Nairac case was another unfathomable quagmire in that it involved collusion between the gardaí in Louth and elements of the South Armagh IRA. Bizarrely in the Nairac case, it looked as if an element inside the gardaí had wanted to help the Provos.

'The only solid bit of information that we have to corroborate your friend Irwin's story are ferry records from 1970. We've verified that the men travelled to Ireland on 2 September 1970 on the *Inisfallon*. Came here directly to Cork from Swansea. There were no return bookings. We've since found a record of James Irwin and Michael Egan returning to England on the Liverpool ferry nearly a week later. So four men came to Ireland from England and only two returned there, which supports Irwin's story.

'That's significant, no?'

'Yes but it's not a lot to go on. The ferry records support the mathematics of Irwin's account. But what else have we? According to James Irwin, he made it back to London with Michael Egan. A while later Michael Egan disappears and is never seen again until his body turns up here in this park, forty years later. No one seems to be able to explain to me why he he was brought back here and not just killed and dumped in London? Have you any theories on that?'

'Only one, but I've no proof for it. I'd say Albert Donnelly had Egan brought back here so he could question him about what he knew and about whether or not there were others involved in the blackmail attempt that they didn't know about. After he had extracted whatever information he could get from him, he had Egan killed.'

Oakes nodded. 'That is plausible all right. To be honest, finding Egan's body could be considered a breakthrough if it was telling a story, but it isn't. We can't determine a cause of death from it. It's a dead end. The other bodies, where are they?' He added, 'That's not a rhetorical question by the way. Without those bodies, this case becomes almost impossible.'

'Which I suppose could explain why you've ended up here.'

'Well, Superintendent Kenny was very keen that we should take a look here. But that's probably optics. A point you'd do well to take heed of, Noelie. Thumbing your nose at the authorities is neither wise nor safe. Just saying now.' After a pause he added, 'We've to spend a few more days here and then we're done. Personally I don't really care. This case hasn't, let me say, caught my interest. Unless, of course, you have something more or new to tell me? If you want me to help you, you'll have to tell me something. Something I don't already know.'

For a second, Noelie wondered if he should give Oakes the benefit of the doubt. Down in Youghal they had covered plenty of ground but they hadn't turned up anything substantial either. There was another half day's work down there but Noelie wasn't as optimistic as he had been about the Youghal Boy angle. They would need to be lucky and he wasn't feeling like they were any more.

'I'm guessing you don't trust me?' said Oakes.

Noelie looked at him. 'That's definitely a consideration. Mind, it's nothing personal. Learning that Special Branch killed Jim Dalton has – how shall I put it? – rocked my faith in the organisation.'

The tension was broken suddenly by a scream of laughter coming from across the canyon – some young girls were rolling bicycle tyres or hoops down the steep hill then running along behind them. It looked like a crazy game, certain to end in injury.

'What about we trade?' asked Oakes.

Noelie looked at him. 'Okay, I'm interested. What do you have?'

'How much do you actually know about Albert Donnelly?'

'A bit,' answered Noelie. 'He's disturbed, I know that.'

'You had the pleasure, I heard.'

Noelie showed Oakes his fingernail-less finger. 'He did that.'

'Do you know he was interviewed by the gardaí about the death of his father?'

Noelie turned sharply towards Oakes, 'I didn't know that.

'Interesting, right?'

'Is it true?'

Oakes nodded. 'I did a little bit of digging and eventually got the name of a garda who was stationed at St Luke's Cross back in those days, in the late sixties. Station's gone now. He remembered the incident well. Old Donnelly walked into a slurry pit on the farm and drowned. Nasty way to go. Drink taken was the explanation. He was an alcoholic so he may not have had a notion of where he was wandering. Very possibly it was an accident.'

'What made anyone think it wasn't?'

'Albert was the only other person on the farm at the time.' Oakes paused. 'There was a housekeeper but she had been told to go home early. Prior to that there had been a bad row between the old fellow and Albert. Apparently they didn't get on and there was a rumour that Albert was going to be disinherited. Anyway this garda said that Albert would've been charged but for who he was and who his family was.'

'Robert Donnelly?'

'I guess. He wasn't high ranking in 1969 but I gather he was favoured in some way. It would've been a big thing to have his brother charged with his father's death. Even a charge of manslaughter against a serving officer's brother wouldn't go down well.'

Noelie thought about this.

'So, you owe me, Noelie. What about you let me see the film that's at the heart of this? That would be really useful.'

'That's what you want in return for what you just told me? It's hardly a fair exchange.'

'I just want to see it. I'm not asking for a copy of it.'

Noelie was suspicious. 'Why?'

'Can you let me see it or not?'

'Well the truth is, we've fucked up. We no longer have any copies of it.' He explained about what had happened with each of the copies. He lied about the hard copy and said they had destroyed it.

Oakes didn't believe him, Noelie could see that. 'I do have something else that might interest you,' he added.

He pointed towards the estates visible on the opposite slope. 'In 1969, the Glen housing project was just getting underway over there. During the site clearance work, human remains were found. There's a report in the local newspaper about it, in the *Evening Echo* to be exact. We've been trying to find out more about it but we've hit a blank.'

'What sort of a blank?'

'There's no coronial records about the find or about whose remains they were. Nor are there any other reports in the newspapers.' Noelie looked at Oakes again. 'We don't know if there's a connection between it and any of this, but there could be.'

Oakes looked over at the Glen estates. The troupe of girls with the hoops were on their way downhill again.

'You're selling me short, Noelie, but okay I'll take a look into it.'

They stood and Oakes put out his hand to shake Noelie's. Gripping it for longer than was necessary. 'You owe me one. I won't forget it.'

'I owe you half a favour.'

'Half it is then.'

14

Noelie found Black Gary in the hospital's quiet room. It was on the ground floor, a short distance from the lifts. The older man was sitting with his eyes closed on an easy chair beside a water fountain. Sitting beside him, Noelie listened to the trickling water too. It was surprisingly soothing.

A woman dressed in a pink dressing gown entered and sat in the corner farthest away from them. Noelie watched her. She looked quite sick and he was sorry for her. She closed her eyes immediately.

Black Gary rested his hand on Noelie's knee, and Noelie put his on top to hold it there.'He's bad, Noelie, worse than I had been expecting. Fuck. And he was in such good form when he came down to me on the island. Looking forward to seeing all of you again. When you and Hannah came to see me that day back in the summer, I knew I needed to help you. It was something I needed to do because I had been in an industrial school. But Martin was different. I don't think his generation really realise what went on. He was just finding out about things and had so many questions: Who did I remember from Danesfort? What happened to me there? Why were they so cruel to us? It was why he came down that bit earlier than you. He wanted to ask me all these questions.'

Black Gary went silent and Noelie thought about his own relationship with Martin. Day-to-day neighbourliness had brought the two of them together. Although they had adjoining flats in the same house on Douglas Street they were generationally poles apart – Noelie was born in the sixties, Martin in the eighties. However, after a series of break-ins on

Douglas Street, things changed: Martin's flat was on the ground floor and vulnerable so he regularly asked Noelie to look in on his place when he wasn't around. In time, Martin reciprocated.

Noelie had worked out early on that Martin was gay. The younger man had moved to Cork to strike out on his own and live his life. Martin never talked much about his life back in Limerick but Noelie worked out that his parents hadn't accepted his sexuality, though his father was much more problematic than his mother. His brother and sister were better about it – his sister, Shauna, in particular.

Noelie had picked up on the family tension the previous night at A & E. Martin's father had been pretty unfriendly, even though he and Katrina had told the family that they were good friends of Martin's. Ollie hadn't fared too well either, although Shauna had intervened and headed off a confrontation.

Noelie eventually broke the silence in the quiet room. 'Notice anything?'

'About?'

'This place.'

Black Gary looked around. He was pale. 'Don't know. What?'

'There are no crucifixes in the room.'

Black Gary looked again. 'You're right.'

'Now, who said we weren't making any progress in this country?'

Black Gary looked askance at Noelie. 'You did, actually'

Noelie put his arm around the older man's shoulders and held him close. 'Come on. Let's get out of here for now. Why don't we take a trip down to Blackrock? It's not that far. We have the address for Let There Be Light. If Martin could talk to us, he'd tell us to keep going.'

Black Gary agreed. 'He would say that.'

★

Black Gary was a slow, careful driver. On their way down salubrious Blackrock Road, they were overtaken by a series of irate motorists. He shrugged. 'City folk. Wouldn't be tolerated on Sherkin.'

Noelie was glad to see that the older man's form had improved. Black Gary also had news on the different seminaries that had existed in the Cork area in the fifties and sixties.

'There were three significant ones: Farranferris, Cloyne and the Vicentians. I gather Farranferris was the key one, although it closed in the eighties.'

'Katrina came across it in the biog she found on Leslie Walsh. So that's something too.'

'And geographically, it wouldn't be far from the Old Donnelly farm would it? I took a look on the map.'

The seminary in Cloyne, in east Cork, had closed in the seventies. Black Gary had found it difficult to find out much more about it. 'Seemed to be smaller and more exclusive,' he told them. 'Apparently the seminary building is still there.'

The final seminary of note was run by the Vincentian Order. 'Now this one's interesting. Guess where it was located?'

'No idea.'

'Sunday's Well. Only a stone's throw from Albert's home, Llanes.'

'You're kidding.'

'Part of the facility has since been acquired by the university. But the original seminary was on the town end of Sunday's Well, about half a kilometre closer to the city centre than Llanes. Ever heard of a Father Donal Gallagher?'

Noelie shook his head.

'Any Tickles?'

Noelie shook his head. 'What does that mean?'

'Gallagher was a bad bit of work. He was known by the nickname 'Any Tickles'. He was named last year in that report

138

on all the abuse in the Dublin diocese. The thing is, Gallagher also spent time in Cork – in fact, that's where he earned the nickname. Ten years in total. In the sixties, and again in the seventies. Serious allegations were made against him.'

Noelie shook his head. 'It's a cesspit, isn't it?'

'Sickening. I saw some pretty bad stuff going on at Danesfort, but you know it was mostly vicious physical abuse, nothing sexual really. At least, not to my knowledge.'

Noelie remembered something that Hannah told him about Leslie Walsh. A rumour had been in circulation that, back in the nineties Walsh had paid compensation to one of his victims to stop him going public. Noelie didn't know anything more about it, nor had Hannah. Apparently it was kept hush, hush, but he wondered if that was another angle to investigate? Hannah's old boss, Fiona, at the *Cork Voice* knew something about the matter and at Hannah's funeral she had offered to help – she was so upset over Hannah's murder.

He was still mulling this over when they reached Blackrock village. Checking the address, Noelie figured their destination was a bit farther on. However when they reached Blackrock Castle, he knew that they had gone too far. They went back the way they had come, then noticed a narrow lane about halfway between the village and the castle. They drove up slowly until, a short distance along, they came to a set of heavy wrought-iron gates. On one of the pillars was a shiny brass plaque that read, 'Let There Be Light'. The emblem with Jesus and the Tree of Life was underneath.

'Bingo,' said Noelie.

From what he could see, there was an old estate with dense mature woodland within the grounds. A sign read 'Private Property – No Entry'. The big gates were locked.

'We could jump it?' suggested Black Gary.

Noelie wasn't so sure he'd be able to. He went closer for a look, then pulled away suddenly on seeing a CCTV camera located on a tree just inside the gate. They agreed that going in by the main entrance wasn't an option. A builder's truck laden with bricks came into view at the far end of the road. It disappeared out of sight again.

'Site entrance?' wondered Black Gary.

'Didn't know there were any active sites left in the city.'

They drove up to where the truck had turned in. A wide opening had been gouged out of the old wall. There was no security around so they followed the truck. A short distance in they were able to rejoin the driveway coming from the locked gates.

It was quite the oasis. Trees lined the road, and there were park benches with plaques on them near the trunks. They passed through the small wood and arrived into a huge open lawn area with flowerbeds, pergolas, trimmed hedging and more seating. The driveway then turned sharply and they saw the main facility arranged in a shallow depression. There were three separate buildings – a new church, circular in shape with a central apex; a building with a part-raised flat-glass roof; and an older, more traditional two-storey building, painted gunship grey, not dissimilar to the main building in Danesfort and with tall narrow windows on both floors, symmetrically arranged on either side of an arched main entrance. Overlooking everything was an impressive, though much smaller, Rio de Janeiro-style Jesus with arms outstretched. A banner underneath proclaimed 'And God Said Let There Be Light and There Was Light.'

'Ground Zero.'

'This is it all right,' agreed Noelie.

'Not short bobs are they?'

'They certainly are not.'

They pulled in to the car park. It looked like it had been recently tarmacked and lined. There were two other cars parked there but it had the capacity for a hundred times that number.

'Are we calling in for tea or is this just a look-see?' asked Black Gary.

'Look-see, I feel,' answered Noelie. 'I'm cautious after what happened when me and Meabh called in to see Albert Donnelly.'

Although it was probably only nerves, Noelie did feel anxious. He wanted to look around but he was really wary too. From what he could see, there was a lot more to Let There Be Light. The question was, how would they be able to find out more?

They went across to the church, which was open and empty. It was quite the structure, with an elaborate circular altar positioned in the middle of a circular seating arrangement. Noelie associated the style with the more ecumenical wing of the church. He wondered if that was how Let There Be Light preferred to be seen: as an open, modern and enlightened body with its conservative heart lurking underneath.

Outside again they passed along the front of the flat-roof building. Through the window, Noelie saw an art room and a small library. There was a man inside in plain clothes. He saw them. Noelie pretended not to notice and told Black Gary that they had been spotted. They walked over to the building site next. It was substantial, sectioned off by a chain-link fence.

Farther on was a series of site notices and an unmanned security box. They went closer and as they did a large Land Rover drove past them at speed. It stopped abruptly and reversed. The passenger-side window came down.

'Can I help you?'

The man at the wheel wore a checked shirt with rolled-up sleeves. He was young, thirty or so, of big build with a treble chin. When neither Noelie nor Black Gary answered he added, 'This is a building site. You're not allowed in here.'

Black Gary was quick off the mark. 'We were wondering if there was any chance of a start?'

Noelie's heart sank – this man was certain to run them off the property now. After all, Black Gary was nearly sixty, Noelie heading towards fifty. Neither of them were builder's labouring material any more.

But Mr Land Rover didn't laugh. 'There's a very long queue and we have nothing at all right now. If you want to put your name in at the office you can.'

'Where's that?'

'Doonpeter. You'll have to go out there. We're not taking any names here.' The man waited. When neither of them moved, he insisted, 'You can't stay here. This is private property.'

When Black Gary explained that they had left their car across in the main car park the man looked surprised and suspicious for the first time.

'Sorry to inconvenience you,' said Noelie quickly. To Black Gary he whispered, 'Let's go.'

They walked casually back to their car and Noelie noted that the Land Rover hadn't moved. The driver was waiting for them to go out ahead of him.

As they fastened their seatbelts, Noelie also saw that the man from the flat-roof building was standing at the main entrance looking at them too. They left by the same route they'd used to come in. Outside the site entrance Noelie asked Black Gary to pull over. He got out. As he did the Land Rover passed and stopped abruptly once more.

Noelie gestured to the site notice they'd stopped beside. 'Just taking down the name.'

The Land Rover waited while Noelie wrote down the details in his notebook.

'Thanks again,' he called to the driver and waved. Getting back into the car he said, 'He's not taking any chances with us, is he?'

Black Gary shook his head. 'We must look suspicious.' He nodded towards Noelie's notebook with a questioning look.

'Just wanted to be sure about something, and I was right. The builders are Moroney and Sons.' Noelie paused. 'I went with my historian friend Ted Toner to take a look at the site of the old Donnelly homestead, out past Ballyvolane. The Donnellys still own the small bit of land that the house used to sit on. It's surrounded by a fence – quite a new one too – but the sign on it said Moroney Fences and this lot here are Moroney and Sons.'

15

Back at Hannah's apartment they met Meabh and Katrina, who had returned from the hospital with the news that Martin was out of surgery. They had been able to see him but only from the door of Intensive Care. He was still on a ventilator and hadn't regained consciousness. According to Martin's sister, Shauna, his condition remained critical.

'We couldn't even see his face,' reported Meabh flatly. 'His head was almost entirely wrapped in bandages ...' She shook her head.

Katrina added, 'They were a bit more hopeful, I thought. More surgery is planned tomorrow. That will tell a lot.'

The mood was sombre. Black Gary insisted that he needed to stay busy and offered to cook the dinner – there weren't any objections. There was a large supply of canned tuna in Hannah's cupboards, and he figured he could do something with it. He tried to make a joke of why she had so much tuna in the house, but no one was in any mood.

At the window Noelie watched him cross Washington Street, heading for Centra to buy some other bits and pieces for dinner. A few days earlier he had been optimistic: their arrangement with Wikileaks gave them protection and they'd had good leads to follow. He had never thought it was going to be easy but Black Gary had assured them it wouldn't be that hard to identify the boys in the film – particularly if he made enquiries through the extensive networks of industrial school survivors. But that had turned up nothing in the end and they were also a long way from working out the identity of this third man. Even with Youghal Boy it was going to take a lot longer than anticipated – a stint in Dublin at the National Archives, or worse still to the Rosminians in Clonmel. The investigation could easily stretch out into weeks of work.

Had Meabh been right after all? Maybe Romania should be the focus? If they could find Albert Donnelly they would reach the heart of the matter. It would be high risk though. He had a network of some type protecting him; they had no idea what that network was or who was in it.

As soon as Black Gary had dinner underway Noelie collected their mobiles and put them in the bathroom. He put on The Fall's *Live At The Witch Trials*, but Black Gary complained that it was depressing. Noelie suggested a Cowboy Junkies album instead – it had been a favourite of Hannah's – but this got voted down as being ineffective as background noise due to its moody melodic. Eventually he chose a Bronski Beat CD and put that on.

'For Martin,' he said and Meabh smiled, acknowledging the choice.

They settled in a circle to eat their food. Noelie told the others about his encounter with Oakes at the Glen and what he had learned about Albert's suspected involvement in Old Donnelly's death.

Katrina shook her head. 'That family is seriously fucked up.'

Noelie reviewed what they knew. 'Old Donnelly had two children, Tony and Robert, by his wife, Clara. She died along with her third in childbirth sometime in the mid-thirties leaving Donnelly a widower. We know that in 1936, he travelled to Spain and fought for Franco, losing a leg in the process. Sometime later we believe he was offered a child to adopt and rear as his own – this was Albert. We don't know if this was some sort of payment in kind to him or if it had more to do with Albert being given up to an upstanding family to be raised as a good Catholic.'

'Could have been both reasons,' suggested Black Gary. 'Kill

two birds with one stone and all of that.'

'Very possibly. Meabh's mother also told us something important when we confronted her in August. She said there was a question mark over Albert's birth or origins. That's as much as we actually know but one thing seems clear: Albert's childhood at the farm under Old Donnelly's rule was not good. To me it sounds like Old Donnelly rejected him and made his life a misery. Meabh's mother implied it was even worse than that and that Old Donnelly regularly humiliated Albert. He also appears to have involved his older sons in Albert's humiliation. To put it mildly, Old Donnelly sounds rightly fucked up.'

'He was a fascist,' stated Meabh bluntly. 'Do we need to say more?'

Noelie continued, 'Basically Albert had motive aplenty to point his father in the direction of the slurry pit.'

'Was that how Old Donnelly died? In a slurry pit?' Black Gary winced. 'Not nice.'

'So where does this get us, knowing this?' enquired Katrina. She was sitting comfortably on a beanbag eating her food; she had also acquired a beer. 'I'm not trying to be smart by the way, I'm just trying to work out where we can go with this information.'

Noelie shrugged. 'It's just another piece of the jigsaw. Sometimes we find two pieces of information that actually fit together and it moves us on quite a bit … but that's rare enough. It's slow progress.'

Black Gary was sympathetic. 'We lack a good source for that time. Someone who was there at that farm during those years. Without that we are at a big disadvantage. We're looking at stuff forty or more years ago, now. Things vanish easily in the fog of time.'

Noelie told the others that Toner, the elderly historian, was on the lookout for someone who might be able to help them.

'If anyone can dig someone up, he can.'

When they had all finished their food, Noelie collected their plates and put them beside the sink, then got himself a glass of water. When he returned, he noticed that Meabh was looking impatient. He had spent a good bit of time with her in Amsterdam and had got to know her better. She was quite positive but occasionally, when she slipped into her own world, she could get irritable and wasn't easy to be around. Sometimes that was helpful in that it drove them on. The downside was that she took risks, and not always the wisest of ones either – as Noelie knew to his cost.

'So give me another piece of the jigsaw' said Katrina.

When no one else replied, Noelie said, 'Well, something Meabh and I were thinking about has to do with the blackmail attempt in mid- to late-1970. You kinda got me thinking more about that again actually, Katrina. You were saying that Albert's response to the blackmail attempt was pretty violent – let's face it, it was vicious. So, what do we know about all of that? Well, we know that the blackmail was orchestrated by four ex-industrial schoolboys. They acquired an amateur home movie showing the abuse of boys at the Donnelly farm. The subsequent blackmail attempt was largely motivated by a desire to get quick money and revenge on Albert but, as we know, it went tragically wrong. Two of the blackmailers were murdered, a third was hunted down and then killed. Only our good friend Jamesy Irwin escaped and he was so traumatised he went into hiding and wasn't heard from for almost forty years. The significant part of all of that–'

Katrina interrupted, shaking her head, 'That wasn't the significant part?'

'Well, it was but there's more. This botched blackmail attempt coincides with the creation of the mole/informer codenamed 'Brian Boru' inside Sinn Féin. Note Sinn Féin *not* the IRA here. Two different things.' He smiled. 'Well, kind of.

Anyway, Brian Boru goes on to become a highly valued asset – I think that's the terminology used – in Special Branch's espionage arsenal. The mole is inside Sinn Féin from its earliest days. With time he becomes a trusted member of the party's inner circle, above all suspicion. The entire time he's feeding information to Special Branch. Through the seventies, eighties, nineties. Right up until recently in fact.' Noelie shook his head. 'That's in part why Hannah was murdered. Branch didn't want to lose such a valuable commodity, and I think that was one of the reasons why they let Hannah walk calmly to her death when they could have intervened and saved her. Brian Boru was someone of very high value. His origins however are in and around the time of the failed blackmail attempt.'

Katrina nodded. 'Interesting.'

'So what do we know about these origins?' continued Noelie. 'As a concept, Brian Boru was Robert Donnelly's idea. In fact for a number of years Robert Donnelly was his handler in Cork. Later, when Brian Boru's significance was acknowledged by Dublin, they took control of the asset. But for a long period of time he was Robert Donnelly's responsibility and one of the reasons why Donnelly rose to a high rank inside Cork's gardaí so quickly. So we know that Brian Boru was Robert Donnelly's idea – Albert confirmed that. But how did this idea to create the mole Brian Boru come about?'

After a pause, Noelie continued. 'At first we thought it had to do with Robert Donnelly simply knowing or discovering that Father Brian Boran was a child abuser. See, in the late fifties and early sixties, Father Boran seems to have been a regular visitor to the Donnelly farm. Maybe he was involved with escorting boys from Danesfort to the farm to help with farm labouring and other activities, and took advantage of that situation.'

'By the way "help" is not quite the right term, Noelie. "Ruthlessly exploit" would be more accurate,' said Black Gary sourly.

'Duly noted. We believe that it was during these visits to the farm that Father Boran and Albert became close. We don't know any more than that, but certainly it seems that there was some sort of bond between them.'

'As in, an item?' asked Katrina.

Noelie shrugged. 'Don't know the answer to that.'

Meabh cut in. 'Highly unlikely in my opinion. It was cerebral. Struck me as church stuff and all of that. But Noelie is right: the two were close. Just the way Albert talked about Father Boran, it was ... there was respect.'

Meabh repositioned herself on the sofa, tucking her legs under herself. 'We talked about this a lot in Amsterdam,' she continued, 'trying to work out what had happened, what had precipitated the decision to force Father Boran into turning informer. One thing we do know is that by 1970, Father Brian Boran has changed his identity to Tommy Keogh. This appears to have followed on the heels of the Rosminians kicking Father Boran out of Danesfort in 1965 because of multiple complaints about him abusing boys. They sent him to Newry in Northern Ireland, and whether it was that town didn't agree with him or something else happened, he moved on to Belfast. But in the move, or shortly afterwards perhaps, he changed his name to Tommy Keogh and was no longer a Rosminian as such. He told us, for what that's worth, that he was very happy in Belfast then. He joined Sinn Féin in the midst of all the sectarian violence that was kicking off in Belfast around this time for, he claims, entirely honest reasons – to help the party. As he said, he was in the process of remaking himself, leaving his sordid past behind. Or so he claimed to us. Personally I have my doubts.'

'Me too,' agreed Noelie.

Meabh continued, 'Anyway, the simple answer that might explain the origins of Brian Boru, is that Robert Donnelly possibly just availed of an opportunity that came his way. He recognised and knew that Father Boran was compromised due to his abusive past and also knew about his change of identity and new life and so on, including his membership of Sinn Féin. He added two and two together and said, "You know, maybe I could make use of this man in the great war against Irish republicanism". The rest then, as they say, would be history.'

'It does seem like a plausible explanation,' said Black Gary.

Noelie shook his head slowly. 'We thought so too but then came around to thinking not. For one, Boran was living in Belfast and had been well out of Robert's Donnelly's eyeline for quite some time. As well as that, Father Boran – aka Tommy Keogh – was a nobody in Sinn Féin in 1970. In fact Sinn Féin were nobodies too. The party was only in its infancy then, and wouldn't pose a real threat for a good while yet. Another thing is this: Father Boran was trying to escape his past but it was not like he was a mass murderer or anything like that. He had beaten the shit out of a few boys at Danesfort. Big deal. Where Boran/Keogh did have something to hide was the sexual abuse of boys at Danesfort. That was – how shall we say? – unsavoury, and Rosminians moved him on because of that. But remember, Boran was never convicted of anything, never mind serious crimes of abuse. Even acknowledging such crimes, let alone securing the conviction of any perpetrators, was, in 1970, still a long way off. You really have to get to the late-nineties, and this decade actually, the noughties, before you see crimes of sexual abuse really being taken as seriously as they deserve. So, the conclusion we came to was that in 1970, Boran wouldn't have jumped out at Robert Donnelly as being the potential great informer he later turned out to be.'

There was silence.

'An option we started thinking about,' said Meabh, 'was whether Robert Donnelly had found out about these Glen murders. Now that would've been leverage. Say in the process of learning about the murders, he also learned about the existence of these amateur films documenting the abuse of children at the farm. Now we are into a much different business, for all concerned.'

Noelie added, 'If Robert learned of the murders, he suddenly had Albert over a barrel and a number of other people too. Including Boran. Robert could, if he wanted to, have all those people locked up until the end of their days for these killings. But he had a very good reason not to do that. If he brought a sordid matter like this out into the daylight his reputation, and that of his family, would be damaged as well. There would be no way Robert could escape without being tainted too. So, he plays thing carefully. Now he has a way of keeping Albert in check. If, as we now know, Albert was a suspect in his father's death then clearly there could've been serious tension between them anyway: a brotherly rivalry further poisoned by how Albert was treated as he grew up. So Robert could have had a real interest in getting something over Albert and keeping some sort of control of him. And now he gets it, via these killings and what he learns about them and about Albert. Furthermore he also catches Boran in the net too. His value is only realised in time as Sinn Féin begin their ascent to greatness.'

'Not wanting to rain on anyone's parade here,' said Katrina, 'but the evidence for all of this is?'

Meabh frowned. 'No direct evidence, as such. What set Noelie and myself to thinking along these lines was the comment Albert made to us the night he was going to bag us up and sink us in the high seas. He said that Father Boran, or Father Brian as he referred to him, had returned to Cork to help him with a problem. He implied it was a serious problem. For me the blackmail attempt comes to mind – that was a very serious problem. We know also that Albert had a few people in the Glen the night he murdered Copley and Spitere. So, was

Father Boran one of those directly involved in the killings? Albert added also that it was at this time or during this visit by Boran to Cork that Robert betrayed him. I couldn't see Albert's face when he admitted this. I was on the floor all tied up but he said that Robert had abused his trust, or words to that effect. And he said it bitterly too.'

Noelie nodded. 'It strikes me that what happened was that Albert sorted out one problem, the blackmailers, only to find himself lumbered with an entirely different one – Robert now knew what he was up to.'

'A question then,' said Katrina. 'How much do Special Branch know about all of this? If Brian Boru was created at that time and as a result of the fallout from the botched blackmail attempt, would they know about the 1970 murders? Would they also know about the abuse at the Donnelly farm?'

'That's the big question,' answered Noelie. 'Robert Donnelly wouldn't have wanted to expose the abuse at the farm. On the other hand, he would have had to prove to his bosses that he had something serious over Father Brian Boran. The abuse films are central in their own way. One of them was in Robert Donnelly's possession for some time. We know this because that film went on to become part of the whistle-blower file compiled by Sean Sugrue.'

'I feel Branch definitely know about the film and what's on it,' stated Meabh. 'When we threatened to publish it in August, they backed off like their hand had been bitten by a Rottweiler. I mean, they couldn't do enough to placate us. At the time – remember, Noelie? – they were trying to fit you up for the murder of that Don Cronin guy. That all mysteriously disappeared too in a puff of smoke, as they say.'

Katrina got up and changed the music to the Talking Heads' album *Remain in the Light*.

'Good choice,' said Noelie. 'That music always lifts my

spirits, and they certainly need lifting right now.'

Katrina sat again and said, 'What you're talking about – moles in Sinn Féin, informers and Branch and all of that – well, it seems to fit with my own thinking that we're dealing with professionals here. It seems to me that someone was listening in on us down on Sherkin. And Martin's accident is looking too inconvenient for us to have been just an accident. Which makes me think the opposition isn't quite Albert league. It's better organised, resourced and more focused.'

'I'm thinking that way too,' said Meabh.

'Me three,' said Black Gary. 'Look, I was naive about those people who moved in. I've seen people come and go at the marine station over the years and he just seemed like one of them too. I didn't look closer.'

'We don't know it was them,' clarified Katrina. 'I think we all just need to be super vigilant now.'

'I should 'fess up then,' said Noelie. 'I gave Detective Byrne a call – the detective from the inquest. You remember, Katrina, the evening of Martin's accident she came by? She's been getting the cold shoulder treatment down in Anglesea Street Station. Some of it to do with the fallout from the Jim Dalton affair in the summer. She's also copping it over this error in the mobile phone record in Shane's inquest. Anyway, to cut a long story short, she said if we needed help, to give her a shout. I told her about Martin's accident and that we were trying to find out some more about what happened. There will be a crash investigation report, although it won't be available for a while yet. But she said she'd go down to Kinsale Garda Station in the morning to ask some questions on our behalf. We might find out something. Right now we know fuck all.'

'Is she trustworthy?' asked Katrina.

'We have to hope so. Anyway it's not as if I'm letting a lot out of the bag by telling her what we think may have happened to Martin.'

'An awful pity that we couldn't call over to Llanes for tea and a chat with Robert Donnelly,' said Black Gary. 'Methinks he has the entire story in his head.'

'In his very confused head,' clarified Meabh.

'What does he suffer from?' asked Katrina.

'Parkinson's, I think,' answered Noelie. 'Maybe dementia. He has a maid and a minder, the works, looking after him now. Who says crime doesn't pay?'

'Do you think you could get any more information from Oakes, Noelie?' asked Meabh. 'I mean if he has a source in the gardaí from back in the late sixties, that person may know a lot more.'

'He said he'd look into this matter of the remains found in the Glen. I guess we could give him a nudge in a day or two.' Noelie thought about the cold case officer. 'You know, Oakes didn't dispute that Branch have a stake in all of this. When I suggested that he should be taking a look at the files in the Phoenix Park marked "Brian Boru", he just laughed at me and more or less said he wouldn't get very far if he tried. Honestly, it amazes me how easily people dismiss a crime once it's covered by the Official Secrets Act.'

Black Gary spoke. 'He's just like a lot of people, Noelie. He's knows what's good for his career and what isn't. He'll have been told about this Brian Boru angle and warned to steer clear of it and he probably will too.'

The constant tension was exhausting and they all felt it. Black Gary made tea and served it.

'Can we get better biscuits?' asked Noelie holding up a nearly empty packet of Digestives.

'You buy them, so,' said Meabh.

'I'm on the dole. I can't be seen buying luxury biscuits. It would be in the *Indo* right away. Can't you see the headline? Above a picture of me choosing All Butter Triple Chocolate-Covered Cookies, the headline "Doley Seen Buying Luxury

Biscuits – Have We Exaggerated the Impact of Austerity?".
Do you know how many are on the dole in this city right now?
Forty-seven-fucking-thousand. And Anglo Irish Bank is still
haemorrhaging money. Too much.'

Black Gary put his hands up, halt style. 'Enough. I can't
handle that now. Although I do agree on the biscuits: I'm a
Mikado man myself.'

The discussion turned to Meabh's visit to see her mother.
Noelie looked over at Katrina. 'Did you have the pleasure?'

'I stayed in the car. I was sort of on-call. If Meabh needed
me, I was ready to come running but I was hoping she wouldn't
and didn't. I'm sure there will be another occasion.'

'She's a cold bitch,' Meabh stated bluntly. 'Not so much
as a "how are you?" or anything from when we last met.
Remember, Noelie?'

Noelie remembered well. He and Meabh had gone to see
Mrs Sugrue to confront her about the Donnellys. Meabh
had demanded to know why her mother hadn't done more
about finding out who had abused her at Llanes. They'd got
nowhere. Mrs Sugrue would admit to nothing. Noelie was
sorry for Meabh. Not only had she been abused, but her own
mother had betrayed her in the worst possible way – that had
to be one of the worst things to come to terms with.

'As I surmised, she wanted something. She wants us to
meet the Walshes. Or more accurately they want to meet us.'

'The Walshes,' said Noelie. 'As in, the family of Leslie Walsh,
the developer? What would they want with us?'

'My mother wouldn't say. She was woefully paranoid about
the entire thing though. Which was amusing to witness. I
wasn't to tell anyone about this either. Well, I was allowed tell
you, Noelie.'

'I knew she'd fall for my charm one day.'

'What do they want?' asked Black Gary.

'My mother didn't seem to know. Genuinely. She's

emotionally and spiritually indentured to the Walshes anyway so it's not like she would be questioning them or anything.'

Noelie was feeling restless again. He went to get a glass of water.

'Is it legit?' asked Katrina.

'I think so,' said Meabh. 'Leaving aside their Catholic faith, the Walshes are serious business people. They have plenty at stake here. My own thinking, but I've not got anything to back this up with, is that they may be worried about what could come out about their father.'

'The film again,' said Black Gary.

'Exactly,' agreed Meabh, 'that film has made a lot of people very nervous.'

'How Catholic are these Walshes?' asked Katrina.

'Very. Noelie saw it for himself when he attended the month's mind service in July with me. They're true believers. There's four children and I wouldn't be surprised if they are all practising Catholics too. No black sheep among that lot.'

'Is there anything in this for us?' enquired Katrina. 'Say with Let There Be Light? It could be worth meeting them in the first instance anyway. We need to find out more about that organisation.'

'I agree,' said Meabh. 'I think this is worth following up, if only to see what they want. It could give us some clue as to the lie of the land.'

'Okay,' nodded Noelie.

'It's you they want to meet by the way, Noelie. In Peter and Paul's tomorrow.'

'In the church? Why there? Bit odd, no?' said Noelie. He knew Peter and Paul's. Admittedly it was very central, just off Patrick's Street.

Black Gary winked. 'Maybe they'll try to convert you?'

'I'm feeling vulnerable but not that fucking vulnerable.'

'It will be one of the Walsh sons also. You know that business about God creating woman from a man's spare rib and what that all means et cetera? Well, my mother and the Walshes believe that shit. So this meeting will be "man-to-man".'

Meabh looked knowingly at Katrina who just smiled.

They stopped a short while later. It had been a long day, but Noelie knew he wouldn't be able to sleep. He had heard about a local punk band playing at Fred Zeppelin's – the drummer was often in Solidarity Books – and he knew they were good. He asked if any of the others were interested in going along.

Meabh shook her head. 'Count me out. I had an early start this morning, remember?'

Black Gary declined too, but Katrina was all for it. 'If I'm going to die soon I might as well make the most of life and live now. Right?'

'Not funny,' said Black Gary.

'No, I guess not.'

There was a small crowd at the upstairs venue, made up of people around Noelie's age, most of whom had gone bald, and a younger more energetic crew with Mohicans and spiky hair. It was how the punk scene was now: the old crew trying to reconnect with a musical experience from a long time ago and a much younger, newer fan base that was creating the tradition anew. As was proved by the support band: an all-woman group wearing t-shirts with 'Repeal!' written across them in punk typeface.

Noelie felt his tension easing. Every song the support band played was political, which was just what he wanted. The Celtic Tiger. The crash. The plight of asylum seekers. Anglo Irish Bank. Granard. Austerity. All the issues got the treatment at a high-octane pace. Whoever was writing the lyrics had talent. The crowd loved the band.

'Total energy,' Noelie declared happily when they finished.

Katrina looked like she had enjoyed it too. They were both covered in sweat. They went downstairs during the break for a pint.

'Hannah said a few times that you were an old punk, Noelie.'

'More in spirit I guess. She was one herself, of course.'

'She didn't deny it.'

Noelie got a Beamish and Katrina a Murphy's. 'So, did she say anything else compromising about me? Nothing too damning please.'

They toasted Hannah and for a moment the reality that she was dead struck them both. They were quiet for a while.

'She liked you a lot,' said Katrina and, after a pause, glanced at him. 'She always described you as a good friend though. I asked her once if there was going to be more and she said she didn't think so. Ready for this? She said once that you were quite closed, that you held back too much.'

Noelie thought about this. It was not untrue, he conceded. 'I wasted years in the States – I was in a relationship there too that was never going anywhere. Don't ask me why I stayed.'

'It probably felt safe.'

He laughed. 'Yes, I guess. When I came back to Ireland I was sure I wanted to live on my own. But that wasn't a cakewalk either. Hannah used to do this review of all the things I was unhappy about and she'd say in the end, "Noelie, Noelie, Noelie, what am I going to do with you?" She really liked what she was doing, her job I mean. She wanted to earn more at it – who wouldn't? – but she loved journalism. I don't know, I guess I didn't want to jeopardise what I had with her. Then when all this shit hit the fan in the summer I started to see things differently. She really looked out for me.' He sighed, 'And I sort of suddenly saw how much she meant to me.' He shook his head bitterly. 'Fuck it.'

After a long silence and a sip of her pint, Katrina said, 'You're the lucky one, actually.'

'How's that?'

'Well, you can still believe something could've happened between you. And maybe it would've. I got my answer from her and it was the wrong one. I really tried to get her to stay in Australia with me. I made my pitch and told her how much she meant to me. But she wouldn't stay ...' Katrina looked upset.

'That's hard. I'm sorry.'

She nodded. 'Ah, it's in the past now. I got over it. I had to if I wanted to keep something there between us, which I did. And I have someone else special now, I think. Not *as* special but you can't have everything.'

Upstairs the main band had just got underway.

Noelie downed the rest of his pint. 'Funny thing is I got the shot in the arm that I needed from that support band earlier. I don't need to see the main band now except I know one of the lads in it so I have to show my face.'

They went up and stayed for most of the set, but Noelie's mind was not on the music – Katrina had made him realise that there was quite a lot he hadn't known about Hannah. She'd told him plenty about her trips to Australia but he hadn't ever picked up on it being more than that. On the way home they talked more about different people they had gone out with.

When they reached the apartment, Meabh was still up.

'Thought you were going to sleep?' asked Noelie.

'Just couldn't. Been thinking and thinking and worrying about Martin. And then you two as well. Now that you're back safe, I'll probably be okay.'

16

A narrow lane left the main road near where Martin had crashed. Byrne pulled her car on to the verge at the junction and switched off the engine. It had rained earlier, just a drizzle, but it was clear again. They were about six kilometres from Kinsale.

'Shall we?' she asked.

They got out. Although it was late morning there was a steady flow of traffic in either direction. They walked a short distance uphill to where the crash had happened. Martin's car had since been removed and, in the process, a number of trees had been cut down and almost all of the undergrowth in the immediate area removed. It was clear where exactly his car had left the road. In the daylight Noelie could better appreciate why the location was a known accident black spot. Coming from Cork, as Martin had been, the road was quite straight and level for more than a kilometre before suddenly dipping into a series of bends. Visibility to oncoming traffic wasn't great in either direction.

However, Martin had been unlucky too. His car had left the road at the worst possible place – where the bend was at its sharpest and the protective boundary ditch close to non-existent. On the other side there was a hollow, a few metres deep, at the bottom of which a stream flowed. In other words, Martin's car, as soon as it left the road, had plummeted to an abrupt and sudden halt. Earlier, on his way to meet Byrne, Noelie had received a new update: Martin had gone back into surgery for the third time in under two days.

Given the bends and location's reputation it wasn't

unreasonable to think that Martin had simply lost control of his car, or that an oncoming car had unintentionally caused Martin to swerve and leave the road. It was, however, equally possible that Martin's car had been deliberately forced off the road. If it had, then the operation would have needed military precision – the stretch of road where Martin had crashed didn't exactly offer an attacker a surfeit of opportunity.

Noelie almost didn't want to entertain this scenario – but in another sense it was almost impossible to avoid it. The problem was, Martin was the only person who knew the location of the digital backup copy of the double-8mm film. He was also their contact with Wikileaks. If their film ever did resurface at the whistle-blower site, they would have no way of finding out, or of accessing the communications. Seen in that context, Martin's accident looked highly suspicious.

Byrne had walked on uphill to where the dip in the road began, a distance of about a hundred metres, where she seemed to be intermittently observing the traffic then checking her phone. Noelie wasn't sure what she was doing or what was up with her. He usually found Byrne friendly, but on the drive to Kinsale she had hardly spoken, despite his repeated efforts to engage her in chit-chat. She had, of course, asked Noelie what had concerned him about Martin's crash. He had explained that there was very little information forthcoming from Martin's family, and that he knew Martin to be a careful driver. He didn't know if Byrne believed him, but she hadn't pursued the matter either. She was preoccupied and he wondered if it was to do with Shane's inquest. Noelie had already heard from his sister that the inquest was expected to resume soon. The matter of Shane's mobile phone trail was the outstanding matter to be settled and Noelie knew Byrne's competency was somewhat hanging on that.

At the crash site, he noticed what looked like a part of the car body in the undergrowth. It was a small section but it was the right colour – red. Possibly a part of the roof that had to be cut away when Martin was being extricated from the vehicle by the fire brigade. He went to have a closer look, working his way down the slope. As he did, he saw something glinting in the sunlight. He reached out until it rested in his palm. It was a gold miraculous medal that had been hung on a branch just beside where the car had come to a stop. Noelie was about to remove it when he realised that a well-wisher, or perhaps someone from Martin's family, had put it there. He left it where it was and instead picked up the small piece of red metal.

Back up on the road he showed it to Byrne. 'Not very thorough, were they?'

Byrne didn't make a comment. She explained to Noelie what she had been doing, taking the timings of the passing traffic, and showed him her results.

'The gaps in the traffic are longer than I had expected. There was one gap of over three minutes; several that lasted approximately two-to-three minutes; and a few that were only about thirty seconds. Mid- to late-afternoon, when Martin's crash happened, could easily have been as quiet or quieter. So, I suppose it's not implausible that no one saw what happened.'

Noelie nodded. 'I thought this road was busier actually.'

'Well, it's the more minor of the two routes into Kinsale from Cork. During the summer, at the height of the tourist season, it would certainly be busier.'

Byrne walked a short distance back up the road. When the traffic quietened, she crossed slowly to the other side looking around at the road's surface. When the traffic cleared again she returned to where Noelie was standing.

'It's difficult to have a proper look without halting the traffic, but I can't see any significant tyre marks on the road that would suggest a near- or partial-collision. It looks quite clean to me.

Noelie walked along the roadside going uphill. He wondered if Martin had lost control earlier at the turn into the bend. But he saw nothing suspicious and returned.

'So all you have,' said Byrne, 'is one possibly suspicious mark on the driver's side of the car. That could've been caused by a glancing collision on the bend. The crash investigators are usually prompt so they'll know down in the station in Kinsale in a few days. I'll keep you posted.'

The other piece of information Byrne had from her visit to Kinsale's garda station, was to do with witnesses – there were none. The gardaí had issued repeated appeals on local radio but so far no one had come forward. She'd told Noelie that, because of that, the gardaí in Kinsale were unlikely to make the crash a priority any time soon.

'Resources are stretched tight right now. The way they see it, they are dealing with a single vehicle incident in which the only victim is the driver. Sorry to say this, but it's a hiding to nothing for them.'

A phone rang in Byrne's car, echoing through the vehicle's speaker system.

'You keep a few phones going too, I see,' said Noelie.

'That's my lot,' Byrne replied sourly, going over to answer it.

Noelie looked around again. If Martin's crash hadn't been an accident it also meant that someone had been watching him for some time. Who these people were, he didn't know but clearly they had done their homework. They may well have had an electronic tracker on his car. It just reinforced Noelie's belief that he and his friends were total amateurs by comparison. He had mentioned this to Katrina and she had just laughed and told him about a conversation she'd had with Black Gary in which she'd asked him if he even kept his door locked down in Sherkin. He had replied no. It hadn't even crossed his mind to.

It was looking more and more likely they were facing off

against professionals, and that meant Branch or people who worked with or for Branch. These days, with the upsurge in sub-contracted security services, all of which were available for the right price, who was to say who was doing the state's dirty work for them.

Byrne needed to head back to the city, although she didn't say why. They got in the car and she pulled out on to the bend with such haste that they narrowly missed having a crash of their own. Noelie jumped in fright, which made Byrne smile.

'Nervous boy.'

'I'm just, you know, safety conscious.'

'You're in the wrong business so.'

'Business?'

'Being a private eye and so on.'

Noelie shook his head. 'You've got that wrong. I'm not in that line at all.'

Byrne gave Noelie a despairing smile. 'I believe you, of course.' She lowered her voice. 'The problem is no else does.'

They drove in silence for a while. In an attempt to spark some pleasant conversation, he tapped Byrne's left hand, which was resting on the gear stick and sporting a huge ring.

'Congratulations by the way.'

She looked at him quickly and smiled. 'So, you noticed?'

'Hard to miss. In Cork that's classed as a serious rock. Who's the lucky man?'

'Jim.'

'A garda too?'

Byrne laughed. 'No. Surprised?'

Noelie thought about it. 'Kind of. I hear your type stick together.'

'Some do but I'm not that sort. I have enough of the job from eight to eight. He's a brewer.'

'A what?'

She told him that her fiancé used to work for a whiskey

company but was interested in going out on his own. He had a start-up company with two others making new stouts and beers. 'Micro-brewing.'

'I read about that. IPAs and that sort of thing?'

'Exactly.' She told Noelie all about India pale ales and the upsurge in interest in them. After a pause and then a short conversation about the likelihood that Byrne would ask for a transfer out of Cork in due course – her fiancé was based up in Wicklow – Noelie got his opportunity.

'How is your career going these days by the way? Any developments?'

'I'm heading back to the station now and then it's over to Dream. The report is ready, it seems. I gather the coroner could reconvene as early as this afternoon. He's in a terrible rush for some reason.'

'Any idea what the Dream log is saying?'

Byrne didn't answer right away. But Noelie gathered from that and the expression on her face that it had not gone in her favour. Eventually, after overtaking a truck at reckless speed, she said, 'It's a fuck up. It just looks terrible. I look terrible. That's all there is to it.'

Noelie waited for the detective to say more. When she didn't, he said, 'Don't take this the wrong way now but is there any way you could have misread the original information?'

She looked at him briefly and then shook her head. 'I am absolutely certain I was always dealing with a document that indicated Turner's Cross. It was an original document too. Or at least I thought it was. It looked and felt totally authentic. No, I'm certain – 100 per cent. But that matters little now, Noelie, because I can't find it. So whether I'm right or wrong, I'm left looking like I made a rookie error.'

Noelie felt bad for Byrne because that was exactly how it did look. He had even thought it himself. However, he knew too that the actual error had preceded her involvement. By

Bonfire Night, Shane had been missing for twenty-four hours. Noelie remembered going around Cork looking for his nephew. It was that evening, as the bonfires were getting going, that he first heard mention of Turner's Cross as the location where Shane's phone had signed off the network for good. His sister had called Noelie to tell him this. Or maybe he had called her, and she had told him – he couldn't remember now. But the point was, Turner's Cross was first mentioned on Bonfire Night, which predated Byrne's involvement by two whole days; officially the detective only got involved with the discovery of Shane's body in the Lee.

Noelie considered pointing this out to Byrne but at the last moment he decided not to. He needed to think the matter through. The thing was, if Byrne was sure the original document from Dream had specified Turner's Cross as the final beacon, it had to mean that someone had altered the document to point the search in the wrong direction. And if so, why?

Byrne didn't say more and Noelie continued to mull over the matter. When they reached Hannah's, the matter was clearly still on the detective's mind.

'Maybe it's for the best that I'm getting out of Cork,' she said pulling over on to double-yellow lines.

'Well, I'll miss you,' he said. 'I guess I'm not the only one disappointed by the sight of that ring.'

She smiled, released the central locking, pointed to the footpath and said, 'Enough, Noelie, out.' She added. 'If you need any more help, give me a call.'

Noelie's burner had vibrated a couple of times on the return drive. He hadn't wanted to answer, figuring that he mightn't be able to talk freely in front of Byrne anyway. Checking now, he saw that it was Katrina's number. He rang her immediately.

'I guessed you were with Byrne, but I was starting to wonder too. Getting paranoid like the rest of you now, Noelie.'

'No harm in that.'

He told her what he had learned about the crash and the growing certainty he had that it had not been an accident. 'If it was planned then we're facing professionals for sure. There isn't even a tell-tale mark on the road down there, and most important of all probably, no witnesses. Where are you anyway?'

'We've just finished in Youghal. We were through the last of the newspapers when the proverbial break we were all looking for walked in the door to talk to us. Did it ever occur to you that someone might have looked into this before?'

'About this missing boy from Youghal? No, not really.'

'You said that Irwin mentioned that this boy's sister had been making enquiries and was actively looking for her brother.'

'Yes, but that was way back, in the late sixties, I guess. After the boy's sister got out of the industrial school. That was how the contact with Copley came about. She found out that Copley was from Youghal and had also been in Danesfort. So she asked for his help. But that was like 1967 or '68 or so.'

'Remember the librarian we were talking to here the first day, when you were with us? Well, as we were wrapping up, we got to talking to her about our research and she remembered helping a woman back in the late nineties who was digging into a story very similar to Youghal Boy's. We've no idea yet if it is the same person but we're on our way to find out.'

It wasn't improbable, Noelie knew that. He had read of a few heart-rending stories connected to Mother and Baby Homes and Magdalene Laundries. Situations where the nuns involved had falsified information on children's birth certificates obscuring the real identities of the babies under their care. Some of these children, when they reached adulthood, spent their entire lives looking for their real families or even one sibling – sometimes successfully but, more often than not, unsuccessfully.

'This woman had been looking for information on a fishing accident in Youghal in 1958. It's a complicated saga, but the word tragedy does come to mind and there was possibly an industrial school angle to the case too. Apparently, the librarian put the woman in contact with a local genealogist who had a side interest in Youghal's fishing industry, to do with his grandfather or something. She still had his number, and we've been trying to call, but he's not answering. We're told that his place is not so far away, on the Cork–Waterford border, so we're heading over there now. We should be able to find out from him for sure if this 1958 fishing tragedy did have an industrial school angle or not.'

Noelie was surprised and delighted. He almost didn't believe it. 'Well done,' he said, happily. 'Don't tell Meabh, but I had more or less given up hope of anything coming of the Youghal angle.' He added, 'Be careful, though. Stay in touch and all the rest. Just in case. I am justifiably paranoid.'

'Likewise. Keep Black Gary close at hand when you go into Peter and Paul's.'

Noelie had spare time before his meeting at the church, so he walked over to Douglas Street. At Sheila's house he looked in the window. The front room was bare and had been swept. There were no longer any puddles on the floor. He knocked on the front door but, not surprisingly, there was no one there. He looked over at where his own flat had been: about seven or so houses along, in the town direction, on the other side of the street.

Why had Sheila been looking for him? He had thought it was just neighbourliness but now he wasn't so sure. Had Sheila noticed something or remembered something and was that why she had wanted to make contact? It was possible. Sheila was one of those characters who knew everything that happened on the street.

The other thing was she was always taking photos. It annoyed some of her neighbours a lot but Noelie refused to take offense. For years, Sheila had been in a dispute with the council over her entitlement to a disability parking space outside her house. The council ruled against her so at one stage, in defiance, Sheila had put down her own road markings. This had caused untold trouble and eventually the council had painted these over and threatened her with court. At the beginning of the summer, Sheila had put the road markings back in place again. 'I'll go to jail over this,' she'd once told Noelie.

To support her case, Sheila had taken to recording traffic and parking transgressions outside and around her front door. She was constantly at the ready with her camera and had amassed an arsenal of evidence that she felt would, one day, overwhelm the bureaucrats – her words – inside City Hall.

Noelie decided to call down to the joiner's workshop at the end of the street. He figured Barry might have a number for Sheila's sister, Nora. He found him busy at work, sanding the corners on kitchen unit doors. He was a gregarious, friendly man who did quality work. Recognising Noelie, he immediately asked if he had seen Sheila's place. They talked about what had happened and what bad luck it was. Noelie didn't learn anything new about the fire, but the joiner did have Sheila's sister's number. He jotted it down on a piece of scrap paper.

As he walked back to Hannah's, he called Nora. He got no answer but left a long message asking about Sheila and how she was. He also asked about Sheila's collection of photos and if they had been saved from the fire.

17

On the steps of St Peter and Paul's, Noelie stopped and texted Katrina to ask if there was any news and to remind her to keep him updated that they were okay. He looked around. Patrick Street, Cork's main street, was a short distance away on his left; in the opposite direction, at the far end of the lane, was the old red-bricked presbytery building that, at one time, had been linked to Peter and Paul's. Black Gary was waiting there, standing in at one of the arched doorways.

Noelie had been into Peter and Paul's as a child with his father and remembered it as a dark, dreary place. Either it had had a makeover or his memory was deceiving him. The altar area, largely made of white marble, seemed drowned in light, which lent the church a warm, bright aura. He caught a vague smell of incense too – a smell he had always liked.

On his right, a woman stood in front of one of the Stations of the Cross, her head bowed. Up at the front of the church, close to the altar, a man kneeled in prayer. Near the entrance to the sacristy, also close to the front of the church, a group of women were standing together. They were talking loudly and Noelie wondered if they were tourists.

He went left to one of the Stations. It was the seventh: 'Jesus falls for the second time'. He walked up the aisle, passed six, 'Veronica wipes the face of Jesus', and arrived at five, 'Simon of Cyrene helps Jesus carry his cross'. There was no one around. He sidled into the pew and sat down. It was a few minutes after 2 p.m.

Checking his burner again to see that it was still functioning, he saw that he hadn't received any reply from Katrina. Earlier he had put Black Gary's number on speed dial and checked that it had worked. If this meeting with the Walsh son produced any unwanted surprises, he would be able to call Black Gary immediately.

While he waited, he looked at the fifth Station. Like the others, it had been hand painted in a simple un-embellished style that was almost childish. He couldn't decide if this was intentional or not. A Roman soldier was directing a pilgrim, Simon of Cyrene, to help Jesus carry the cross. Jesus looked troubled, in pain and was bleeding around the forehead from the crown of thorns on his head.

A figure came into view over at the main aisle. He was using a Zimmer frame on wheels. Noelie watched him for a while – he looked young, no more than forty – but he didn't make eye contact or look in his direction. Eventually he shuffled out of view.

Noelie checked his watch again, it was gone five past. A phone rang, and its owner answered it, without any apparent compunction that he was in a church. A country accent explained for all to hear that he was here and, yes, he was waiting. That was something Noelie had noticed about mobile phones. People lost all decorum once they had one in their hand. Even he was miffed: really, answering a call inside a church was just not on. The voice grew fainter however and then couldn't be heard at all. Silence returned.

A man crossed up near the altar, genuflected and continued onwards, temporarily obscured from Noelie's view due to the large pulpit. Noelie hadn't seen him come into the church and wondered if he had entered via the sacristy. He reappeared and came down the side aisle towards Noelie. He was in his early thirties, well dressed, clean-shaven with heavy-set eyebrows and dark hair. He didn't make eye contact.

At the fifth Station, the man stopped and blessed himself. He appeared to say a prayer, genuflected and then sat in the pew beside Noelie. 'Thank you for coming,' he said.

Noelie turned to get a better look at the man. Up close he wasn't as impressive as he had first seemed coming down the aisle. His eyes were small, and his facial skin seemed stretched. Clearly the man was too young to be using Botox but there was that look to him that Noelie didn't find satisfying. He caught the whiff of money though: the suit and overcoat were high end.

'There was nowhere else we could meet?' Noelie asked him.

'This is safe.'

'For you, maybe.'

As if on cue the man looked around. 'For now, it's better that no one knows I'm talking to you.' He put his hand out to shake Noelie's. 'Stephen Walsh.'

'So, what is it you want?'

'Let me explain. Meabh probably told you something about me. She wouldn't have known that I was close to my father, but I was particularly so in his last years. We didn't live with my dad, hadn't done for many years, but I wanted to keep some sort of connection with him and I did that of my own volition. My mother had severed all her connections with him, apart from her commercial and business links. But they had effectively been separated from the mid-nineties.'

There was a pause. Noelie glanced uneasily around. The church was quiet.

'I don't know how to describe my father,' Stephen went on. 'I actually don't know what to think about him. As you can imagine I'm conflicted. I felt very sorry for him and he was quite alone at the end. In case you are wondering, I didn't know he was going to kill himself. I knew nothing at all about what led to that. Afterwards there were rumours, that it was because of the crash or some bad investments, but these were all wrong. I believe I know now why he did what he did.'

'Why?'

172

'The film that you found. Perhaps not so much the film, but what it represented and the possibility that it might be made public. I think he decided that if it was made public – and he expected that it would – that the damage to his family would be significant. Whereas if he was dead, we would be spared some of the fallout. So he killed himself, for our family.'

'So noble.'

'I gathered over a long while that there were two parts to my father's troubles. He was personally contrite, riven by regret, disgust and shame. He came to understand, and he said this to me at one stage, that he couldn't be other than who he was. He knew he had done wrong. He accepted he had taken advantage of people.'

'Children.'

'I'm sorry?'

'It wasn't *people* he took advantage of, it was children. Let's not fudge the matter here.'

For the first time Stephen Walsh looked annoyed. 'I don't think we are talking about the same thing here. If you gave me a chance to finish, perhaps that would become clear.'

'Go on so,' said Noelie looking pointedly at his watch.

'Do you have somewhere to be?'

Noelie looked at Walsh. 'Yes, actually and soon too.'

There was silence. Stephen Walsh's face seemed to glaze over for a moment. Noelie regretted being rude. At the same time, he was alert. He heard the Zimmer frame man moving about again – it was quite a distinctive shuffle and Noelie suddenly realised that he was near, behind where they were sitting. He looked around but he couldn't see anyone.

'There was a case, in the nineties … it was effectively what ended my parents' marriage. It related to something that had happened a number of years earlier, but it came back to haunt my father. He was forced to face up to what happened and, I think, it affected him hugely and led him, for the first

173

time, to appreciate that what he wanted had very damaging consequences for others.'

'We know there was a case he paid to keep out of the public domain back around then. Was that that case?'

Stephen Walsh looked at Noelie, 'There were two such cases. But I can't talk about either.'

Noelie moved away a little. 'You wouldn't think, would you, that that's part of what's at issue here? There's cover-up after cover-up going on. If people like your father, for all his supposed insight, actually showed an ounce of integrity and told the truth we might not be in this mess right now.' Sharply, he added, 'Well?'

'I was trying to say that there were two parts to my father's troubles. The other part, the second part, was what he really couldn't get away from and it involved Albert Donnelly. He would tell me nothing about this matter, but I came to understand that it was much more significant for my father than everything else.'

Noelie had already been thinking along those lines: the lingering impact of the killings. The failed blackmail may well have exposed Albert to his brother Robert's wrath but it may also have ensnared a number of other men, among them Leslie Walsh and possibly this mysterious third man too.

'I never did find out what my father was alluding to. I tried to get more information out of him, but he wouldn't talk about it and I left it. My attitude while he was alive was to keep in touch and to keep talking to him. I figured that perhaps at some stage in the future he might come around and tell me more. Or everything. I was prepared to bide my time and anyway he was a bit like that. Closed sometimes, talkative others. But then he killed himself.'

There was a pause. 'In a way that was the end of it, until I realised that my father may have left something behind, an account or a record perhaps. So, in due course, I began looking. My father had his personal possessions, of course, but I found other things too. Things that I think are significant.'

'What did you find?' asked Noelie more impatiently than he had intended.

'This is why I'm here, Noelie. Our family has some idea of what may be in the film that you have. We were wondering,' he said, turning to face Noelie, 'if you could find a way to remove any evidence of my father's involvement. We could arrange something in return if you would give us your word that you would do that.'

Noelie's temper rose. 'So really,' he said as calmly as he could, 'this is like one of those cases that you and your family have paid to have kept quiet. You want us to play the same game now too. You want to get your dad and your family out of this ugly picture before it goes on public view. Let the shit hit the fan, but only when you're not around to catch any of the spray.'

'This is really for my mother,' said Stephen Walsh quietly. 'It isn't for me.'

'Have you a violin?'

'What?'

'A violin. Because if you have, we could play something for her. A duet?'

There was silence. Noelie noticed that the other man was chewing his lower lip.

'We're not interested in that sort of a deal,' Noelie hissed. 'Get it? That's not what this is about ...'

'And what about what happened to your friend?'

Now it was Noelie's turn to be surprised. 'What?' he said in shock. 'Who? What are you talking about?'

'Wasn't the man you shared a flat with on Douglas Street in some sort of an accident?'

Noelie heard the words that were spoken but he also heard something more in Stephen Walsh's voice. It took him a moment to identify it – smugness? Surely not. If there was one thing that he found objectionable about well-heeled Corkonians, it was when they acted smug when they had no right to be. He grabbed Stephen Walsh by his coat collar, stood and hauled him up at the same time. There was no resistance from the younger man. He actually looked afraid, which made Noelie back off immediately. He let go of Walsh. The other man half sat, half fell off the pew.

'My father kept a record of those involved in all that trouble with Albert. I don't think you should pass up on this opportunity, Mr Sullivan.' Arrogantly he added, 'For your own sake even.'

He stood then and brushed past Noelie. He stopped in the aisle, genuflected once more and walked back in the direction he had come. Noelie remained there a moment longer. He was annoyed he had lost his temper, but he was incensed too. A part of him wanted to run after Walsh and chase him through the streets of Cork. But Noelie knew already who would be arrested if he did that. Instead he walked to the back of the church and out through the main doors.

He felt immediately better in the sunlight. He checked his mobile but there were no messages. He hoped the others were okay. Black Gary had seen him and was walking towards him. They met at the corner of Paul Street.

'You all right?' asked Black Gary.

Noelie realised he was quite shaken. He began to explain but Black Gary interrupted him.

'Something's come up. Your sister Ellen was on to Meabh when she couldn't get a reply on your phone. Meabh gave me a call then.'

'Please don't fucking tell me something has happened to them. Meabh and Katrina, are they okay?'

'They're fine. It's nothing like that,' said Black Gary calmly. 'Meabh wouldn't say anything because we were on the ordinary phones but something positive has happened down there, I gather. At last, right?'

Noelie nodded.

'The message from your sister is that the inquest has resumed at the courthouse.'

Noelie went directly there. The inquest was on in dreary Court 1; there were only a few people in attendance. Noelie looked around for his sister – she was on her own in the front row of the public gallery. He sat down beside her, and she immediately held his hand.

'Byrne submitted the official log from Dream. It was the Father Mathew Quay beacon all along. Shane never went anywhere near Turner's Cross.' Ellen shook her head in disbelief. The expression on her face was a mixture of anger and incredulity. 'Is she stupid or what?'

Byrne was no longer on the witness stand and Noelie couldn't see her anywhere in the witness gallery either. Taylor was talking. Noelie realised that he had missed Taylor's cross-examination of the detective as well – worse luck.

The family's solicitor was requesting more time, a further adjournment so that the family could consider what they had just learned regarding the mobile phone trail. It was a smart move. Noelie enquired after Arthur.

'He's away,' answered Ellen. 'This took us by surprise, especially as this is apparently just a formality. There's to be another adjournment, there isn't any doubt about that, although I don't know if it will make any difference.'

Noelie heard the sadness in his sister's voice and squeezed her hand again. In essence, she was right and Noelie understood the futility. What good was truth or justice in a way? If they ever got it for Shane – or for Hannah for that matter – and it was debatable if they ever would, what difference would it actually make? They weren't coming back.

Everyone was waiting. Taylor had concluded his point and was sitting again. The coroner then informed them that he had also been petitioned for further time by the pathologist, Canning. Although she wasn't present to explain what this was about, in view of the evidence regarding the Dream log and Taylor's request on behalf of the family, he was disposed to agree.

The inquest would adjourn until early the following week. The coroner would update all the parties once he had communicated with the pathologist. Noelie watched him lean over to speak to the jurors. He wondered why Canning wanted more time. He sat there with Ellen for a moment.

'I don't know what to think or say,' she said finally, wiping tears away. 'I mean, what if we could have saved him? I remember so well when we got that information. We were looking all around our home area and then suddenly we upped sticks and went over to Turner's Cross, where no one had seen him at all. It was so dispiriting out there. I remember trying to work out what was going on. He didn't have one friend out that way. He probably had one in every other suburb of Cork but not in that one. It was awful. I felt useless and now we know it actually was pointless too. Damn them, Noelie. Damn them, damn them, damn them.'

Noelie held his sister. He remembered that day all too well. He could safely say that, in what had been a summer of many desperate experiences, those days helplessly searching for Shane ranked with the very worst of them. Never again in his life did he want to search for a missing person. It was hell.

Ellen wanted to speak to Taylor. She dried her eyes and spent a moment fixing her make-up. Noelie saw Black Gary standing by the courtroom door, his expression indicating that something was wrong. He thought about Meabh and Katrina in Ardmore. He didn't like it that they were off doing that search on their own. They'd call him sexist if he said that to them but he didn't care.

He followed Ellen across the courtroom floor. She stopped abruptly to deliver one final comment, 'And do you know this as well, Noelie? You can't actually sue the police. They're protected from that too.' She bristled, shaking her head, 'I mean, really.'

Noelie liked that his sister was angry. He figured anger was a better emotion than hopelessness. He said hello briefly to Taylor and thanked him again. Taylor made little of it all. Noelie got the impression he was shyer than his occupation allowed for.

He went to find Black Gary who was no longer by the door. He went out into the corridor and saw him by the stairs.

'What is it?'

'Shauna phoned ... a few minutes ago.' He shook his head. 'Martin.'

18

Arriving at the hospital, Noelie and Black Gary went directly to Martin's room. Some of the bandaging around his head had been removed and it was now possible to see most of his face. His complexion was no longer rosy and he looked peaceful, as if he was asleep. Family and friends were gathered outside, around and along the corridor adjacent to the room. Martin's sister, Shauna, came over. She told Noelie and Black Gary that Martin had had to go for more emergency surgery first thing that morning.

'From the beginning they were worried about his liver, but it was worse than they expected. Multiple lacerations. He was transfused a few times but in the end they couldn't stop the bleeding.'

Noelie could hardly contain his grief. Seeing Martin lying there on the bed, hearing Shauna's breaking voice and knowing the background: it was awful. He held her tightly. He didn't know if Martin had ever told Shauna anything about their investigation, but he got the impression she knew more than she was saying. It was different with Martin's parents and his brother; they kept their distance. Noelie wanted to offer them his condolences but Shauna suggested that another time might be better. Black Gary agreed. He led Noelie out into the corridor where Ollie, Martin's boyfriend, was being minded by friends. He was distraught.

Black Gary chatted ably to those who were around. Noelie was envious of his easy way with people. There was an honest directness about him that people responded to. In contrast, Noelie found it hard just being there. He wanted to get away and, when he saw a priest arriving, he took his opportunity. He told Black Gary he'd be downstairs and that he'd keep an eye out for Meabh and Katrina who were expected at any moment.

On the ground floor he couldn't face the canteen, which, as usual, was full to capacity. Although it had rained again, he went out and stood under an awning. It was cold though. Taxis came and went, collecting and dropping off patients and visitors. Periodically a tannoy sounded, reminding everyone that these were hospital grounds and that no smoking was allowed under any circumstances.

He went back inside. Visitors, patients, staff and ambulance crew mingled in the busy foyer area. He walked up the main hospital corridor. An old man hobbled past him using a frame. He looked quite ill but determined to get to wherever he was going. Noelie thought of Martin: now he would never reach old age. There would be no Berlin, no big love in his life, no children, no so-many-things. Tears came to his eyes.

He looked around for a seat and instead saw Andrea Canning – she was wearing jeans and a long green cardigan, quite different to when he had seen her last at the inquest. She noticed him too and immediately her expression changed to one of concern. She was with colleagues but she left them and came over.

'Noelie, what's up? Are you okay?'

He looked dreadful and he knew it. He wiped his eyes. 'I'm fine,' he replied.

'You don't look fine. Really, what happened?'

He told her about Martin. 'He was in a car crash a few days ago. We really thought he would make it.'

She asked if he would like a coffee or a glass of water and he nodded.

'I can get them from the staffroom. It won't take a moment. What's it to be?'

'Coffee.'

She suggested he wait near the lifts. Noelie watched the pathologist head over to a small side corridor. A group of young doctors passed with stethoscopes around their necks. Andrea returned carrying two cups. She nodded to him to follow and led him back out into the foyer area.

'I know a spot,' she said and winked.

He followed her past reception to a low window ledge. Others were sitting there but a few spaces were still free.

'Let's perch there.'

She sat down and he sat beside her.

'Thank you,' he said.

'You're very welcome. I've been lucky in my life,' she added, 'so far anyway. No one close to me has ever died. Both my parents are still alive. Rickety but still going. In the business I'm in, I sometimes feel like I'm cheating. Tell me about your friend.'

Noelie explained how he knew Martin and what had happened – without the context of the investigation. It was simpler that way. He also told her that Martin was gay and that his parents hadn't respected that, though he immediately regretted bringing the matter up, even though it stuck in his craw. He went on, he knew, but she listened and didn't interrupt. In the end she said in an even-handed way that families often didn't really know what they were doing when someone close to them died.

Noelie was silent after that. He knew he was fending off the grief he felt by getting angry at Martin's parents. It all felt strange. A hospital didn't seem to be the right place to grieve. You came to a hospital to be saved, to be made better, but that hadn't happened for Martin.

They sat for a moment watching the activity. Noelie was glad he had met the pathologist. There was something reassuring about her, although he didn't fully understand what that was.

'After we last talked, Noelie, outside the courthouse, I remembered something. I'll confess I looked it up on the Internet, to be certain I mean. It's to do with Hannah Hegarty and what happened in the summer – about that mole inside the IRA and all of that.'

'In Sinn Féin actually,' Noelie corrected her.

'Well, in Sinn Féin then. I was so shocked when I heard. About her being murdered. It was just terrible.'

Noelie wasn't sure if he wanted to talk about Hannah – it was another death he'd had an unintended hand in – but Andrea continued anyway.

'She came out here to CUH to do a story once. It was about this private hospital that was setting up nearby. Staff and resources were being poached by this place. It was quite rotten. Hannah did a very good article on it. She interviewed me briefly, which was when we both realised we had a mutual connection through UCC. Strange isn't it? You and her. Me and you. You knew her quite well though, right?'

'I did. We were very close.'

Canning's pager went off then, breaking the moment. 'I should be getting back,' she said. 'Anyway I just wanted to let you know.'

He watched her drain her cup of tea. 'Thanks,' he said, 'for remembering Hannah. And for the coffee too.'

She nodded. 'Where will you go now?'

'Me?' he said. 'I have friends. They should be arriving soon. I think I'll stay down here for another bit though.'

'Okay.' She stood. 'Mind yourself. And we'll talk in a while anyway. I'm determined to catch up properly.'

He watched her walk away. 'One thing, Andrea?' he called. 'I was in the courthouse earlier. The coroner said you asked for more time too. Has something come up?'

She came back over. 'Not as such. I just want to double-check everything. In the circumstances I think it's best.'

'The circumstances?'

'Well, the mobile phone error.'

'But the mobile phone error was only confirmed today.'

Canning looked slightly uncomfortable. Noelie was immediately sorry for putting her on the spot.

'I'm sorry, Andrea,' he said. 'Don't mind me. I'm all mixed up.' He held up the coffee again. 'Thanks for this.'

Back at the apartment, Katrina went to her room and Noelie to his. Meabh sat near the riverside window and talked occasionally to Black Gary who had decided to service Hannah's old radio. He worked on the corroded contacts, polishing them until they shone again like silver.

After a while, the silence became unbearable and Noelie went back out to rejoin the others. He found Meabh staring at the river and he wondered if she was thinking about their own brush with death that summer. The Lee had almost killed them twice but it had also brought them to safety too.

'How are you?' he asked.

'I feel like shit. How're you?'

'The same.'

Meabh sighed. 'I just don't know. It hasn't sunk in … Did we do this, Noelie?'

'Don't go there,' said Black Gary.

She stood suddenly. 'We need to tell you what we found out in Youghal. Or Ardmore to be more precise.' She went to the main bedroom and asked Katrina to join them. Black Gary collected their phones and placed them in the bathroom. It was his turn to choose the music and he put on Moving Hearts. Only Noelie had heard of them. Hannah had been a fan, which was why a number of their CDs were in her collection. Moving Hearts defied easy categorisation but they blended Irish traditional, rock 'n' roll and jazz. Hearing them now brought Noelie back to a time and a place that felt very far away – the early eighties in Cork.

Katrina began. 'We actually made progress on this Youghal Boy matter – which I guess is something. But, as you'll realise, it's disturbing what we found out. So first off, via the librarian in Youghal, we got an address for the genealogist who was in and out of the library there quite a lot a few years back. It turned out the address for him was for his mother's place. This guy's only in his mid-thirties and his genealogist business went kaput in the crash. About a year ago he emigrated to Canada.'

'We explained to his mother what we were after and that it was urgent,' said Meabh. 'In the end, after a lot of pleading, she gave us his number in Canada.'

'It was around breakfast time there. He was pretty nice and was interested immediately. Remembered the case well and the surname. The person he was thinking of was named Corrigan. He told us she lived in Ardmore, just on the far side of the Cork–Waterford border. The surname was not the one we were working off but the industrial school angle was apparently right – he confirmed that – so we decided to head over there. We didn't have an address but we asked around. Ardmore is small so the second person we approached knew who we were talking about. Off we went. I have to say, the moment the door was opened to us I kinda felt we had the right person. Mary Corrigan's her name and she's never been married. Her missing brother's name is Paul.'

'She was like a little bird,' added Meabh. 'At first I thought she was ill, she was so thin and scrawny. And she smoked the entire time we were there. I haven't been in a house like that for a long time.' Meabh smelled her jumper. 'Yep, it's still there.'

'We told her who we were and why we were there,' continued Katrina. 'She stared us down for about two full minutes with a look that said, "I'll fucking murder ye if ye are having me on here". I thought she was going to slam the door on us actually.'

'What age is she?' enquired Black Gary.

'She was nine when she was put into St Francis's in Loughrea in 1959,' answered Meabh. 'So sixty now and looked it too. I don't know if she's had a hard life or what. I guess so.'

Katrina continued. 'We gave her the whole story. She listened, didn't say anything until we mentioned Copley. She remembered him. She got out of Loughrea in 1967 and went looking for her brothers and her sister. There were five of them and she found them all except for Paul, the youngest. It seems that they were all sent to different places when they were taken into care.'

Meabh shook her head. 'She got quite upset telling us about it.'

'I think by 1968 or so she had managed to trace Copley and she wrote to him. She got a few letters from him saying that he would help her and then the connection went dead. She never heard from him again. She had no idea, of course, that he'd been murdered.'

'I'm sure she was pretty shocked when she found out.'

'We didn't tell her,' Meabh cut in. 'Look, Noelie, it wasn't straightforward down there. Just wait a minute, hear us out and you'll see what I mean.'

Noelie wasn't sure what was going on, but he nodded. 'Sure.'

Katrina continued again. 'She was dogged for a long number of years looking for her brother Paul. When one line of enquiry dried up, she tried another. Apparently he disappeared from Danesfort within a couple of months of arriving there. She eventually got to see his full record at the Rosminians' place in Clonmel. We asked her if the record looked authentic. She was surprised by the question – she wasn't suspicious in that way. As far as she was concerned the record she saw looked legit.'

'She mentioned Father Tony Donnelly and that he had helped her a lot,' added Meabh. 'She described him as very helpful. Apparently he paid for adverts to be placed in local papers in west Cork, Clonakilty and Bandon. She also said that Father Tony, as she called him, had always been totally helpful in every way. But she never turned up anything. All her searching came to nothing in the end.'

'Did Tony Donnelly ever tell her about Ballyvolane?' asked Black Gary.

Meabh shook her head grimly. 'She never heard mention of the place until this afternoon from us. She did know that boys from Danesfort were loaned out to farms as free labour but she never knew that her brother could have been sent to work as far away as the Donnelly farm in Ballyvolane. Never heard the name Albert Donnelly either.'

'What did his file in Clonmel say?' asked Noelie. 'About him going missing, I mean?'

'Only that he ran away from Danesfort,' Meabh replied.

Katrina continued again, 'She gave up for a long time after that. She's another of that generation of Irish people who worked abroad for long stretches. Over in Manchester mainly, she said. She'd come home occasionally to one of her brothers here and go at it again. She paid for adverts in the papers in Australia and America at one stage. She had a picture of him. In 1983, I think she said, she came back to live here again and that's when things got interesting once more. She got to know of a solicitor over in Dungarvan who had defended someone charged with IRA membership. Apparently this woman had a thing for taking on unpopular cases. It was this solicitor who forced the Rosminians to open their files to Mary Corrigan. She also pursued the gardaí in Bandon. She threatened them with court about their lack of action on the case and suggested that they had been negligent at the time in not doing more to find the boy. That seemed to get them moving. A bit, anyway. Basically, the solicitor in Dungarvan had to keep writing letters to the gardaí in Bandon for updates. They'd get a polite letter back to say "we're working on it" and then nothing more. That went on for a few years. Then something strange happened, which to this day Mary Corrigan doesn't understand. A detective showed up at her house in Ardmore. Knew all about the case and asked her to tell him everything she knew all over again. Mary Corrigan was delighted. Finally something was being done. He asked for all information that she had, some letters and a few photos of Paul and she gave them all to him.'

Meabh continued from here. 'But this detective then vanished. She didn't hear anything back from him and so, after a bit, she went and asked about him. All she had was his name. Bandon cops said they didn't know him. She went to her solicitor and she hadn't heard from this man either. Got the total run around and has no idea even now who he was.'

'Was he legit?'asked Black Gary. 'Did he show her ID and all the rest?'

'Yes,' answered Katrina. 'Mary Corrigan said he showed her ID and seemed knowledgeable about her brother's case. She assumed he was from Bandon. He had a Cork accent, she remembered. But was never seen or heard from again.'

Noelie shook his head incredulously. 'Did that make her suspicious at all?'

'I would've thought it might but …' Meabh looked at Katrina. 'What did you make of her?'

'It was strange. I found the entire meeting odd in a different sense. See, here we are doing our damnedest to find this woman and her brother, and we have all this context for why and what may have happened to him. The Donnelly family and Albert and all of that. But she wasn't coming from the same angle at all. Her brother went missing and that was the beginning and end of it for her. I think Mary Corrigan still fundamentally believes that her brother ran away. All these years she's been thinking along the lines that he might have stolen something at Danesfort. Her theory is that her little brother went off the grid, to use a modern parlance, so as not

188

to be found. It sounds mad but apparently it happened.'

'Oh it did,' confirmed Black Gary. 'Survivors have never had it any good with the gardaí. The rule was you kept out of their way. Back in the old days, the gardaí would deliver you back into hell right fast. And kids did steal. They stole because they were kept hungry. So if you robbed something and ran away, you would keep away from the authorities. If you were caught, the punishment could be severe.'

Meabh nodded. 'I don't like to be saying it but I found Mary Corrigan a bit gullible too. Absolutely determined, don't get me wrong – I mean she has searched high and low for her brother – but, at the same time, gullible.'

'With the loss of her personal items through this probably bogus detective, her search for Paul seemed to fizzle out,' added Katrina.

'And the solicitor?' asked Black Gary.

Meabh answered. 'She kept at it for another while. Bandon gardaí made a song and dance about checking the migration records from that time. But nothing turned up there either.'

'It was sad in the end,' added Meabh. 'As we talked to her, you could see she was getting to trust us more and then she said, "Oh I wish I had a photo of him to show you." She put her hands out. "But I have nothing any more. Just my memories of him." She told us a bit about him. She was heartbroken when you got down to it.'

'We take photos for granted nowadays,' said Katrina. 'We have too many, but back in those days, one photo mattered a huge amount. The loss of the photo of her brother really brought her search for him to an effective end.'

'When did this mysterious detective appear on the scene as a matter of interest?' asked Black Gary.

'It was 1996 or 1997,' answered Katrina. 'She remembers seeing the documentary on Goldenbridge orphanage on RTÉ and this detective appearing not long after. That documentary was aired in 1996. I remember watching it myself. It was ground-breaking and it set a lot of people thinking for the first time about what had gone on in the past in Ireland. Anyway, Mary Corrigan thought there was a connection. That the detective had arrived because someone in the gardaí had woken up to all of these old injustices. Fat chance.'

Noelie got up and opened the window. The night air was refreshing. He heard the river and traffic. Far away, a siren was going off.

'How did the Corrigans end up in the system in the first place?' asked Black Gary.

'Her father's death was the source of it. He was on a boat that got into trouble. They were fishing off Helvic Head and were returning to Youghal when conditions deteriorated. There was a rumour that they were smuggling something and the boat was overloaded, a rumour that apparently did the surviving families no good in terms of their relations with the constabulary. Sounded to me like none of the men on the boat that sunk were favourites with the local gardaí. Anyway, the three men onboard drowned. But Mary Corrigan's dad was the only one whose body was never found. I think that caused them a lot of anguish and, obviously, that was very difficult for them. Mary said that was why she wanted to find all her brothers and sisters again. Anyway they were impoverished afterwards, and it sounded like they didn't have a lot first day. Their mother didn't or couldn't cope and the rest, as they say, is tragic history.'

They took a break to make tea. Noelie couldn't stop thinking about Martin. Everything had happened so suddenly and so quickly. He looked at each of the others – at Meabh, Black Gary and Katrina – and wondered who would be next. If anyone was to be the target he wanted it to be himself.

He took his tea over to the window that looked out over Washington Street. One thing was very clear, someone was going to extraordinary effort to hide what had happened in the past. It wasn't just the brutal attack on the blackmailers all those years ago, it seemed to Noelie more and more that there was an ongoing effort. It was like someone, or a few people even, were alert to all possible threats. Like this detective who had called to Mary Corrigan's and had taken all of the personal material about her brother. It seemed very much as though someone had heard about Mary Corrigan's enquiries and had decided to nip the matter in the bud. It had worked too.

Which drew Noelie back to the other, larger question: what was the real crime that they were on the trail of? He had thought for a long time that it was the films and what the films revealed. Then he had thought that it was more about the men in the films. Was there someone particularly important among them who was in danger of being compromised? A politician or someone like that?

The other issue was what should they do next. Getting the name of Youghal Boy was a breakthrough, no doubt about that. But what could they do with that information? And was it connected in any way to the remains found in the Glen in 1969? Whose remains were those? Noelie had heard nothing back from Oakes. He had left a message for him, to nudge him along but nothing so far. Anyway, where were those remains now? It wasn't clear what had happened to them or where they were even buried. Could DNA be extracted from remains that were over forty years in the ground? As far as Noelie knew, they could be but the remains would still have to be located. If they were, could they be linked to Paul Corrigan? Did his sister have anything of his any more that might be useful, DNA-wise? Probably not, which meant that this entire angle was turning into another dead end.

'Fuck,' he said loudly and the others looked at him. Maybe he had been rash dismissing the Walsh son after all. Maybe that offer wasn't so bad? The old story: it was all relative. He could look down his nose at Stephen Walsh but he potentially had a way to get them right into the heart of this matter once and for all.

Time was everything now and he felt that. The longer this went on, the more likely it was that another attempt would be made on one or more of their lives. Any one of them could be next and it could happen at any time.

They sat in close once again. Black Gary pointed to the plate of Mikados. 'Ask and you shall receive.'

Katrina savoured one. 'Along with Tayto, Mikados are a cornerstone of civilisation that they don't have Down Under.'

Noelie took one too and ate it slowly.

Eventually Meabh looked up. 'So we thought we were done but we weren't.' She looked at Katrina. 'You tell them, will you?'

'After we learned about this detective that came and took away her brother's photo and so on, our meeting kind of ran out of steam. Mary Corrigan was quite upset. We were upset too and for her as well. I asked about exchanging numbers. We both wanted to leave it there. Earlier Noelie you asked about us telling Mary Corrigan about Copley. I had been intending to but I hadn't the heart for it really in the end. We were thinking another time we could come back and tell her a bit about what we knew or suspected. Slowly, slowly, you know.'

'We had actually gone out the door and down to the front gate …' said Meabh. 'Then I just thought about Boy A and Boy B. I was standing there. Deflated wasn't the word. Anyway, I have the photos of the two boys on my phone. Just head and shoulders crops. So I put the battery in and powered up, brought up their pictures and went back up to the front door and knocked again.'

'I was watching from down at the gate,' said Katrina. 'I saw Mary Corrigan falling down. Meabh shouted at me, "Jesus, she's fainted."'

'Christ,' said Noelie.

'She recognised him,' stated Black Gary.

Meabh nodded. 'Exactly. Boy B, the skinhead one, is Paul Corrigan, her brother.'

Noelie and Black Gary looked at each other.

'So we went back in,' said Katrina. 'She was all questions then. After she got over her shock she was happy. But she couldn't believe it either.'

'We had to do some quick thinking. I just couldn't tell her what we knew,' said Meabh. 'I just couldn't.'

'We explained that the photo was a still from an old film we had found,' added Katrina. 'We told her as well that we hadn't access to the film any longer. We mentioned Ballyvolane and asked if she knew anything about that side of things. She had never heard of the place, as I said. I felt bad but I didn't want to go into the details of what we know … I just couldn't bring myself to tell her. It was awful because we could both see that her hopes were up again.'

Noelie hadn't seen Katrina lose her composure before but she did now. She excused herself quickly and went to the bathroom.

'I don't think this is as bad as it looks,' said Noelie quietly. 'I mean …'

'He's dead, Noelie,' said Meabh. 'Don't you see? That kid's not missing, he's dead and he's dead because of what he was put through in those films. Now, just tell me which part of that is not as bad as it looks.' Meabh stood up. Her voice rose. 'Just forget about the investigation for a minute and just see. See what we're seeing? Aren't I right, Gary?'

Black Gary wouldn't say. 'Noelie didn't …'

'They killed that poor boy and they've probably killed others too.' Meabh shouted. 'The only question is how fuckin' many?'

She left the apartment slamming the door behind her. Black

Gary nodded to Noelie. 'I'll go after her.'

Noelie watched him leave.

Katrina returned from the bathroom. 'I heard that,' she said coming over.

Noelie nodded and gave a long deep sigh. 'I'm going to crack up soon.' He looked at Katrina. 'Are you okay?'

'For the first time since I came here – since we talked that day, Noelie, here in this apartment, remember? – I've thought about quitting and maybe heading back to Australia.'

'But you won't, will you?'

She shook her head. 'I guess not. Not yet anyway.'

Noelie got up and went over to her. They held each other.

Black Gary returned. He scratched his head. 'She'll be all right … She's sorry, Noelie. She said to say that to you.'

Noelie nodded unenthusiastically. 'Oh fine, no problem.'

'No, really, she meant it.'

'It's fine,' he said again. 'Look I'm pissed off but I may as well admit it, it won't last. Meabh saved my life. She could call me every name under the sun and I'd probably still smile for her.'

Katrina got beers and passed one to Noelie. Black Gary refused and said he'd go back outside and sit with Meabh a bit more. 'She's on the mooring downstairs looking out at the river.'

After he left Noelie took a slug from his beer. Katrina did the same.

'I think she knew something was wrong, Noelie, Mary Corrigan I mean.'

Noelie looked confused. 'I thought you were saying the opposite. You know, that she was sort of naive and all of that.'

'She was like that and I think she is or was naive, but when she ID'd her brother, I sensed something different in her. And she knew as well that we weren't telling her everything.'

Katrina drank more of her beer and continued. 'The call came through to us around then from Black Gary to say we were to come to the hospital, so we left in a bit of a hurry. Meabh had already gone out to the car, but as I was leaving, Mary Corrigan stopped me to tell me one other thing. She said that this old guy calls to see her once in awhile, very irregularly. She hasn't seen him for a few years actually, so she doesn't know if something has happened to him or if he'll ever even come back. This guy's living rough – kind of a vagabond. Lives somewhere up in Clare, in the woods. Moves around a lot. She also said he's totally mad. He's into all sorts of Celtic mysticism stuff and all of that. He found her though, that's the thing. He knew who she was and about her missing brother. He told her that he used to know her Paul. This guy's age kind of tallied with Paul's so she sort of half-believed him. He told her that she was never to tell anyone about him visiting because he said that people were trying to kill him.'

'Who was trying to kill him?'

'He wouldn't say and she didn't know. He would always shut up if she tried to get any info out of him. In the end she'd just give him tea and something to eat. He was harmless enough, she said. But she said that he once told her that something bad had happened to Paul.'

There was quiet for a while as they drank their beers.

'Hard to know what to make of it,' Katrina said. 'But she told me all about this man in the end without any prompting.'

Noelie nodded. 'She has no way to contact him?'

'I don't think so. Look, we are going to have go down there again anyway sometime and tell her all that we know. We can ask a bit more then. But I'll tell you this now, I am not looking forward to telling Mary Corrigan about what we think happened to her brother.'

Noelie shook his head. 'Me either.'

Graveyard of
the Celtic Tiger

19

Shortly after 6 p.m. Noelie arrived at the hospital. The car park was full so he waited in line for nearly half an hour for a space to come free. Once inside, he drove around looking for Canning's silver Volvo. When he spotted it he pulled in a short distance away, out of view.

Martin's removal had been the evening before, his burial that morning. The two halves of Martin's life – his growing up on the outskirts of Limerick and his years in Cork – were both represented by large numbers of mourners. Although Noelie recognised a lot of Martin's friends from around Cork and from his work, he felt – as did the others – on the margins of the funeral service. Martin's family's grief and shock took centre-stage and Noelie was reminded that he had only known a small part of his young friend's life, even though at times it had felt like he knew much much more than that. Martin might have been living in Cork and getting on with his life on his own terms, but people from his earlier life – his extended family, his schoolfriends and his former GAA teammates – clearly hadn't forgotten him and he still mattered to them.

In the evening between removal and burial, Noelie drank heavily in a way he hadn't for years. He'd still been feeling the worse for that on his return journey to Cork earlier that day, when he'd received further bad news. Oakes had called to tell him that the file on the remains found in Glen Park in October 1969 couldn't be found. He was reassuring though.

'Don't jump to conclusions just yet,' he had told Noelie. 'It happens. They'll keep looking and it might be nearby, just stuffed in the wrong box. I'll keep you posted.' Noelie thanked Oakes and then told the others.

'That's a real fucking surprise,' commented Meabh. No one else said anything.

He waited impatiently in the car park and after nearly an hour, Andrea Canning appeared with a colleague. They stood near her car chatting for a while and then he left. She got into her car and checked her phone before pulling out of the space. Noelie followed her on to the motorway where, a short distance beyond Douglas, she took the Rochestown exit and continued on the main road through Passage West and Glenbrook. For much of the journey the deep narrow channel connecting Cork's docks to the harbour expanse was on his left. Just before Monkstown, the Volvo took a right and climbed a narrow country road into the hills overlooking the channel.

There was little traffic so Noelie dropped back and then lost sight of the pathologist to one of the houses situated on the hillside. He backtracked, narrowing his options to three gated properties. Eventually he spotted the Volvo parked in a short, wide driveway alongside a white hatchback with L-plates. He pulled in nearby and tried the gate, entering quietly.

There were other houses behind and further along the hill on the same level as Canning's. The location was pretty and a lot of work had been done to the garden, which had been levelled around the house. Lower down on the slope, terraced flower beds and a rambling rockery had been used to manage the hilly location.

He was uneasy. Following a woman to her home and then calling to her door in the late evening was not ideal. At least they knew each other, and their fortuitous meeting at the hospital the evening Martin had died would also help. He rang the bell and heard footsteps in the hall. A porch light came on.

Recognising Noelie right away, Canning's expression changed instantly from neutral to concerned.

'I know how this looks and I apologise,' he said immediately. 'I just need a couple of minutes of your time. I promise that's all.'

What seemed like a long moment passed. Finally Canning stepped back to allow him in. 'All right,' she said with measured reluctance. 'Go to the kitchen. Straight ahead.'

It was a modern, open, split-level kitchen-dining area with a marble-top island at one end around which the cooking and prep counters were arranged. The dining-sitting area was at right angles, down a few steps, with French doors at the far end. As it was nearly dark the lights of Rushbrooke and Cobh, on the other side of the harbour channel, were bright and visible. He decided it was probably not a good idea to comment on her house or the view. He stood there, feeling nervous.

'You followed me?'

He nodded slightly. 'It's not something I normally do. I'm sorry. It's just there's something I need to ask you ...'

'You could've contacted me at the hospital.'

'I didn't want to do that. It's where you work and there's Shane's inquest ...'

'And this isn't about the inquest?' she enquired warily.

He hesitated. 'It is and it isn't.'

'Look, Noelie, I can't talk to you about that or tell you anything about it. Isn't that clear?'

'It is – 100 per cent.'

Canning pointed to one of the seats at the island counter and Noelie walked over. The seat was very heavy and he was hardly able to move it. She noticed but didn't say anything. He perched on its side.

'Tea, coffee?' she asked coolly.

'Water.'

'Only water?'

'Water's fine.'

She filled a heavy tumbler with tap water and put it in front of him. She stood facing him with her back to the counter. 'You have the floor.'

Although Noelie had thought about this meeting and what he needed to say, he still felt unsure about how exactly to begin. He couldn't start with the inquest, he knew that, but at the same time the subject simply couldn't be ignored. He needed to find some way to give her more context – maybe then she would help.

'Shane's entire family, all of us basically, haven't been able to understand his death. The situation remains that way. Look, worst-case scenario he did commit suicide. Another possibility is that he died accidentally, and no one is ruling that out either. He may well have fallen into the Lee and, despite his ability to swim, perhaps he was overcome in some way and just drowned. Obviously suicide or accidental drowning fits with the evidence. He wasn't subjected to any obvious violence in the period preceding his death – your testimony verifies that.'

This was borderline and Noelie knew it. Canning stared at him but she didn't stop him. He continued, 'Around the time he drowned I had trouble of my own. You told me you'd read about what happened to Hannah. Well my trouble was related to that. I stumbled upon information, a statement in fact, which alleged that Special Branch had been involved in the death of a missing man, Jim Dalton, back in 1990, twenty years ago now. The reason, it is believed, that they took this extraordinary action was to protect a mole that they had inside Sinn Féin. Some of this was in the papers.'

Canning nodded.

Noelie continued. 'This informer was known to Branch by the code name Brian Boru. He had lived in Cork for years under the alias Tommy Keogh. His real name was Father

Brian Boran. He was a former Rosminian priest who had worked at Danesfort Industrial School. Shortly after Shane's body was found, I spoke to the detective investigating his death, Byrne, whom you know, and told her about the trouble I had been in. You might recall from the inquest, I was actually the last family member to speak to Shane on the morning of his disappearance. Naturally I was asked to account for my movements that day and I did this to Detective Byrne. Subsequently she was able to verify what I said.'

Noelie sipped his water.

'In effect that was it. I was no longer of interest in my nephew's death. For me, too, other things had also come to the fore, to do with this matter of Jim Dalton and what to do about what I had learned. That's another story that I won't go into now. In the meantime, Detective Byrne continued with and eventually concluded her investigation. Which, as I said at the outset, left us, as a family, with a difficult choice to make for our future peace of mind: had Shane committed suicide or did he just accidentally drown? And so matters remained, until this inquest. Now, suddenly – and I think it is fair to say, unexpectedly – there is a question mark over what happened again.'

Canning nodded again and then spoke. 'Well, there are a number of hours, anywhere between two and eight say – dependent on when one sets the time of drowning – where we don't know where he was. I guess it is true to say that there is more confusion now than there had been.'

Noelie nodded. 'But we've also learned something else significant. Shane's phone was in the area of George's Quay, Douglas Street, Mary Street just before it was disconnected from the network. Prior to this, it was thought he had been out around Turner's Cross. A different locality entirely.'

'Okay, I accept that,' said Canning, 'but what difference does that make?'

'I'll explain. See, Byrne is adamant that she checked the mobile phone beacon assignations when she began her investigation into Shane's death. She says that they pointed to Shane being in the area around Turner's Cross when his phone was switched off. That corroborates what I remember too. On the afternoon that the search for Shane got underway, I had a conversation with the then Inspector Lynch – he's since retired – about Shane's disappearance. I was meeting Lynch to do with a different matter – the whereabouts of Jim Dalton. Anyway I told Lynch that Shane was missing and he said he'd make enquiries. Lynch then came to me and told me that the news on the garda wires was that Shane's mobile had been tracked to Capwell Road area in the period just before it went silent. Only a few hours later, I was in touch with my sister and she said the family had additionally been informed by gardaí that Turner's Cross was where the phone had signed off the network. As a result we all trooped over to that part of town to look for Shane.'

Canning moved. She went to the cabinet and took out a wine glass. 'Do you mind? It's been a very long day. I guess you're driving, at least I hope you are, so I won't offer you any.'

'No problem.'

Noelie watched her half fill the glass with red wine. She came over and pulled out a seat diagonally across from him and sat too.

'So the error made regarding Shane's final phone location preceded Byrne's involvement. Which would suggest that either Dream provided an incorrect record or that it was misread at the garda station or that it was altered there. We know, however, that it wasn't misread because a copy with the incorrect information on it is in circulation – this was the copy that Byrne produced when she was giving her evidence. So, in effect, we are left with the other two options. Since Byrne or nobody for that matter can produce the original document given to the gardaí by Dream, we cannot know for sure if an error was made that first time by Dream. Notwithstanding, it is equally plausible that someone in Anglesea Street Garda Station altered the original data – that possibility now has to be considered.'

Canning looked at Noelie for a moment and then rose to go and stand by the French doors. He tried to work out what she might be thinking. Her expression gave nothing away. At the same time, he had anticipated some push-back, scepticism even – accusing anyone in the gardaí of malpractice was nearly always controversial – but it hadn't materialised. It made Noelie wonder again why she had asked for more time from the coroner. To a large extent, everything still hinged on that and it was why Noelie was there. If Canning had found something, anything that could help them, he wanted to know what it was – if she would tell him.

He followed her down the steps into the sitting area, and waited. There were brochures on the coffee table. One had a 'Toxic' hazard label emblazoned on it – a leaflet about the controversial positioning of an incinerator in the centre of Cork Harbour. Noelie realised that Canning's house was an area that would be directly affected by a noxious plume of smoke emitted by the incinerator.

He picked up one of the brochures and looked at it. Canning noticed but didn't comment. Without looking at him she said, 'You came here to ask me something. What is it?'

'Why did you ask for more time at the inquest?'

Canning looked immediately at Noelie. At the same time a young woman came into the kitchen. She looked with surprise at Noelie and stopped. Canning went over to her quickly.

'I didn't realise you had visitors, Mum.'

Canning talked quietly to her daughter who got a glass of juice from the fridge and left again.

'Exams. Leaving Cert.'

'Commiserations.'

Canning had hardly touched her wine. She looked annoyed and Noelie sensed she was about to call time on his visit. He knew he had overstepped the mark. He also knew his only chance was to continue. He spoke quickly.

'When I found this statement about Jim Dalton, as I said, the central allegation in it was that Special Branch were involved directly in an innocent man's death. By the way it was a former member of Branch that was making this allegation not me – a decorated officer at that, Sean Sugrue. As the significance of that allegation was making itself felt, I was brought in for questioning by the gardaí about an assault that took place around that time. I didn't really understand what was going on or what I had stumbled into so I just told them everything I knew. I had no involvement in the assault anyway and eventually the gardaí accepted that and a while later I was released without charge. However, later that same day, I had to disappear for a few hours. Some people seemed intent on catching up with me – I believe in connection with the information I had discovered about the murder of Jim Dalton. I think they thought that I had other material or information and they wanted to get that back. So I hid myself out of the way. All this information I subsequently told to Detective Byrne and she verified this. But my point is, as soon as I felt it was safe again, I returned to my flat only to discover that it had been trashed. I wasn't sure right away who had broken into my place but my housemate, Martin, encountered a man around the time when my place was smashed up – someone he didn't know, who asked to see me. Later on, we were able to identify this man. His name was Andrew Teland. He's a former priest who was convicted of a number of crimes in the States. Subsequently he was defrocked and he came here to Cork, where he has been living quietly since around the turn of the millennium. Although there was an extradition warrant outstanding for him from the States no one appears to have been too bothered to follow that up. It's unclear how much was known about him or his existence here in Cork but this Teland character was living in a house, Llanes, which is up on Sunday's Well Road. It's just alongside the Lee actually. A beautiful property.'

Canning sat down on one of the long sofas and suggested to Noelie that he should sit too. He perched on the edge of the smaller sofa. There was a set fire but it was unlit. She wasn't looking at him, so he took the opportunity to study her, wondering what it was that he liked about her.

Eventually she looked at him. 'I'm under a lot of pressure, Noelie. I'm overrun with work. Which is partly why I asked for a delay in your nephew's case. I'm not sure what you think I can do here. In a day or two I am going to report what I've found. The coroner is a good man. He won't steamroll things and your family have a very able solicitor to fight your corner. I think this is all in safe hands, if you just trust the process. I really do.'

'Look, Andrea, it's possible that my nephew came to my flat that afternoon when I wasn't there. I'd found those punk records and, as I said in my evidence, I invited him over. I was quite excited about the find, I really was. It was stupid of me really. I probably went on about them too much to Shane. I think he got enthused. He was on his school holidays, see. He should be like your daughter there, getting ready for his Leaving Cert now. He had time on his hands. It wouldn't have been like him to come over and visit me, but the records … he may have come for those.' Noelie shook his head very bitterly. 'I wish I had never mentioned them to him.'

Noelie got upset. He had buried deep the possibility that he could have had a role – no matter how unintentional – in Shane's death. He didn't want it to be true in any way. It was bad enough as it was: for his sister to have lost her only child. For Noelie to even have an incidental link to the tragedy would be awful. And he was worried that there was more and worse to find out. Noelie didn't like what he had heard about Teland and he feared that the teenager had been assaulted. How would he face Ellen if that was true?

'Look, sit down,' Canning said. 'Sit properly on the sofa. It's okay.'

Noelie did as he was told. It was way too soft, though, and he felt himself sink too far. He tried to sit upright but it was nearly impossible.

'Your friend's funeral was this morning, wasn't it?'

'Martin, yes.' Noelie nodded.

'You're under a lot of pressure and you don't come across to me like someone who looks after yourself.'

Noelie decided not to say anything to that. 'I'm fine.'

'Have you taken time off work?'

'I was made redundant,' he answered sullenly. 'Lost my job over a year ago now. It's shit, excuse the language. When this is over, I'm going to have to go away. It's a mess.'

'It's okay, Noelie,' said Canning calmly. 'Really.'

'If you can tell me anything … it might help.'

Canning went back to the counter to get her phone, which she then put on the mantelpiece. Noelie noticed a row of silver-framed family photos, including a picture of Canning and a man he assumed was her husband. She sat down on the large sofa again and looked at him. He met her gaze. A moment passed. It looked to Noelie like she was trying to decide something. Finally, she spoke. 'You did chemistry, right?'

'I did.'

'Then you'll understand this. There was a query regarding Shane's bloods – from the inquest. Taylor asked about it? So to be thorough, I did go back and have all the test results looked at again. I put through another full batch and included the one for GHB that Taylor asked about. The report is now back on those.' Her tone changed. 'So before I go any further, take note that this is not to be spoken of, Noelie. I am warning you, okay? If I hear that this was leaked in any way, I won't speak to you again under any circumstances. Understood?'

Noelie nodded. His heart was beating. Had she found something in Shane's blood? It could change everything – and could mean the investigation into Shane's death would be reopened.

'His bloods are clear. There was nothing in them that would suggest anything out of the way. I guess that is good to know. I'm glad now that the request was made about that test. I think it is important for your sister to know that finding.'

Noelie nodded. He felt dazed. He had convinced himself that he would hear the opposite and that this would be it – the breakthrough. It would be horrible, but a breakthrough nonetheless.

'The thing is there's something else. It's odd and I don't quite know what to make of it.'

Noelie did his best to focus. 'Can you tell me what it is?'

'I looked over Shane's entire file again as part of the re-submission for testing. There was a small amount of material trapped under his fingernails: grit. Bits of grit really. What's odd is that there is an unusually high percentage of atomic chlorine present. Do you understand what I'm saying?'

'I think so.'

'It was the chemist at the lab who brought it to my attention actually. We were chatting about the tests and how long they would take to redo and she asked me what had I made of this high chlorine result and did I want that re-checked too.'

Noelie was glad he was still sitting down. He stared, trying to understand what the pathologist was telling him. So it wasn't GHB. That made sense in a way: Albert was much too careful and organised to be caught using such a notorious sedative. So what did the high chlorine result mean?

Noelie worked it out then.

Canning spoke again. 'I guess I'm worried. I'm seeing something here I don't understand and, combined with the other things I'm hearing about this case, it just doesn't feel right.'

She stood up and got her glass of wine. 'I think it's best that I don't tell you any more. But there is one other thing that you could possibly help me with.'

'No problem. Anything, I'll do it.'

'It's not directly related to Shane's case either so it's even better. I'm not breaking any rules.'

'You never were one to break the rules, were you, Andrea?' said Noelie smiling.

'Very funny. Anyway I'm caught for time, as I said. But to cut a long story short, the chemist who alerted me to this chlorine issue remembered another example of it from quite a while ago. She thinks it was 2002 or 2003. Eventually she found a name and that's all I have. I haven't had the time to look it up. It won't be relevant to my report anyway so it's low priority.'

Noelie had his hand out. 'I'll do it.'

Canning went back over to the counter and wrote the name on a post-it. Handing it to Noelie, she said, 'Daniel Murray. Might be worth looking up. If it was a drowning from that time, there should be information on the Internet about it. A lot of newspapers were online by then. Maybe it will shed some light on what this chlorine result is about.'

Noelie thought for a moment. 'What will you do now with this information, about the chlorine, I mean?'

'The inquest is going to be called to order very soon, perhaps tomorrow. The day after at the latest, I feel. Right now, if I had to go into the court, I'd report precisely what I've just told you. It's odd. On its own, one might not take it much further but considering that there are other oddities about your nephew's case I think the coroner will be open to allowing the family more time again to explore the matter further.'

'Do you think what you have found would be sufficient to

reopen the garda investigation into Shane's death?'

Canning shook her head. 'Not in itself is my guess. Everything else confirms a river drowning. The marks on Shane's body are very typical of what happens if a drowned person is pulled back and forth along an uneven river bed. And the water in his lungs, as I was saying, in terms of the freshwater-to-seawater mix matches what you'd expect of the Lee. So, I'm thinking not. But I could be wrong, of course.'

Noelie stood. Canning too. He wanted to hug her but he decided that that was probably not the best thing to do.

'From the bottom of my heart, thank you,' he said. 'I really mean it.'

She smiled. 'Not a word of this can leak out though until I give my evidence, right?'

'You have my word.'

Canning showed him to the front door.

'I'm going to need a way to contact you,' he said.

'Do you want my mobile number?'

'Better not. Is there another way?'

Canning frowned a little. 'I won't ask. Look I have a pager – if you just send your name to it, I'll know to ring you.'

They swapped contact information then, Noelie giving her his burner number.

'Only ring this number from a landline,' he told her. 'Don't use your mobile.'

She frowned good-naturedly. 'Okay.'

20

At Hannah's the smell was atrocious. Noelie held his nose as he entered. 'Oh boy, that is bad.'

Most of the furniture in the kitchen-sitting area had been moved to the far end of the apartment, around the riverside window. The large open space that remained had been covered in old newspaper. Meabh, Black Gary and Katrina were kneeling beside heaps of photos and photosets, ordering and sorting them. The pictures were all from Sheila's fire-damaged house and so they smelled strongly of smoke.

Black Gary looked up shaking his head in agreement. 'Tell me about it. My nose is nearly dead. Actually, it probably is dead.'

Meabh and Katrina stopped what they were doing. Katrina got up and came over. 'How did that go? Any luck?'

Noelie shut the door behind him and went directly to the music system – the Cure were playing – and turned up the volume. He gave them all a big thumbs up and indicated to them to gather around. He spoke in a low voice.

'Albert seems to have made a serious mistake at last. This could be it.'

He told them precisely what Canning had said. Meabh and Black Gary didn't understand the significance of the chlorine levels but Katrina did immediately. Noelie explained.

'I reckon Albert's been using bleach, sodium hypochlorite to be precise, in his under-garden cavern. Probably just to keep it clean and to control algae growth. Of course, bleach is also useful for a different reason. It's perfect for degrading human tissue residue. My guess is that Albert has being using concentrated bleach – industrial grade even – and probably over a long time too. As a result, the stone and concrete in the cavern has become impregnated with residual chlorine.'

Black Gary still looked unsure.

'Okay, so to go back to basics,' continued Noelie, 'the chemical formula for bleach is NaOCl. "Cl" is chlorine, "Na" is sodium and "O" is oxygen. If bleach is left around for a while, it breaks down into more stable chemical compounds. Which ones are formed will depend a bit on the exact conditions at the time – the temperature and so on. I won't go into that now. But the by-products over time will contain a lot of chlorine and those by-products will deposit as tiny crystals on any surface that the bleach is used near. Which is probably what happened in Albert's under-garden cavern. The inside surface has become impregnated with higher than usual levels of chlorine.'

Meabh nodded. 'When Noelie and I were imprisoned in Albert's cavern in the summer we had no idea where we were or what was happening. We found ourselves lying on a slope in the dark. Gradually the cavern filled with water and we had to scramble up the incline to stay above the waterline. Naturally we used our hands and, because it was slippy, we found that we were scraping the rough surface with our fingers and fingernails. Grit probably got under our fingernails too. I remember Noelie's fingers looked very sore afterward. Mine weren't as bad.' She grimaced. 'Basically what Noelie is telling us is that this chlorine that's been found under Shane's fingernails is probably definitive evidence that poor Shane was held in the same under-garden cavern. Shane probably died in there.'

Meabh went to Noelie and held him for a long while. Noelie knew she was right. It was pretty awful to think that this might have been how Shane's life had ended. He didn't want to dwell any further on that and tried instead to focus on getting at the truth.

He said, 'During the recheck of Shane's bloods, a chemist in the hospital lab drew Canning's attention to the chlorine. Apparently it's a very unusual finding. Neither Canning nor the chemist really understand what it means but Canning knows enough to know that it isn't right. I guess you could say alarm bells are sounding. Also, now with the error in the mobile phone records confirmed, she's beginning to get suspicious too. I think this is the breakthrough. I was always worried that something like this might turn out to be the explanation for Shane's death. I guess I was right.'

'Did you tell Canning what you think happened to Shane?' asked Katrina.

'No. None of this can be spoken of yet. She's going to bring the finding to the inquest. She thinks another adjournment is now very likely. She isn't sure if the chlorine finding in and of itself is sufficient for the garda investigation to be reopened, but she believes that that's where things are heading.'

Black Gary hugged Noelie too. 'I'm sorry,' he said.

Katrina did the same. Noelie went and sat down. On the drive back to town from Canning's place he had been thinking that sometimes finding out the truth isn't all that it's cracked up to be. Of course he needed to know and he'd had to find out but it was a miserable discovery. He was already wondering how he'd tell his sister. He didn't know if he could.

'There's more,' he said.

'More, how?' asked Meabh.

'Well, this chemist remembered that there was another example, quite a few years back, of a similar sort of thing. Some people are just on the ball, aren't they? This woman deserves a medal in my book. Anyway, another high chlorine reading. She's since found the name of the person involved. A drowning too. Daniel Murray. From around 2002 or thereabouts. Canning thinks we should be able to find something on the Internet about it. She's intrigued herself now, too, I think.'

'Will I take a quick look?' asked Meabh going for her laptop.

'Let's not use the Internet here,' suggested Katrina. 'We'll go over the road.'

'I'll second that,' said Black Gary, nodding at the chaotic heaps of photos on the floor. 'And anyway I need a break from that. Not sure about this one, Noelie. I'm all for looking in places one shouldn't be looking in but those photos – what I've seen of them - are fairly mundane. The ones that you can actually see that is. Most of them are stuck together like glue from all the water as well.'

It had taken Noelie a couple of attempts to finally make contact with Sheila's sister, Nora. She told him that Sheila was still in an induced coma at CUH. Doctors were happy with her progress and were planning to bring her out of the coma shortly to make an assessment. It was still possible that she would be returned to a coma for another period but Nora had been told that, in the long run, the doctors were hopeful Sheila would make a good recovery. She'd need quite a lot of surgery – skin grafts and so on – but they were optimistic there too.

Noelie had raised the matter of Sheila's photos with Nora. He'd learned that most of them had been saved and put in refuse sacks. Some unfortunately had probably been dumped in the general cleanout that took place after the fire. Noelie offered to take a look at them and, at a minimum, to help dry them out. He pointed out that if they were left lying in the sacks they'd just rot.

Nora was surprised and clearly doubtful that there was any point in even trying to save them, but Noelie had insisted, passing off his offer as him returning a favour to Sheila. Sheila would actually want the photos to be saved – Noelie knew that – so it wasn't as if he was doing anything wrong. He hadn't wanted to field any other questions about his motives; in particular he didn't want to alarm Nora about the fire at her sister's. And, as things stood anyway, Noelie had no evidence at all that there was anything sinister about it.

After returning from Martin's funeral in Limerick he had gone to the house on Douglas Street and collected the five refuse sacks. It was useful that they were already bagged up and ready to be taken, but they had already turned mildly rancid.

Katrina selected a photo from the floor and showed it to Noelie. 'One useful thing,' she said pointing to the numerals printed in a corner of the photo. 'Most of the shots I've looked at are all date-stamped. So, all we'll need to do is find one readable picture in each bunch. Once we find that, it allows us to put a photoset in its appropriate year. We'll be able to rule out 98 per cent of what we have here almost right away. The only photos we are interested in are from June 2010, right? Easy-peasy.'

'Late June actually will do,' clarified Noelie.

'Well I still think it's mad,' said Black Gary rolling his eyes. 'A needle in a haystack comes to mind, people.'

'I'm with Black Gary,' said Meabh. 'All I've found so far are photos of car reg plates, exhaust pipes, cars parked up on pavements, and a few full-on shots of very irate motorists. Your Sheila sounds like she was not to be messed with.'

'Salt of the earth,' countered Noelie defiantly. 'She would not allow herself to be walked on … and, please note, she stood alongside me when we tried to stop the privatisation of the bin collection service. Back in the day.'

'Probably just to get at the council,' said Black Gary.

Noelie was about to reply but Katrina interrupted. 'Could we leave that argument for another time and just go over to the Internet cafe?'

Noelie nodded. He wasn't as sure himself any more about the photo search. It had looked more promising when they were desperate – as they had been in the immediate aftermath of

Martin's death. However, now with the chlorine breakthrough, he was less inclined to put any more of their time into it.

On the other side of Washington Street was a narrow lane called Little Hanover Street. The Internet cafe was a short distance along, past Penny Dinners. Hannah had occasionally used it in the early days of the Internet when her network connection had been poor.

Katrina had been there a few times already and was friendly with the owner, who reminded Noelie of a well-past-his-sell-by-date hippy; nerdy was not what came to mind at all. Clearly, he liked Katrina a lot and had arranged for her to use a separate computer in one of the back rooms. It had a Tor browser installed, which Katrina seemed to be familiar with.

She spent a moment authenticating the browser. 'Nothing's 100 per cent secure but Tor is as close as we'll be able to get.'

Noelie was impressed. He watched as Katrina typed quickly. Dialogue boxes opened and closed on the screen.

'Impressive,' he commented to Meabh.

She shook her head. 'You're easily fooled, Noelie. That could mean nothing what she's doing. She could be working for the Russians for all you know.'

'Spoilsport.'

Just as Noelie was about to ask why they were going to these lengths to hide a simple person search on the web, Katrina began. She entered 'Daniel Murray death' and got a result immediately. It was clear too from the short *Irish Examiner* report why his case was linked to Shane's.

Latest: Body of missing tourist found in River Lee
Friday, May 6, 2004 – 7.40 a.m.
The body of a man believed to be missing tourist Daniel Murray was located during a search of the River Lee in Cork

late yesterday evening. A member of Sunday's Well Tennis Club reported seeing something suspicious in the river near the clubhouse earlier in the day.

A public appeal was launched yesterday to find Mr Murray, who is believed to have been in his mid-forties, after he failed to return to the Metropole Hotel, where he was staying. He left the hotel on Monday afternoon and didn't return. He was last seen leaving the hotel on Monday afternoon and the alarm was raised on Wednesday. Efforts to contact Mr Murray's next of kin have been unsuccessful. Gardaí are expected to issue a further appeal for information later today.

There were a few more articles like this, including an update in the *Echo* that noted that the gardaí had again issued a new appeal for information.

'Odd,' commented Noelie. 'Try adding "inquest" to the search terms.'

That produced a new link, dated September of the same year.

A Cork man who had returned to his native city for the first time in over twenty-five years is believed to have drowned tragically after getting into difficulty close to Cork's Shaky Bridge on the evening of 2 May. Daniel Murray had arrived in Cork on the previous Saturday and was staying at the Metropole Hotel on McCurtain Street. He had booked into the hotel for a week and was due to travel on to Dublin and Belfast. He left to take a short walk on Monday afternoon. When he hadn't returned by Wednesday, the alarm was raised.

Recording an open verdict, Coroner Dr Kevin Crinnon said Mr Murray's death was particularly sad to record as he had returned to Ireland after a long absence. Initially the gardaí had difficulty identifying Mr Murray. His current address was finally traced to Chicago. A statement by one of his neighbours in Chicago, read into the record at the inquest, described Mr Murray as a private man. It is believed he left Ireland at a young age. It was established that he had no living relatives in the Cork area.

Mr Murray was last seen alive, captured on CCTV walking near the old Cork City Gaol late on Monday evening.

Det. John O'Mahony of Bridewell Station, Cork, said it had not been determined why or how Mr Murray had ended up in the Lee. The only explanation offered was that Mr Murray had accidentally fallen into the river. It was a sunny spring evening and it has been speculated that Mr Murray may have slipped or fallen into the river where the bank is exposed and unguarded.

Mr Murray died of acute cardiac respiratory failure due to drowning, assistant state pathologist Dr Con O'Hare told the inquest. Dr O'Hare said many of the findings were in keeping with an accident, but the lack of evidence meant that an open verdict must be returned.

Noelie pulled over a seat and sat down. He read the inquest report again.

'Same area of the river as Shane's drowning, isn't it?' said Meabh. 'Where's that tennis club on Sunday's Well, Noelie? Do you know it?'

'It's right on the riverbank,' he answered. 'Lovely spot actually, and not a hundred miles from Albert's either. In fact I'd guess about a hundred metres downriver of it, on the opposite bank.'

'So, same area of the Lee, a drowning too, and now this chlorine factor in common as well.' Katrina looked around at them. 'That's a match in my books.'

Noelie agreed. He shifted in his seat and read the report on the screen for a third time.

'Out with it,' said Katrina.

'I wonder has he killed others this way, using a method facilitated by the under-garden cavern. I think he has. Meabh, you once asked me why did I think Albert had that place in his garden? I mean it's a hidden space under a very well-kept, immaculate garden. As we know to our cost, to access it you have to use an elaborate electronic control device. Serious planning has gone into this. He's killed this way before.' Noelie knocked his knuckles off his head. 'Stupid. Why didn't we realise this before now?'

Meabh put her face near to Noelie's. 'Because we've been obsessing about the past. I told you, Albert's where this is at.'

'She never lets up does she?' said Noelie to Katrina who just smiled and replied, 'She's got a point.'

Black Gary spoke. 'There's something else. We said this before too. Why has no one come forward complaining about the abuse that happened at that farm? This is 2010. People are prepared to talk about abuse finally, thankfully. If there were survivors, why haven't we heard about them? From even one, I mean?'

'We're nearly certain that Paul Corrigan is dead,' added Meabh.

Black Gary nodded at the screen. 'So is Daniel Murray one of Albert's victims too? Was he abused at the farm, at one of those "gatherings"? Is he like Jamesy Irwin: left Ireland afterwards and went as far away as he could? That's what a lot of survivors did … Murray seemed to have no family here either.'

They wrote down all the details and then Katrina scrubbed the history. Walking back along Little Hanover Street, they stopped on Washington Street and waited to cross over. Further along, a large crowd had gathered outside a pub. The area was popular with students. A huge cheer went up from outside the pub. Black Gary wondered if some important football match was on; no one knew.

They crossed over and went to the door of the apartment block. Noelie asked them to wait a moment. He spoke in a quiet voice again.

'You know a while back we talked about going into Llanes?

I wonder should we strike now while we have the opportunity. I think having an actual photo of the entrance area to the under-garden cavern could be very useful. Getting a photo of the actual cavern itself would of course be excellent too – but that's probably not feasible. But there's another reason too. If Shane's inquest starts to move in the direction of foul play, anyone with a connection to Albert Donnelly is going to dive for cover. The remaining films in Llanes will disappear and for good too. I think we should strike now while we have the chance.'

'Makes sense,' said Katrina.

Black Gary reminded them that the property was empty for a few hours most afternoons. 'It's a question of waiting for the right moment, and then going for it.'

'What do you think, Meabh?' asked Noelie.

'Honestly, I'm not wild about going back in there, but if it has to be, it has to be. Count me in.'

'Okay, I'll check with Ciarán at Solidarity Books about the canoe and if that's available. I don't think there will be a problem though. Tomorrow?'

'Tomorrow it is,' said Black Gary.

21

Noelie spent much of the night – too much – thinking about Albert Donnelly. On a sunny summer's afternoon in July, he and Meabh had called to Albert's home only to find themselves, less than an hour later, fighting for their lives. Their trip to Llanes that day hadn't been planned, yet there was nothing haphazard or hesitant about how Albert had come after them.

They were very lucky to have escaped and for once Albert had been unlucky. However, the more Noelie thought about it, the surer he was that Albert must have attacked and killed in a similar way before. Albert was certainly capable of the surprise attack and clearly, if presented with an opportunity, he took it. But there was preparation and planning too – as proven by the under-garden cavern at Llanes. The question was, did anyone else know what he had been up to?

In the morning, Noelie contacted Canning via her pager. She was a bit abrupt with him but then agreed to a meeting. She suggested The Wilton, a large pub across from the hospital. Noelie arrived punctually at 12.15 p.m. The Wilton was another of those suburban bars that had had a makeover during the good years of the Celtic Tiger. It was full of oversized armchairs, annexes and alcoves. There were no other customers.

Canning was dressed casually again and looked well. Although she didn't make it obvious, it was clear to Noelie that he had only a narrow slot in her busy schedule. She didn't like the table Noelie chose and moved to one beside a window. However, that looked out on the local church. Noelie sat with his back to it.

'Do you have a phone?' he asked her, then explained how smart phones could easily be converted into listening devices. 'Someone would have to be suspicious of you to want to make the effort, so hopefully no one is. But I prefer to take every precaution if I can.'

Canning had an iPhone. Noelie's brother-in-law had the same one.

'Can't remove the battery from these,' she said.

'Could you shut it down so?'

Canning did. If she was still doubtful about Noelie, she wasn't showing it any longer. He told her about Daniel Murray. 'He drowned in 2004. He was from Cork but had lived in the States for years, ever since his late teens, it seems. He didn't appear to have family here. Eventually he was tracked to an address in Chicago and a neighbour there said he had been planning a trip to Ireland for some time. But it isn't known who, or why, he was visiting here. It's early days so we'll look into it some more. I might call to see the garda who was involved. But right now, I can't see a connection.'

This wasn't the truth, of course. Noelie and the others now had a theory and it had become more obvious to all of them overnight. But Noelie didn't want to overload Canning, at least not right away – it sounded like she had plenty on her plate as it was.

Eventually Canning asked, 'You still here, Noelie?'

'What d'you mean?'

'You seem to have gone off somewhere. Are you day-dreaming? Did you have something more to tell me or is that it?

'No, that's it.'

'Lucky then I have something more to tell you. Otherwise I might be thinking this was just a social call.'

Noelie smiled. 'Well ...'

'Let's not.'

She was hassled, he could tell.

'First the inquest is going to resume in the morning. I'll probably present the evidence as I told it to you, and we'll see what happens then. I think Taylor will be on it like a shot. He doesn't miss anything. That would buy us all a bit more time.'

Noelie noted Canning's use of 'us' and liked it. It was considerable progress, more than he had hoped for.

'Secondly …' She pulled a memory stick from her front pocket and gave it to Noelie. It was branded Viagra. She noticed him notice.

'Never mind that. They're flooding the hospital with their material. I think I'm targeted because I work with dead people a lot. "Even dead people get erections with Viagra" and so on and so forth. A hospital joke. So, the analyst in the labs can't remember there being anyone else, apart from Daniel Murray that is, who had this type of chlorine under the fingernails but I think we probably need to look further. It's impossible to go through all the post-mortem files, there are just too many, but if we could narrow the search it would be feasible. So,' – she pointed to the memory stick – 'on that drive is a database of all river-based deaths in Cork going back to, I think, 1965. Someone researched it years ago. There's not a huge amount of information with each entry but there should be enough for our purposes. I was thinking that you and your …' She paused.

'Colleagues?'

'Exactly. I guess that's what they are, that you could take a look at it and narrow it down. Like with the Murray case, there should be info in the newspapers on most of the drownings. If you could narrow down the list, I could then get access to the relevant PM files.'

'Consider it done.' Noelie looked at the drive again. 'This is really great.'

'It's not for public consumption, Noelie, as there is some personal information on it. So don't make copies. Don't let it out of your sight. And I need it back as soon as you're done. Right?'

'Absolutely. You have my word.'

Canning finished her tea and got ready to go. 'No rest for the wicked.'

'At the risk of causing an international incident and all, what made you decide to put this information' – he held up the memory stick – 'our way? I mean it's great, don't get me wrong.'

'Well, it's not connected to Shane's inquest. And I guess I've come around to the belief that something's not right here. And … I took a look at that Teland character. I checked online. I didn't like what I read.'

A short distance down from Wellington Bridge, the embankment flattened to a narrow gravel shore. It was an easy place to access the Lee from and the canoe had been left at the far end under an overhanging tree. Indian in style, the canoe had recently been painted: lacquered brown inside and out, with red tips fore and aft. There were paddles, life vests and a flare gun, which Noelie examined.

'Not sure we'll be needing this, but it might be worth taking anyway,' he said.

Meabh shook her head, moodily. 'Don't make this any worse than it is.' She went down to the water's edge, close to a few Fresher students who were taking advice from an instructor on the dos and don'ts of canoeing on the Lee.

Noelie watched her and knew she was unsettled. He was anxious too. He went to the river's edge where the water lapped calmly on to the shore. Occasionally the clouds parted and the sun shone, but it was only for short spells. The area further downriver from where he was standing was known as the Mardyke. It was easily the most beautiful part of the city. When he was at college, he had dated another student and they'd often walked around this area when they'd had free time. Noelie liked it a lot.

Katrina looked at her phone for the umpteenth time and then smiled at Noelie. She seemed the calmest of them. Noelie wondered if she was relishing the boat trip. She had kind of taken charge.

'By the way,' she said, 'that Ciarán guy said to tell you it's not called Wellington Bridge any more. It's called Thomas Davis Bridge now.'

Noelie pursed his lips. 'I guess that's progress. He ask what we were up to?'

'No. He was diplomatic. Just enquired how far up or down we were going and warned me about the weirs. He suggested a few places farther along where we could leave the boat if we needed to. There's another embankment like this where he can get his van up close. So he said it would be as easy for him to collect there as back here. It's two bridges on, just beyond the second footbridge. Near a place called "bum hole". Is that an actual place?'

'It is, strangely enough. Don't know how or why it got that name. Could have been some kid winding up their parents, but it has stuck. It's by the skate park.'

'He said he wanted a word with you about something else too. I told him we'd text him when we're done and he said he might try to come over if he had the time.'

Noelie wondered what it could be about.

He asked Katrina what she thought about the current. It looked strong to him and he knew that this was the case sometimes on the Lee, depending both on the tidal pull and if water had been let out upriver at Inniscarra Dam.

'It's grand. It'll make it easier to get there. We'll just have to guide ourselves across to the far embankment. We'll be there in a few minutes, believe me.'

The Shaky Bridge was the next bridge on. Just a footbridge,

but it had iconic status in Cork – people loved to jump up and down on it and cause it to shake. Llanes was only a short distance on from it.

Katrina's burner lit up. Black Gary had texted – *Robert D and nurse just left.*

She nodded to Noelie, 'Let's go.'

She got them each a life vest from the canoe and had the boat down on the water's edge in no time. 'In,' she ordered.

Noelie went first but Meabh remained on the bank. She looked pale.

'I can't do it. I thought I'd be fine, but I can't.'

The look on Meabh's face was desperate.

'At all?' he asked.

'I mightn't think straight if I go in. I just … I don't want to put any of you in any danger.'

She looked at Noelie. He felt she wanted him to support her. 'It'll be fine,' he said. 'Nothing will happen. It's just a look-see, Meabh.' He actually wanted Meabh to go in with him – she had been there with him before. She might wobble, but she would come good when needed. He had no doubt of that.

She shook her head again. Katrina waited, looked at Noelie and then at Meabh again. 'We need to make a decision. Time is everything here.'

'Would you go?' Meabh asked her.

'You mean into the house?' asked Katrina. Meabh nodded. 'Sure. Of course. If that will work. I'll go in with Noelie and you can stay with the canoe. Would that be better?'

Meabh nodded unenthusiastically. 'I think so.'

'We have a plan, so.'

Katrina steadied the canoe while Meabh got in, then she waded in to the river up to her knees and jumped onboard. They were out in the mid-river flow almost right away. She guided them deftly to the far side. She was right about the current too. It was in their favour and they moved quickly.

Stopping will be the issue, thought Noelie.

Katrina took them in close to the embankment and, for some reason, that slowed their progress dramatically. It was autumn and many of the trees along the riverbank had turned various shades of brown and yellow. Across on the other side Noelie saw pedestrians on the path alongside the university's sports complex. Although it wasn't common to see boats on this section of the river, it wasn't exceptional either. People were probably looking at them, but they wouldn't wonder what they were doing.

They reached the Shaky Bridge and went under. Noelie pointed to a protrusion of concrete farther along which suddenly came into view. 'That's our spot. There.'

Katrina guided them in perfectly as Noelie reached for and held on to a branch from a nearby bush. He jumped out on to the old concrete step and tied up the boat, pulling it alongside. The others disembarked.

'Look at all the trees,' said Meabh.

Noelie nodded unhappily. A dense line of poplars and bushy shrubs had been planted along the end of the garden forming a natural screen. Before the planting it had been possible to look right into the garden from the opposite riverbank. It was a worry and Noelie hoped that they hadn't left it too late.

They had agreed earlier to message each other every five minutes. They went over this arrangement again. If Noelie and Katrina didn't re-emerge, the plan was for Meabh to continue back to safety and link up with Black Gary who was in the car on Sunday's Well Road. If contact couldn't be re-established after one hour, they would alert Detective Byrne immediately.

'Ready?' asked Katrina.

Meabh took Noelie by the arm and squeezed it. 'Be careful. Don't take any chances.'

The garden was in a poor state and that surprised Noelie. It had been like a showpiece when he'd last seen it. He soon realised why there had been such a deterioration. Two new large flower beds were now positioned exactly where he figured the entrance to the under-garden cavern should be. These were raised, bordered by pretty stone walls. The work was of such quality that, if Noelie hadn't known better, he would have said the beds had been there for years.

'Fuck,' he said, squatting beside the nearest one. 'Looks to me like Albert's covering his tracks again.'

There was nothing to be seen now – which was, in part, why Albert's under-garden cavern was ingenious. Who could imagine anything like it existed under the lawn in this beautiful setting? Noelie suggested that they move on. They went up the garden, past the lily pond and then down the gravel path that led to a door into the lower basement. Noelie tested it with his shoulder but it held. There was a window alongside. He jimmied it with a short crowbar he had brought with him and looked in. It was dark and empty inside. Meabh had told him the room was full with garden chemicals and tools – from when she had been through the basement area in the summer – but it was as bare as the state coffers now.

Katrina offered to climb in. He held her arm a moment. 'Thanks for not even asking me to try.'

She got in with a squeeze and unlocked the door from inside. The area smelled bad. Noelie took a few pictures and they continued into the next room. Meabh had given them the layout of the basement area beforehand. Noelie understood that the area they were now in had been the part of the house that Andrew Teland had been living in. It was totally empty. All the furniture had been removed and the floors swept clean.

'We're too late,' Noelie said dejectedly.

'We'll see what we see.'

They stopped a moment to do a text check with the others and then looked in the adjoining room. It too was empty.

'We'd better go upstairs. No point hanging around here.'

They went along the hall. Noelie was bitterly disappointed. He had considered breaking into Llanes around the time of Hannah's funeral, before he had left for Amsterdam, but he couldn't bring himself to do it. Meabh wouldn't have gone with him then anyway, whatever about now. But he realised now it had been a mistake to delay. Albert had realised the danger and had acted accordingly.

They arrived at a lift with metal concertina doors. It was old style and looked it.

'I'm not getting in that,' said Noelie.

'Me neither.'

They looked along the short hall for the stairwell. Katrina found it finally behind a heavy metal door. They went up one floor to the upper basement level. Climbing the next set of stairs, they reached a door and Noelie opened it carefully. He saw bright sunshine and a side hall and knew where he was. He and Meabh had been brought along this part of the hall in the summer; it connected the front door and the back area of the house.

They stepped out into the brightness. It was quiet apart from the loud ticking of a clock. Noelie gave Katrina an idea of the house plan.

'The back area with the terrace looks out over the garden, and down on to the Lee and Fitzgerald Park. To our right is the hall that leads to the front door and the front entrance leading out to Sunday's Well, where hopefully Black Gary is keeping watch.'

He pointed to a large portrait hanging on the wall. 'There's Old Donnelly in all his splendour. Policeman in the Irish Free State, Blueshirt, mercenary for Franco and possibly the root cause of this entire ugly mess.'

'Irish Brigade flag there,' nodded Katrina at the staff with the white and red flag draped from it.

'You know your history.'

'Emblems, flags and all of that. Once I see one, I never forget it.'

'Keep going?'

They texted again and received replies; all was fine. Noelie led Katrina to one of the nearby doors, which he guessed would take them into the library. He was right.

'This is where the films were. Maybe we'll be in luck.'

'Put on the light?'

Noelie shook his head and went over to the window; he pulled the curtains open. The room looked as impressive as when he had first seen it. Beautiful, dark wood shelving on two walls filled with books and book collections. In two corners were glass cabinets containing different memorabilia.

He checked the cabinet near the door. It had been, and still was, full of white boxes, all carefully labelled. His plan, in the interest of justice was to steal the lot – well, borrow them for a period anyway – but when he lifted the first box, his heart sank. It felt light and he knew it was empty.

'Fuck.'

They checked every box, but they were all empty. Noelie fumed. There were drawers under the cabinets and Katrina looked through these, but there was nothing in any of them.

'Keep looking, Noelie.'

He went over to the worktable. There was something sitting beside it covered by a yellow sheet. Noelie removed this and saw a wooden carving underneath. It was strange but it seemed to be a cross in two parts – too large and cumbersome to stand as one piece. It was unusual in that figures and scenes were partially carved on to the upright. Whoever was working on it was a talented woodworker. Some of the scenes were elaborate, but it was incomplete. Noelie remembered seeing something like this when he had been in the house that afternoon with Albert but that cross had been colourful and much smaller – not like the usual type you'd see in Ireland. For the most part,

Irish crosses were either plain and brown, or they were Celtic Crosses. This was more like an ornament.

He opened the worktable drawer and found drawings inside. He took them out and called Katrina. She examined each one, opening the curtains even more to allow in extra light.

'Best to photograph them,' she said.

She flicked through the selection, holding each one out for a moment so that Noelie could take a shot of it. There was also an old faded print of Da Vinci's 'The Last Supper', and an old black and white photo of a group of men in suits, standing in two lines, one behind and higher up than the other.

'Maybe we should take that photo?' asked Noelie, examining it some more. 'It looks interesting. Like, who are all these people?'

Katrina thought it would be better to leave things undisturbed, so instead Noelie took a few close-ups of the picture. They found one other photo as they were putting the drawings back. It looked like an old picture of Robert Donnelly in uniform. Katrina held it up. He looked very dour. Noelie photographed that too. Finally, he took some shots of the two-piece cross from a few angles.

Katrina texted again to report that they were fine. Noelie photographed the cabinet with the Blueshirt uniform in it. He took a couple of other photos, then they pulled the curtains closed and left.

'What is it Kevin Kline says in *A Fish Called Wanda*?' asked Noelie. '"Disssappooiiiiiinted" isn't it? Well fuckin' "disssappooiiiiiinted".'

'You got me thinking about Jamie Lee Curtis now.'

That reminded Noelie of Albert's infamous film room. There wouldn't be anything in there to see, but Noelie was drawn to it for no other reason than to confront his own fears. It was in that room that Albert had drugged him. But the door was locked. Maybe it's as well, he thought.

'Look upstairs?' asked Katrina.

Noelie nodded. He wanted to see Albert's bedroom. He would have laid a bet that it would reveal something significant about Albert's person. Although what exactly, he didn't know. They climbed the stairs. The first two doors they tried were locked.

'Shit.' said Noelie.

The next one was open and they looked in. Noelie figured immediately that it was Robert Donnelly's room. There was a folded-up wheelchair in a corner. The bed was an ancient four-poster, unsympathetically fitted with protective rails on two sides. It was already made up with a pale blue quilted cover.

'His underpants are probably blue too,' said Noelie.

Katrina looked around. 'In need of a makeover I think.'

Noelie nodded. 'I'm generally well disposed to people who are ill, but Robert Donnelly leaves me numb. In one way I'd like to know more about him, in another, I'd almost prefer to have my teeth pulled without anaesthetic.'

'Take a picture anyway.'

Noelie looked around but there wasn't much. On the wall were two largish photos. One was of Old Donnelly with a well-dressed woman – Noelie wondered was it Robert's mother, the woman who had died in childbirth – the other was of a man he didn't recognise. He photographed both.

Out on the landing again, they tried another door. Locked too. Noelie walked towards a large window at the far end, that looked down over the back garden and on to the Lee. He was able to see as far as the university. He looked to see if he could spot Meabh, but he couldn't. He couldn't even see the canoe. The line of trees at the end of the garden was an effective screen.

Katrina called him over. 'Look at these.'

Along one wall was a series of framed old photos. They

looked like a collection in terms of style, subject matter and framing. They were all of places. Noelie recognised the old Donnelly house out past Ballyvolane. It was a much better photo than the one he had got from Toner. Beside it was a photo taken from almost the exact same place as the previous, except that now the Donnelly house was just rubble. A small part of one side wall remained standing. There were piles of stones nearby. The interior of the ruin was also just visible with what must have been a basement now exposed to the daylight.

'An odd photo isn't it?' commented Noelie.

'Why do say that?'

'Just the idea that you would photograph your old family home after it had been demolished.'

They looked at it some more. There was a group of men in the photo, and behind them, a builder's truck. Noelie peered closely at the logo on the side of the truck, but he couldn't make it out. He photographed the photograph.

Katrina said, 'Photograph them all, Noelie, but look at this one.'

Noelie took the shots. When he got to the one that Katrina was looking at, he saw immediately why it was of interest. It was quite an old picture and it was of Llanes. It was hard to put an exact date on it, but Noelie guessed it was from the early 1900s based on how the men in the picture were dressed – some were ready to go swimming and were wearing those one-piece bathing suits that were fashionable long ago.

In the photo, chairs and tables were set out on an immaculate lawn. The centrepiece of the photo was a long rectangular swimming pool. At one end was a diving board and some of the men in the photo were watching someone getting ready to dive.

'So that was Llanes once upon a time,' he muttered.

Katrina read the text in the bottom right hand corner with difficulty. 'Marshall House, 1919.'

Noelie took a few pictures of it.

A text came in. It was from Black Gary. 'They're coming back,' said Katrina.

Noelie took a few remaining shots and then they quickly went down the stairs, through the bottom basement and out into the back garden.

'Those last photos may have made this visit worthwhile, after all,' whispered Noelie. He was pleased with them. The photo of the swimming pool in the property as it had once been might also suffice for Canning. It was a find. Did it explain the origins of the under-garden cavern in Llanes? Was the cavern itself the remnants of an old outdoor swimming pool?

'And don't forget that photo of those men from the library either. That's an interesting one too.'

They walked quickly along the side of the garden, crouching as they went. A lawnmower was running nearby, possibly in the adjoining garden. They reached the fuchsia bushes at the end of the lawn and Noelie immediately saw that the canoe wasn't where it should be – it was on the river floating away. He looked all around but he couldn't see Meabh. 'Where is she?' he hissed.

They went down the steps to the water's edge. 'Meabh? Meabh?' Noelie called in as loud a whisper as he dared. He turned to Katrina. 'What the fuck?' he said. Her face had turned ashen.

They decided to split up to check the two neighbouring gardens – going as close to the boundary of each as they could and calling Meabh's name. There was no answer. They returned to the spot where the canoe had been tethered. Noelie felt like he was going to get sick.

Katrina called Meabh's burner and got a 'cannot be connected at this time' message. She tried her main phone and they heard a faint vibrating sound close by. Noelie followed it and saw the phone discarded in a flowerbed, partially covered by fallen leaves. There was something wrapped around it.

His hands were shaking as he showed it to Katrina. He recognised what it was – a miraculous medal. She took the phone from him and undid the silver chain.

'There was one of those at Martin's crash site,' Noelie said in a low voice. 'It was hanging from a tree branch near where the car left the road. I didn't think much about it because I thought someone religious might have left it there. Martin's mother or father or someone like that. But this is different.'

Katrina examined the medal. 'The chain's new but the medal itself is quite old.' There was a motif of Our Lady on one side and the letter 'M' over a cross and bar on the reverse.

'Well, whatever about where Martin crashed, this medal isn't here by accident.'

'For sure,' agreed Katrina. Looking at Noelie, she said, 'Maybe it isn't Branch who we're dealing with after all?'

They couched close together out of view of Llanes. Noelie called Black Gary on the burner. Thankfully he answered immediately. He hadn't noticed anything up on Sunday's Well Road. Noelie asked him to check along the street. 'Be careful,' he added.

Katrina was still examining the medal. It was hallmarked and she showed Noelie the indentation but it was too small to be made out without magnification.

'Fuck, fuck, fuck' he said.

They remained there for a moment looking around.

'Contact Byrne?' asked Katrina.

Noelie shook his head immediately. 'We'll have to tell them what we're up to here … and more. I don't want to risk it, not yet anyway. What do you think?'

'I agree. Let's keep looking for now.' She nodded at the river. 'We need to get that boat. I'll swim out.'

They went down to the water's edge. The canoe was quite

a bit away but it hadn't been pulled into the main current. Noelie watched as Katrina quickly removed her clothes and slipped into the water. She swam quietly towards the boat. He could see that it wasn't easy for her to drag the canoe back. Eventually she made it. Noelie helped her to get out and tied up the boat.

22

At Hannah's, the smell was worse. Noelie opened the windows in the apartment to let in fresh air and stood looking out on Washington Street. After a while Black Gary joined him.

'What are you thinking?' he asked.

'I'm trying not to think about the worst-case scenario.'

'We have to stay hopeful, Noelie.'

They had searched for Meabh for a long time. The occupants of the home upriver of Llanes were happily gardening so it seemed safe to rule out the possibility that anyone had entered from there. However the other garden, downriver of Llanes, appeared empty. It was a large property too with lots of untended bushes, shrubs and mature trees. There were opportunities aplenty to hide. While Katrina dried herself off, Noelie climbed over the fence and took a look. He searched everywhere but he saw no one or anything suspicious.

They checked around the lower garden area of Llanes once more in case there was anything they had missed but they found nothing. After checking again with Black Gary they left. Katrina paddled the canoe up and down the embankment on the same side as Albert's property. It wasn't easy due to the current so Noelie helped. They looked everywhere they could without attracting attention, but there was no sign of Meabh or of who may have taken her.

A while later they stopped searching and took the boat back to the embankment near the skate park. Katrina called Ciarán and left a message for him. They met up with Black Gary next and circled around Sunday's Well to see if they could see anything. The three of them hardly spoke the entire time. Black Gary hadn't known that anything was amiss until they had contacted him. Until that moment he had thought the break-in had gone very well. He hadn't seen anyone acting suspiciously on the road outside Llanes either.

Noelie noticed that Katrina was another person who liked to remain busy when she was under pressure. He watched her prise apart blocks of water-damaged photos. Everything from the refuse sacks from Sheila's house had now been sorted and dried. However a lot of the photos were stuck together as if glue had been used on them. Katrina was patient, and she took her time as she carefully peeled two pictures apart. When she realised he was watching her, she smiled dejectedly. Noelie knew she was badly unnerved by what had happened.

'I think we should go over what we know,' she said after a while. 'What we do next is important. And if we do hear from whoever has Meabh, we need to be ready.'

Noelie wasn't enthusiastic. He was too worried and afraid But Black Gary agreed with Katrina. 'Come on, we need to do it.'

Noelie brought the old radio over to the table and switched it on. An African mask of Hannah's was hanging off-centre so he straightened it. Black Gary collected their phones and put them away. That was another issue: Meabh's burner was missing. Her ordinary phone had been found but not the one she used to communicate with them. They decided that they needed to change all their SIMs immediately.

Katrina showed Noelie a photo from Sheila's haul. 'Finally one from June of this year. Early June, mind, but it's close. Maybe we'll find something after all.'

The photo was of a white van that had mounted the kerb

just outside Sheila's. It was where the pavement on Douglas Street was quite narrow. The owner of the van had parked far too close to Sheila's front door. It was clear why Sheila had taken the photograph.

Noelie was glad of the diversion. He took the picture and looked at it. 'Crazy isn't it?' he said, shaking his head. 'Some people would actually park on top of you if they were able.'

'There are actually very few photos from 2010,' said Katrina. 'Which is a bit odd, isn't it? Maybe Sheila had moved to digital, Noelie, or had she stopped taking photos?'

He shook his head. 'She hadn't stopped. Before I had to move out in July, she was still snapping away happily. I often slagged her off about it. So they should be about.'

'Could have been the ones that went into the skip,' said Black Gary, taking his turn to look at the photo.

They had retrieved quite a few CDs too; they were in the refuse sacks with the photosets. 'Anything on those?' Noelie asked.

'Meabh went through most of them early this morning. Nothing. They're just random collections. A couple are unreadable. I'll take them over to my man across the street and see if he can help with those. CDs are a pain, frankly.'

'Did you find out if Sheila had a computer?' asked Black Gary.

Noelie shook his head. 'Not yet.'

Black Gary gave the photo back to Katrina and she put it with a few others in a folder labelled '2010'. Then they went over what they knew again. First the remains found in the Glen and the news, courtesy of Oakes, that the file into that matter couldn't be found. Linked to that, they now had the identity of one of the boys in the double-8 film – Paul Corrigan. In time, there might be some way for them to revive a missing persons investigation into Paul Corrigan. In addition, if they could find a record from Danesfort – if one existed – indicating that

Paul Corrigan had been sent over to the Donnelly farm at some point, they might have something tangible to work with linking the missing boy to Albert. Katrina wondered as well if Mary Corrigan could be interested in doing more once she was fully apprised of what they thought might have happened to her brother.

'That woman has spirit, no doubt there. If she finds out that something happened to Paul, she'll want to pursue it, I feel.'

'The next significant matter we've looked at,' continued Katrina, 'that we've made no further progress on, is to do with the death of the blackmailers in 1970. We have a theory that the discovery of the murders could have brought Robert Donnelly into the conspiracy, in that he aided and abetted a cover-up in order to preserve his family's good name but also to keep control of Albert. The huge payoff to Robert Donnelly was Brain Boru, his informer inside Sinn Féin.'

Noelie spoke. 'Meabh reminded me of something else–' He stopped abruptly and looked at the two of them. There were tears in his eyes. 'What if they've killed her?'

The question hung there. It was on each of their minds but no one wanted to face the possibility.

'We have to hope, Noelie,' said Black Gary.

Katrina nodded. 'We have to stay focused. It's important. It's about keeping ourselves sane as well. What did Meabh remind you of?'

'Well, when we confronted her mother in August about all that had happened and about her not helping her daughter, she defended herself by saying that she had told Robert Donnelly about the abuse linked to Llanes. She said that Robert wanted to help but that he was afraid of Albert. I challenged her saying that that couldn't be true – due to Robert's senior rank in the gardaí – but Mrs Sugrue was adamant. If that was true then it meant that the tables had turned again. Now Robert was living in fear of Albert. The thing is,' asked Noelie, 'how could that be? Had something else happened that we don't know about?'

There was silence.

Black Gary shook his head and looked at Katrina.

'Could be just the simple impact of time,' she said. 'Robert Donnelly was a youngish cop in 1970. He uncovers these murders and the abuse. That gave him the upper hand with Albert. But part of the deal involved Robert keeping quiet too. Fast forward twenty years or so and now Robert's a senior figure in the gardaí, in Cork society too. Except his closet is bursting at the seams. Who also knows this? Well, dear Albert of course. Albert's worked out how vulnerable Robert is, now that he's a person of higher standing. Maybe he's taken to reminding Robert of the fact every once in a while.'

Black Gary nodded. 'Considering that there was never any love lost between them either, it's plausible.'

Noelie agreed as well and nodded. At the same time his mind had veered on to something else, similar but not directly related. It had to do with seeing the photo in Llanes earlier of the swimming pool as it had been in the old days. He felt another bit of the jigsaw was moving into position. He wondered if the blackmail attempt and, before that, the discovery of the human remains on the Glen building site had acted as a warning to Albert that the past was going to come back at him with a vengeance. The crimes of abuse from the sixties had happened. In time, those victims would find their voice. Albert might have wondered how he could insure himself against the problem that was bound to materialise at some point in the future. Had the move to Llanes given Albert his solution? Noelie didn't know if Llanes was chosen by accident or design but Albert might have seen its potential in the early days.

Far better to end someone's life by constructing a death that has all the appearances of being an accident. Old Donnelly walking drunkly into the slurry pit was a perfect example: all

Albert may have had to do was point his father in the right, fatal, direction. Whereas the botched blackmail murders in the Glen were at the other extreme. Those were violent, full-on assaults that had left the killers with a lot of cleaning up to do afterwards. Had the swimming-pool-under-garden cavern in Llanes emerged as the perfect solution? Albert must have known after the botched blackmail attempt that other trouble would turn up at his door again one day.

Out of nowhere Katrina said, 'Maybe we should to the Walshes after all?'

'Why do you say that?' asked Black Gary.

'Well,' she said, 'what are our options right now? We've made progress. I mean in time, if we are all still alive, I think we might well break this open. But Meabh's life depends on what we do in the next twenty-four hours.'

Noelie nodded. 'Our hard copy of the double-8 film is in Australia. It is the one thing that we have that everyone else wants. It's valuable, no question. But when I last spoke to Irwin on the phone, he sounded worried. He'd had his house professionally checked for listening devices and two were discovered. He's afraid, but more for his family than anything else. I'm really sorry now that we sent the film back with him. What were we thinking?'

'We weren't to know what was going to happen,' pointed out Black Gary.

Noelie wondered also about the low-res digital copy that Meabh had told him about. However that was in Amsterdam. He could call her friends there and ask them to look for it for him but she had probably put it somewhere safe, which would mean it would be difficult to locate.

He swore and then said, 'I think we have to consider the Walshes' offer too. Breaks my fucking heart to do it, but if it means Meabh will be safe, there's no question for me. But it still means getting the hard copy of the film here as soon as possible.' He shook his head in despair. 'Easier said than done.'

'We could still go to the cops,' Black Gary reminded them. 'Should we make contact?'

Noelie had already given this more thought. He figured Byrne wouldn't be able to do much personally because they hadn't a definite suspect in mind – other than Albert of course, and he was nowhere to be found.

'They'd probably treat it as a straightforward missing-person case,' he said. 'I'm not sure how much use that would be.'

'I agree,' said Katrina. 'If we want them to take us seriously, we'd have to tell them what we know – about the Donnellys, the Walshes, Let There Be Light, everything. If we do that we risk having our information leaked to the very people we're after. I'm reluctant for now.'

Black Gary nodded. 'I think that means we're back to the Walshes' offer. With so little time, it really is looking like the best way to go.'

Katrina nodded as well. 'Although, when the Walshes find out, if they haven't already, that Meabh is missing, things will change. They'll know that we are desperate. Our bargaining position is now a lot weaker.'

Noelie nodded. 'Yes, it will be the full film in exchange for help getting Meabh back. Any notion that we might also get the list of names they claim to have, is frankly pie in the sky. I'll talk to Irwin,' he added. 'I think it's best he comes here personally with the film. It's the safest thing to do.'

'Before we decide for definite on the Walsh move, what about Shane and the inquest?' asked Katrina.

'We're on to something, no doubt there,' answered Noelie. 'But we have to let things happen naturally. We can't pile in, I feel, making wild claims until we have proof. What will happen next will depend on whether the present evidence pushes the coroner in the direction of reopening the garda investigation or not. It's definitely edging in that direction. A further adjournment is likely. Look, it's like with everything else: we have to hope and we have to keep pushing.'

In the end, they were unable to reach a final decision. Reluctant though he was to do it, Noelie figured that they had no choice but to ask Irwin to travel to Ireland with the double-8 film. The home movie was their strongest bargaining chip and getting it to Cork as soon as possible was their best hope.

Later, alone in his room and feeling exhausted, Noelie put the battery back in his main phone and waited for it to power up. If someone was going to communicate with them about Meabh it would be via his main phone – they had just replaced their burner SIMs.

He waited to hear the tell-tale sound of a message coming in. What he feared most now was that Meabh would suffer the same fate as Hannah. Hannah had almost certainly been killed almost as soon as she was taken. It was quite possible that the same thing would happened to Meabh. Maybe it already had? He dearly wanted someone to make contact and propose an exchange. Whatever they asked for, he was going to agree to it too. He no longer cared about getting justice and finding out the truth. Too many people who mattered to him had lost their lives over this already.

He waited and waited. Minutes went by – sometimes the network was slow, he decided – but no message came in.

23

There was still no word by the morning. However, Noelie received a message from his sister to say that the inquest was resuming at 10 a.m.; he knew he needed to be at that.

He and the others had discussed whether they should call to see Meabh's mother to tell her what had happened. Noelie wasn't sure if she would help as she had shown little motherly interest to date. All the same it could be worthwhile. Even if she pretended that she couldn't do anything, she might make contact with someone in Let There Be Light. Maybe they could watch her in case she went somewhere in particular with the information? Noelie didn't know if it would be worth the effort.

Oddly, Canning came to mind. If he sat down with her and told her everything, she might provide a different, objective view, so to speak. She'd probably tell him to go to the police, and maybe he would do just that. He was feeling drained and out of ideas.

Katrina and Black Gary had finished looking through all of Sheila's photos, working late into the night. They had also finally managed to view all the CDs, including the ones that had been damaged. Katrina's friend at the Internet cafe had managed to repair the two discs, but these had just contained photos from 2006 and 2004. It was another dead end.

Noelie was getting ready to leave for the courthouse when Katrina enquired about Irwin. He was forced to admit that he hadn't contacted him yet.

Katrina was angry. She called Black Gary over and told him the situation.

'Noelie, you have to do it,' said Black Gary. 'Get it moving at least. As it is, it'll be forty-eight hours minimum before he gets here. We have to get our hands on that film.'

Reluctantly, Noelie agreed. The others were right, he knew – they had to do everything they could. Privately though he was much more pessimistic than he would admit to. Maybe that was what was stopping him from dragging Irwin into the fray. Albert and his people were killers and they would relish a chance to finally get Irwin.

'So do it then,' said Katrina. 'And I'm not leaving until I see you send the message.'

It was not straightforward, of course. He would need to text Irwin first. Their communication plan involved Noelie alerting Irwin that he needed to talk to him and when Irwin replied, it would be with an online phone number where Noelie could ring him. It wasn't so much a secure means of communication as one that made it very difficult for anyone to monitor.

Noelie sent the message. Katrina actually looked over his shoulder while he did it.

'Done,' he said.

'About time,' she retorted.

After that, she announced she was going to go to the library. She'd work for an hour on Canning's database of the Lee drownings. If Irwin hadn't been in contact by 11 a.m., she told them, she going to see Meabh's mother after all. Under the pretext of wanting to get Stephen Walsh's contact details, she would tell her what had happened to her daughter.

'You better come with me, Black Gary. I might not be able to stay calm dealing with that woman.'

Noelie and Black Gary exchanged glances.

On the way to the courthouse Noelie detoured to Henderson's Photography to order prints of his Llanes photos. The technician who had helped him in the summer was still working there and recognised him. She was off to Australia after Christmas, she said – a lot of her friends were out there already. He was envious.

He explained what he needed, and she offered to crop and touch up the images for him, in particular the photos he'd taken of the framed pictures on the first floor of Llanes. These had been taken in haste and weren't great. She told him to come back in an hour.

At the courthouse, proceedings had just got underway. Noelie joined Ellen and Arthur in the front row of Court 1.

Ellen whispered, 'Taylor says something significant has turned up.'

He could see that she wanted to tell him more but it was difficult with the inquest already in session. She looked hopeful, though, and Noelie was glad. Canning was to testify again. She was wearing a grey trouser suit and a dark blue blouse. Once she was in the witness stand, she put on glasses. She took a moment and then spoke quietly into the microphone. Whatever about the antique appearance of the courtroom, the sound system was top notch.

'Coroner, I'd like to report a clarification to my earlier evidence to this inquest and, secondly, I'd like to bring an additional matter to the court's attention. Firstly, in relation to Mr Taylor's query on the presence of gamma-hydroxybutyrate, or GHB, in Shane Twomey's blood, I can confirm that I expedited a test for this and the result was negative.' Canning paused a moment.

'Thank you,' said the coroner.

'However, in order to provide the most thorough picture possible, I requested that the lab revisit all the findings in Mr Twomey's case. In doing so, my attention was drawn to an anomalous reading that I am not able to explain.'

Noelie looked around. The courtroom was nearly half full. The only sound was the distance buzz of traffic.

'Scrapings from the index and middle fingers on the left hand and from the middle, ring and little fingers on the right hand revealed small amounts of lodged granular material. What is pertinent here is the higher-than-anticipated level of chlorine present on these grains of concrete. There is a variation in levels but to summarise, all results report a chlorine level in the region of three to four hundred times normal levels. At present I am at a loss to explain this finding.'

When it became clear that Canning had nothing further to add, the coroner asked, 'Are we sure that these quantities of chlorine are associated with Mr Twomey's drowning?'

Canning looked unsure. She leaned closer to the microphone. 'I don't follow, Coroner.'

'Well, could these deposits have been present due to some activity that took place prior to Mr Twomey's disappearance?'

Canning thought about her reply. 'The short answer is that it is possible. We cannot rule that out. However, I did re-examine the photos taken of Mr Twomey's hands and there is visible evidence of higher-than-usual levels of wear and tear at the fingertips. I commented on this in my original testimony. It has been speculated that Mr Twomey may have attempted to climb from the river to safety but was unable to do so. Such efforts could possibly account for this appearance.'

'What do we know about these granules as you describe them?' enquired the coroner.

'Well as you may know, the Lee has been scrutinised in detail over the years and much is known about its limestone walls and the river basin itself. There is a database on file courtesy of University College, Cork and I have consulted this, although to no avail. I should add that this does not mean anything in and of itself. All sorts of stones and rock types have been used around and along the Lee over the years. So, in terms of the stone type, I cannot say right now where these granules came from. They are certainly not similar to the limestone predominant along the Lee in the city area.'

Taylor indicated that he wanted to ask a question but the coroner directed the pathologist to continue.

'Coroner,' she said, 'I should clarify one matter here. Saltwater obviously contains salt, or what is more accurately called sodium chloride. So a body of tidal water like the Lee will have a certain amount of the chlorine present as it is subject to the regular ingress of seawater. For example, if we were to analyse the walls of the Lee, we might expect to see higher-than-usual levels of chlorine than we would in, say, a wall protecting the edge of an inland lake, which would only be in contact with fresh water. However there is a quite a different level of contamination in the grains found under Mr Twomey's fingertips. The only explanation I can suggest for these levels would be if he had been in a place that used high concentration, perhaps industrial-grade bleach. Depending on its strength, bleach can contain high levels of sodium hypochlorite, traditionally used as a disinfectant and to keep mildew at bay, et cetera. It was once commonly used in swimming pools, although less so now.' Canning hesitated. 'My earlier evidence, Coroner, given to this inquest last week, suggested that Mr Twomey had died by drowning in a body of water similar to the Lee in terms of its freshwater-saltwater mix. And that finding still remains true. However, this anomalous result regarding chlorine possibly suggests a non-river drowning location.'

Ellen was shaking her head. She spoke to her husband and then to Noelie, 'Am I hearing right? Why wasn't this brought to our attention before now?'

There was now complete silence in the courtroom. The coroner, too, looked surprised. Taylor stood up again and the coroner allowed him to speak this time.

'Was this information brought to the attention of the gardaí?' he asked.

'The data and results were in the file,' said Canning. 'However I don't think it was brought specifically to the notice of the investigating detective. I would describe it as a moderately technical detail. In other words, I am not sure that someone would take note of the chlorine level unless it was specifically pointed out to them. Most people wouldn't know what the finding actually meant.'

'Why has it taken until now to bring this matter to the court's attention, Dr Canning?' asked Taylor.

Canning looked directly at the coroner. 'I take full responsibility in this matter. The result was in the report I received from the laboratory back in late June. I didn't appreciate its significance. May I take this opportunity to apologise to the Twomey family and the court, Coroner?'

Ouch, thought Noelie. To his sister he whispered, 'Honest.'

'Incompetent you mean.'

'So, just to clarify,' stated Taylor, 'it was not brought to the attention of the investigating detective at any stage?'

'Not to my knowledge.'

Taylor waited a moment before continuing. 'You have just said in your explanation that the evidence is suggestive of a non-river drowning location. How are we to make sense of this? What sort of a location would be consistent with this type of finding?'

Again Canning hesitated. It seemed that she was trying to frame her answer properly. 'I would expect to see this level of chlorine in surfaces exposed to prolonged contact with concentrated sodium hypochlorite. So we are talking about an enclosure where the surface is regularly treated with this chemical, probably to maintain a hygienic or algae-free environment. However we must add the caveat that this enclosure would also have to have a regular influx of river water, since, to repeat, the constitution of the water present in Mr Twomey's lungs was consistent with what we find in the tidal Lee.'

Taylor looked at the coroner who looked at Canning. 'Can you shed any light on this matter?' he asked.

'Coroner, one possibility, for example, is the city's water treatment facility further upriver of where Mr Twomey was found. This facility has a number of treatment pools that the Lee is diverted into. However, access to this facility is strictly prohibited and I believe furthermore that it is monitored on a twenty-four-hour basis for obvious security reasons. The only other type of similar structure that comes to mind is, say, a swimming pool or something of that nature. But again, I do not know of any such facility along the Lee since the closure of the Outdoor Baths at the Lee Fields in the eighties, I believe it was.'

'So, a pool? A swimming pool, an aquarium or … ?' clarified Taylor.

Noelie noted that for once the knowledgeable solicitor was lost for words.

'Possibly,' answered Canning. 'But I cannot actually say. I don't know.'

A short while later the inquest was adjourned. Noelie had hoped to get a quick word with Canning but she left immediately. He stood with the others outside the courtroom. Although he didn't make any direct contribution to what was being said, Noelie sensed something had changed for Ellen and Arthur. Ellen in particular had rejected the explanations of suicide or accidental drowning from the outset and now it was beginning to look as if her belief would be vindicated.

He decided he would call to see Ellen later. Maybe she was the one to talk to about Meabh. He'd check with the others first, but he felt that they needed to get fresh counsel to advise them on what to do next.

He returned to the flat, talking to Black Gary by phone along the way. Noelie reported that he hadn't heard from Irwin, which was odd as it was evening time over in Melbourne and that was the best time to contact him. He would try again. There was positive news, however, from the examination of the drowning database. Black Gary wouldn't talk about it over the phone but it was evident from his voice that he was pleased.

Back at Hannah's, Noelie texted Irwin again while moving all of Sheila's boxed up photos downstairs to take back to Douglas Street. He repeatedly checked his main phone for any messages about Meabh. It was odd and it didn't bode well that no one had been in contact. What was going on?

He called Nora on the way to Douglas Street. He asked if there was a neighbour on the street who would have a key to Sheila's – that way he could leave the boxed photos back without having to trouble Nora to make the trip to Douglas Street. Noelie was hoping Nora would go along with that plan because it would allow him to have a look around the house to see if there was a computer about. He didn't understand why they couldn't find any photos bar a single print from 2010.

Nora told him there wasn't any spare key lying about and that she'd meet Noelie at the house – she wanted to have a word with him anyway. She wasn't there when he arrived so he stacked the boxes near the door and called to Solidarity Books. Ciarán was there but so were a lot of other people. Some sort of meeting was about to get underway.

Noelie thanked Ciarán again for the loan of the canoe.

'Any time, Noelie. No bother.'

'There was something else? Katrina mentioned it.' Noelie prompted.

Ciarán remembered. He was a big man and didn't do a quiet voice easily. 'Let's go outside,' he said. They stood in front of the window display of the US troops at Shannon Airport.

'There was a cop around here, about a day or so ago. A female detective. It was to do with your nephew. She had a picture of him with her. Flashed the badge, the usual. Byrne's her name. I think that was it anyway.'

'That would be right,' agreed Noelie. He was surprised to hear it though. So Byrne had jumped to the same conclusion that he had: that a deliberate attempt had been made to divert attention away from Douglas Street. She was wondering too, if someone on the street had witnessed something.

'It all seemed above board in one way. But we weren't sure about her either. One of the others in the shop recognised her. From up in Mayo at the time of the Corrib gas protests. Shell2Sea and all that. She was one of the watchers up there, seeing who was active and who wasn't. People are wary of her. Is it legit her asking about your nephew or is she nosing into something else and us?'

Noelie was taken aback by what he heard. But he answered, 'I do think it's legit. There's been trouble at my nephew's inquest. It looked straightforward when it began. In fact we thought it was going to be over in just one day, but it's still going on.'

Ciarán seemed reassured. Noelie thanked him again and said if he learned anything more to the contrary he would let him know. It was unsettling news all the same – about Byrne's involvement up in Mayo. In the early 2000s, Shell2Sea had formed the main opposition to a controversial pipeline that would link the offshore Corrib gas field to Shell's inland refinery. The gardaí had acted as glorified henchmen for the Shell oil corporation, but what had disturbed many of the people who had been there at the time was how much the gardaí seemed to relish the work.

Nora arrived by taxi. Noelie heard her calling to him so he went down to her. There was a free parking space adjacent to the pavement. The taxi driver had been able to pull in close and set down the ramp easily. Clearly Nora knew him well. She told the taxi driver she'd need him again in a short while.

Noelie never knew if he should offer to help push people in wheelchairs or not, but before he could work out what to do,

Nora had the front door open and she was rolling down the hall of her sister's house.

He followed her in and they both remarked on the terrible smell. The damp was rising off the floor and walls too. Noelie carried in the boxes of photos and put them in a room at the back of the house that hadn't been damaged by the fire.

'Thanks for doing all of that,' Nora said when Noelie was finished.

They talked about Sheila. Nora was expecting to hear any day about when she would be taken out of the induced coma. She told Noelie how much she missed her.

'At least, Noelie, she's alive,' said Nora.

The comment got to Noelie. With all that had happened, he understood only too well what that sentiment really meant. If only … for Martin, Hannah and Shane.

'I'm looking forward to seeing her too,' he said. 'Will you let me know when she regains consciousness? If visiting is allowed, I'll be in the queue to see her.'

Nora got ready to leave again. At the front door Noelie enquired as casually as he could if Sheila had a computer. The second he opened his mouth Nora had him. She snapped on her wheelchair brake and rocked backwards a little. 'What do you really want, Noelie?' she asked. 'Out with it. I mean, it was kind of you about the photos but most people agree my sister's daft. Her photos … well, *Hello!* magazine won't be looking for them, let me put it that way. Now you want to look at her computer too.'

He put his hands up. He figured he was lucky he got on well with Sheila; Nora was more miffed than really annoyed with him.

He told her that Sheila had been asking for him in relation to his nephew's inquest. He explained how the inquest was not going smoothly and that there was now a question mark over Shane's final whereabouts.

Nora nodded. 'There was a bit in the *Echo* about it. I'm sorry, Noelie. Really. It's not easy.'

'Did she mention anything to you in relation to the inquest?' he asked.

Nora shook her head. 'No.'

'Could I take a look at her computer anyway just in case? It's above board, I swear.'

Nora told him she'd had it moved to one of the smallest rooms upstairs where she had figured it would be safe. Noelie found the room but there was no computer in there. He returned downstairs. 'Would it have been thrown out?' he asked her.

'Course not.'

Noelie went up and looked again, and looked in one of the other rooms as well. But he couldn't see it anywhere. He returned again. Nora said she'd ask the builder in case it had been put somewhere, but she didn't think it had. 'Are you sure you looked properly?' she asked Noelie.

'I did look properly,' he replied as calmly as he was able.

Nora was sounding like her patience with him was running out too. Diplomatically, he decided to wait with her until her taxi arrived. She asked him some more about the inquest and he told her about the error in the mobile phone records. She asked Noelie if he had a picture of Shane. He had, on his main phone. Noelie opened it and flicked down through a few photos. He showed her one. It wasn't one of the best ones so he flicked down a few more to a photo of Shane holding his guitar. It was one of Noelie's favourites. He had a big broad smile in it.

'Terrible,' commented Nora. 'So young.'

'Only sixteen.'

After a moment she said, 'How do you know that other man in your photos, the one with the white hair?'

Noelie returned to the first photo of Shane and scrolled back

256

down again slowly. He reached the picture of Albert Donnelly.

Nora asked warily, 'You're not a friend of his, are you?'

'That man, Albert Donnelly? Definitely not. How do you know him?'

Nora shook her head. 'I don't know him, I don't know people like that. But he was the one we had all the trouble with.'

'What trouble?'

'There was an argument here on the street between him and Sheila. I just came in at the end of it. It's complicated, but I was due to visit and Sheila had put out no-parking cones to reserve the space outside her front door. The space has her disabled markings on it too, but a lot of people know they aren't the proper ones so they ignore them. I had been a bit sick. This was in the summer now and I'd had an operation, so Sheila was just trying to mind me. Anyway, that man, what did you say his name was?'

'Albert Donnelly.'

'Well, apparently he came early this particular day and took the spot. Just pushed the cones out of the way. Sheila was a bit annoyed about that. But she asked him would he move later on as I was coming. I wasn't coming until after lunch. Well, he wouldn't move. He was horrible. It was a bit strange too as he had a disabled-access car of his own and there was an older man in it. He was all up on his high horse about his rights, that fella Albert. I don't mind telling you, it was quite bad.'

Noelie leaned against the window ledge beside the door. 'You said this was in the summer, do you remember when?'

'June, I'd say. Around then.'

'Any idea when in June?

Nora opened her handbag. 'It'll be on the video.' She looked at Noelie. 'The date, won't it?'

Noelie was now very glad he was, at least, partially sitting down. He felt a bit light-headed. Nora's phone was the slider type. Fancy enough. He watched her peer at the screen.

'I took a video,' she said. 'They didn't know I did. When I arrived, Sheila was having a full-blown argument with that Albert man and another man was involved too. He was horrible to Sheila. She could give as good as she got, but I thought it was going to get out of hand. He wouldn't give way and neither would Sheila, so I began videoing it. I was sitting there in my wheelchair just looking on. People don't pay much attention to you when you're in a chair. I held my phone close and pressed record.' She held out her hand. 'Here it is.'

The video played. It was taken from a lopsided angle. Noelie watched. 'Jesus Christ,' he said.

'Now, now, Noelie, I go to Mass.'

'Sorry.'

He checked the date on the film – it was taken the day before Bonfire Night, 23 June, the day Shane went missing.

The film was a few minutes long. In the main it recorded Albert. Noelie worked out from it that Nora was in her chair out on the road. Her phone captured a lot of what happened. Sheila was remonstrating with Albert about taking the space. Albert looked angry. Clearly, Sheila was harassing him and he was not liking it. At one point, Andrew Teland appeared in view – seen talking quietly to Albert. Teland seemed calm. Then Noelie saw something else, something he simply didn't expect to see. He went completely cold all over.

Nora noticed his glazed over expression. 'Are you all right?'

'I'm not actually,' he said. He shook his head. Composing himself again he asked about the film. 'Could I make a copy of it, Nora?'

'No problem.'

Next he called Katrina on her burner. He called it four times and it didn't answer. He was incensed. He called Black Gary and he got an answer immediately. He told him quickly what had happened and that he needed to talk to Katrina. It took a moment as she was immersed in newspaper folios again.

'You all right?' she asked immediately.

He told her about the film. 'How do we get something like that off her phone? We need to copy it immediately. Like a hundred times. Put it on YouTube or something. I don't care, any place.'

'Calm down,' said Katrina. 'Head for our Internet cafe. They'll have a cable for the phone there. That man's got everything under the sun somewhere on the premises.'

Noelie asked Nora if she would be okay to do that and she said she would. When the taxi came they went straight to Little Hanover Street.

24

Noelie entered the Imperial Hotel on Pembroke Street, crossing through the restaurant to the main foyer. He looked around – a couple were chatting at reception – and continued to the front doors. The rush hour was over and South Mall was quiet once more. Katrina was across the street, near the Passport Office. Black Gary was more difficult to locate. Noelie eventually saw him in a doorway on the corner of Father Mathew Street. Returning to the foyer, he looked around again and then went into the cafe. He ordered a coffee and sat at a window table.

There was one other customer. He was nervous. This was a gamble and he had no idea how Lynch was going to respond. The former inspector appeared as Noelie's coffee arrived. Lynch had a good look around. He was in a grey two-piece suit with a dark jumper underneath. It took Noelie a moment to work out what was different about him. Then he realised that the Saddam Hussein style moustache was gone.

Lynch came over, stood with his hands in pockets and looked at Noelie.

'Have a seat?'

'What do you want, Noel? I've only got a few minutes. I'm on my way to a show.'

'Really? Which one?'

'Does it matter? What do you want?'

Noelie nodded. 'Okay then. As I said when I called, I've new information about how my nephew died. I'm giving you the opportunity to look at it first. If there's a reasonable explanation for what it suggests then fine, no harm done here.

If there isn't one, then maybe you can help me with a problem I have.'

Lynch continued to stand.

Noelie added, 'I'm doing you a very big favour here.'

Lynch sat down, looking at his watch at the same time, presumably for Noelie's benefit.

'My nephew drowned. He ended up in the river and that, as they say, is that. Except it's not. They've found something. I know you're following what's going on at his inquest, so you'll know that I'm not bullshitting you. It'll be in the papers tomorrow anyway. Albert's fucked up. It's just one of those weird things really. A quirk of life, I suppose. A lot of killers, even ones as good as Albert Donnelly, get caught out by things that they've never even considered.' Noelie paused. 'So it is with Shane's drowning. This morning at the inquest it was reported that Shane probably drowned in a non-river location. What do you think "non-river" actually means? Do you happen to know of any non-river locations? Maybe you don't but I certainly do. I happen to know that there's one at Albert's house, in the garden there. It's only a matter of time now before all this comes out. Shane was murdered in Llanes by Albert Donnelly and Andrew Teland. The only questions will be why and did they have any other help.'

The waiter came over to ask if Lynch wanted anything. He shook his head and the waiter left again.

'Am I meant to say something? I mean, what am I to say?' He shrugged at Noelie. 'This is news to me. I'm sorry to hear it actually, if it is true what you are saying about your nephew. Really, it's not easy for anyone, in particular for a family to deal with a situation of murder if that is what this turns out to be. I'm surprised, I must say. You are right, I did attend the inquest once but that was only out of courtesy, nothing more. You are quite wrong to say that I am following the proceedings. I just wanted to show my face at the courthouse for your sister and brother-in-law's sakes. Sometimes it is hard to leave a job like mine behind. It was my life. I do feel for them and what they have gone through.'

'How well do you know Albert Donnelly?'

'Never met him.'

Noelie raised his eyebrows. 'At all? Are you sure? Never been to his place in Sunday's Well? To Llanes? To see Robert even? I mean, Robert and you were colleagues, right? Until Robert went into decline?'

'Robert Donnelly was my boss, Noel. I don't know what you know about the gardaí, but it's not the kind of job where they encourage you to visit your boss at home. So no, I haven't had the pleasure.'

'What about the child abuser, Teland, that ex-priest? Detective Byrne showed me the file on him. He had been living quietly in Llanes for nearly ten years. Ever meet him?'

'Have you a hearing issue? I said I was never at that place, Llanes or whatever it's called.'

'Remember the month's mind Mass for Leslie Walsh? I was there with Meabh Sugrue. You remember Meabh, don't you?'

If Lynch had seen her recently it didn't show on his face. He continued to stare at Noelie.

'I saw you at that. You were there with a bald-headed man. You looked very cosy with Robert Donnelly that day.'

'I don't know if you know this, but Robert Donnelly is unwell and has been for a long time. I very much doubt if he even knew where he was that day. Or who I was even. And anyway, so what? Is it a crime, going to a month's mind?'

'Okay then, so what's your connection to Leslie Walsh?'

Lynch sighed heavily. 'Look, Noel. I've done you a favour, out of courtesy, to come here. But I'm not answering any more questions. If you have something to show me let's see it. Otherwise I'm going.'

'I'm just trying to understand why you were there. What's

your connection to these people? I mean, you're not actually one of them, are you? Because one could get the wrong idea.'

'The wrong idea? Them? What are you talking about?'

'Teland was a convicted abuser. Leslie Walsh paid off two victims to keep quiet. That sort of idea – that type of people'

'I'm going.'

As Lynch stood to leave, Noelie produced a photo envelope with Henderson's logo emblazoned across it. He put the first picture on the table.

'Albert Donnelly's car: an olive-green Berlingo. It's wheelchair adapted too, I guess for Robert. If you look closely, you can make out a figure sitting in the car. According to my source, the Berlingo was parked on Douglas Street for a few hours on the afternoon of 23 June, which is the day before Bonfire Night by the way. Coincidently it's also the day my nephew went missing.' Noelie looked more closely at the photo on the table. 'It's hard to say who that is in the Berlingo, but I believe it could be Robert Donnelly. What do you think?'

Lynch sat down again. He looked suddenly wary. Noelie guessed he knew what was coming. He put another photo on the table. Although taken from a skewed angle and of low quality, it showed Albert Donnelly's face mid-grimace. He looked angry. Noelie had seen the video that the images were pulled from so he knew the shot's context – it had been taken at a moment when Albert and Sheila had been exchanging insults. The time was 3.17 p.m. and Noelie wondered if Albert and Teland had already encountered Shane by this time. Was that why Albert was more than usually agitated? Were they in the middle of attempting to get Shane away from Noelie's flat without being seen?

Noelie put down another photo. This one was only of half a face but Andrew Teland's large ear was hard to mistake.

'Andrew Teland,' said Noelie pointing, 'since you don't know who he is.' He looked around then. No one had come in or out of the cafe. The waiter was watching them though. Noelie put the final photo out on the table. Again, it was an odd shot, taken as Nora had moved in her wheelchair. For the few seconds that she was in motion, the camera had panned across the street, along the line of parked cars, capturing a shot of Lynch as he talked to Teland.

'And there you are,' he said. 'Take a closer look. All these photos, by the way, are still frames from a video taken on the day that Shane vanished. If you take note of the times, they tally precisely with when Shane disappeared. Did you put them on to it, to my place I mean? Did Shane just surprise them? Saw the door open at my place and went up to my flat and saw them there tearing it to bits. Is that it? But why kill him?'

Noelie shook his head because he still didn't understand that. And then of course he did. Albert Donnelly would never take any chances. He had almost been caught before, he was never going to make those sorts of mistakes again.

'All that Shane probably ever did wrong was to look them in the eye, I guess.'

Before the meeting, Noelie had worried how Lynch would react. The ex-garda had a notoriously short fuse. But he didn't look dangerous to Noelie right then. Lynch looked more bewildered.

'Shane's not in these photos,' Noelie continued, 'so it will take a bit longer to put the final bit of the jigsaw in place. The woman in the argument with Albert is Sheila Carroll. Her house caught fire just before the inquest, strangely enough. She had been trying to make contact with me. She's seriously injured in hospital, but she'll make it. I wonder now did she see my nephew on Douglas Street that day. She wouldn't have known who he was and it probably didn't seem important to her because the investigation and search for Shane was deliberately directed away from Douglas Street. Your work, I guess. You almost succeeded too. All of us have my sister to thank that you didn't. She never believed that Shane had killed himself. I guess that's mothers for you.'

Lynch picked up the photos and looked through them. There was a far away expression on his face. Noelie wondered what he was thinking.

'Before you ask, I don't have the video that those photos came from on me. I need your help, and if you work with me, I'll give you the only copy. Otherwise, you're going to be done as an accessory to murder. And your bosses, or ex-bosses as they are now, are going to hang you out to dry. They probably want to be rid of you anyway. I mean, you must know a lot of things that are probably best not talked about in polite circles. You're looking at a long spell in jail. Or maybe something more sudden and terminal will happen.'

Their eyes met. Noelie thought of Lynch standing over him back in 1984, beating him around the head with a baton as he lay helpless on the floor. In those days, people like Lynch didn't even care if you left the station with bruises. You were a walking advertisement for their work and Lynch was proud of his reputation. It was a memory Noelie found difficult to dissociate from the face he was staring at.

'I hate to do this, but I'm going to offer you a way out. Your only hope now is to take this deal. We'll lose this video – there's only the one copy – in return for the safe return of Meabh Sugrue. And don't tell me you know nothing about that. Dropping Miraculous Medals about to throw me and everyone else off the scent is fucking gauche. Produce Meabh, and these photos and the video will vanish for good. And if I hear that anything has happened to her, you're done for.'

Noelie kept his eyes fixed on Lynch. Eventually he spoke. 'In the summer,' he began, 'that first time I interviewed you, I had a bad feeling about all of this. The way that Sugrue file on the killing of Dalton turned up. It was already bad when this' – he held the photos up – 'happened. It's as you say. Your nephew did turn up. By the time I got to Douglas Street, it was already too late. According to Albert, Shane came into your flat and saw him. He went to run but Teland was behind him and stopped him. He was put out right away. It was never going to end any other way after that.'

'There was never any need to kill him.'

'Calm down.'

'Don't fuckin' tell me to calm down.'

Lynch held up the photos. 'You're forgetting when this happened. You and your friends fucked up the entire Brian Boru matter. It's over and done with now. Everyone's living in the new reality thanks to you. How many lives will that stupid act of yours cost? The likes of you never factor in how many lives Brian Boru actually saved, do you? How many bombs never went off because he was talking to us. No, you don't think about that at all. It's plain "right and wrong" to you, isn't it? I'm wrong because of my uniform and you're right, why? Because you have some chip on your shoulder about … about just about everything from what I hear.'

The waiter moved close to the table in a blatant reminder to quieten down. Lynch glared at him. Eventually he looked at Noelie again and spoke in a calm voice. 'Perhaps your nephew could've been allowed to live. Maybe he could've been threatened to such a degree as to never have mentioned what he saw at your flat again. But with the future of Brian Boru at stake, as it was in June, was that risk ever going to have been taken? No. Absolutely not is the answer.'

'But how did helping Albert cover up what he did to my nephew help anyone?'

'Because if Albert went down everyone and everything went down. And that's been the way for quite some time now. So, I had to help Albert. That's why I questioned you that morning at Anglesea Street Station. I was the one who kept tabs on it all.

So when Albert got himself muck deep in trouble over at your flat, I was the one who had to go there and clean things up.'

Lynch's phone rang then. Noelie eyed him warily as he reached into his jacket pocket to retrieve it.

'My wife. I really was going to a show.'

'Well, you're going to have to change that plan.'

'Can I answer this?'

Noelie shook his head. 'Fuck off.'

'I'm going to have to speak to her soon. You know how women are. She'll keep calling until I answer.'

'Then turn the phone off.'

Lynch obeyed, then, as if there had been no interruption, said, 'I've been involved in all of this for twenty years – drawn in over Jim Dalton's death. I was a close colleague of Robert's and he'd told me about Brian Boru. A mole of that calibre inside Sinn Féin at that time was priceless. Totally above suspicion too. I tell you this, there was no hesitation upstairs when it came to the killing of Jim Dalton. The real mistake was bringing Sean Sugrue into the matter.

'It was thought that Jim Dalton had already told people what he knew and that he had seen Father Brian Boran in Cork. So, it wasn't just a matter of getting rid of him, they had to destroy his good name too – make him appear unreliable, disreputable even. So rumours were circulated around the city that he was an informer. Sugrue was needed for that part of the plan. By the way, he's not the saint everyone makes him out to be either. Scott Medal or no Scott Medal. Anyway, as you know, that all went tits up and I was brought in for the clean up. And then one thing led to another. Before Sugrue died, he came to me and asked me to help him to expose the rot around Brian Boru. It was already a fucking cancer seeping into everything by then. But I was compromised. I had to keep going. You see, Noel, you are right about one thing. They'll throw me to the wolves tomorrow morning and I know that.'

'Who tipped Albert off about my place? Who told him that I had found some of the Sugrue file? You? It had to be.'

'No, it wasn't. I was sent in to clean up the mess but I wasn't the one who put him on to you. I've spent most of my life in Branch. My loyalty is to the gardaí first and foremost. I've only ever done what I've done strictly on the assurance that it has been necessary. It has meant dealing with people like Albert, but they don't own me.'

'You have a swanky house I hear, so I guess it hasn't done you any harm either?'

Lynch sneered. 'You think this has been easy?' He shook his head. 'What happened to your nephew was the bottom of the barrel. Dealing with people like Teland. I'm glad to be out of it.'

It had started to rain heavily outside. It was much darker looking too. Black Gary had warned Noelie that a downpour was expected.

He had one last question. 'If you didn't tip Albert off, who did?'

Lynch had recovered some of his composure. A condescending smile crossed his face. 'Who else is out there, is that what you want to know, Noel?'

'That's exactly what I want to know.'

'There's been cat and mouse going on for years. Albert's always wanted to get that film back because it's something that Branch had over him. He wanted the film to free Boran too. Albert's totally deluded, by the way. Did he seriously think they'd let Brian Boru retire one day? Obviously Branch wanted the film for itself – it would safeguard Brian Boru and act as insurance against Albert. But there are other films, maybe you know that, and there are other people involved. Which means that there's an uneasy peace. It's like with you and me here. It looks like I am going to have to accept your terms, right? And maybe at the end of the day it will all turn out satisfactorily for both of us. I don't go down for murder and you get to see your sweetheart again.'

Noelie ignored the jibe.

'But if the opportunity came my way to get one over on you, I might do just that. And, let's face it, if you got the same chance, you'd take it too. I mean, I'm sure you'll regret it if I get off on this matter to do with Shane.'

Noelie didn't move or say anything, but Lynch was on the nail and he knew it.

'It's the same with Branch and the people around Albert who are tied into the films. When there are common problems to be dealt with, it's fine; peace reigns. But every once in a while, the other side attempt to gain the advantage. When news came suddenly in June that the Sugrue file had turned up, there was an almighty scramble to get to all of the material first.'

'And my nephew died because of that.'

'I regret it Noel, I really do. It wasn't supposed to happen but it did.'

'It had to have been someone in the cops who tipped Albert off though. You reported what you found up the chain of command. So, is there someone higher up the garda chain who is an abuser?'

'Is Albert one? Seriously, I don't know. The question has been asked many times but no one has ever given me a straight answer. Frankly, no one understands what makes that man tick. Except he's fucked up. All are agreed there. Look, Noel, there are people in the gardaí – and I thought you of all people, given what you believe, would know this – who have other allegiances. I've been approached a number of times and I'm not even God-fearing. These people look out for each other. I don't think Albert is particularly admired, but he's one of their own, warts and all. Only the other day I was reading about the Pope, Ratzinger, that he has apparently known for a long time about all the abuse going on under his nose. Apparently he knows who the senior people involved in it are too. He doesn't let that get in the way of business. He has other fish to fry. You know, Noel, one thing I've realised about people like you, you're very fucking naive sometimes.'

'I told you I don't have the film with me, but I will arrange for the people who do have it to meet us here in a moment. The deal is we go directly to where Meabh is now and make the exchange immediately.'

Lynch shook his head. 'How do I know you haven't made copies?'

'You have my word.'

Lynch looked sceptical. A moment passed. 'Okay, I suppose I have no choice …'

'Exactly. You don't.'

'But it can't be right now, right away I mean.'

'It has to be.'

'It can't be.'

'Why?'

'Because I'm being watched. We both are right now. You'll walk us all into trouble.'

'And even more if we wait and meet you later.'

'Look you said something earlier, that my bosses would throw me to the wolves. Well, it's true, they will. I have as much at stake in this as you. Maybe even more. I'm not trying to pull one.'

Noelie couldn't decide. A delay would mean more of an opportunity for Lynch and Branch or whoever was out there to regroup. He and the others had the element of surprise on their side, but that wouldn't last.

'I'm not even sure I know where she is,' Lynch said. 'She's not in the city. But I do know that she hasn't been harmed. The plan is to ship her out to Romania, to Albert. Use her as bait to draw you all out there. You're too difficult to get rid of here and I guess that's even more true now.'

Noelie was taken aback at the idea of Meabh ending up in Romania. How would that be done? But he was relieved too. There was a possibility she was alive.

'You have an hour.'

Lynch looked at his watch. 'Not enough time. Make it 10 p.m. As soon as I get her, I'll make contact again. Bring the film. It has to be somewhere quiet.'

'Not too quiet though. How about across from Llanes? Just there at the Shaky Bridge. There's space for two cars to pull in and around. We'll do the exchange there at 10 p.m. And come on your own.'

'You're giving me your word there is only one copy of the film?'

Noelie never thought he would be doing this. 'I'm giving you my word.'

At that moment another phone began to ring. Lynch stood up.

'Not mine,' said Noelie, 'and I saw you switching yours off.'

Lynch's expression was inscrutable. He made no effort to answer the call and just said, 'I'm sure you don't work off one phone, Noel, do you?'

Noelie didn't reply.

'Can I contact you on the phone you used earlier?'

Noelie nodded.

'You need to leave it on.'

'Okay.'

Lynch left immediately and Noelie went to pay the waiter. He was worried, though: he didn't like the sound of that other phone going off.

25

Katrina and Black Gary crossed South Mall and sheltered with Noelie at the entrance to the hotel. The rain poured down.

'He got into a blue Audi,' reported Black Gary. 'Parked near Bank of Ireland. There was no one else in it but he was on his phone the entire time. He took off like a bullet.'

Noelie told the others how it had gone – quite well, he'd thought until the final arrangement, which he felt he had been forced to accept. 'I don't like it,' said Black Gary. Katrina shook her head too. Noelie was reassured; he felt the same.

'I think we have to follow him now and hope he leads us to Meabh,' said Katrina.

Noelie called Colin Dalton, who was currently in his mother's car following the Audi. Noelie had spoken to him before the meeting with Lynch, knowing that Colin would do anything to make the retired cop's life difficult.

'Lynch has this other car stashed out in Douglas but he's not heading for there,' Colin told him. 'We've passed the Commons Bar and are now on the road to Mallow. I'll keep with him, but you'd better get moving too.'

They travelled nearly forty kilometres on the Cork–Limerick road, passing through Mallow and Buttevant. A short distance past the town, Colin called again to say that Lynch had finally left the main road. He gave them directions – to look for a fork in the road – and, a few minutes later, called with a further clarification. 'There's a sign saying "Surplus Building Equipment". I've driven on past and you should too. It's too small a road to follow him on, but that's where he is.'

They missed their turn-off and had to pull in. The rain was

torrential and it was difficult to see around. As they tried to work out where they were, Noelie's main phone rang; it was Lynch.

'I need to push the time back another hour, to 11 p.m. I won't make 10,' he said.

Noelie agreed. 'But this phone is almost out of juice. I'm switching it off now. So no more changes.'

Noelie didn't wait for a reply, ending the call. He took out the battery. He realised that he had made a stupid mistake agreeing to leave his phone on. It was a number that he knew was being traced. If Lynch was operating on his own, it wouldn't matter but if he was planning to double-cross Noelie and the others, then they had probably given their location away – it would be evident they were following Lynch. He cursed his stupidity and told the others.

'We have to go on now, Noelie,' said Katrina. 'Look, it's only 8.30 and just forty-five minutes back to Cork. He could make 10 p.m. if he really wanted to, but he doesn't. So he's up to something all right.'

It sounded like that to Noelie too. Still, he knew he'd made a stupid error.

The rain was unrelenting and road signs a rarity. They were nearly back in Buttevant when they got their bearings. This time they saw the fork and only a short distance on they arrived by the building supply sign. It was hilly around: farmland interspersed with woodland. Noelie remembered that the area around Glenville – where the month's mind had taken place in July – looked similar. But Glenville was much nearer to Cork and farther to the east.

It was nearly dark and visibility very poor. Colin Dalton found them anyway and showed them his secret: night vision glasses. Noelie was impressed. Colin had found a concealed track that led into the forest and suggested they leave the car there out of view.

Once they had parked, he had them moving immediately. They walked back to the turn at the building supply sign and then on about a hundred metres, arriving at a clearing. Higher up there was more woodland; commercial plantings.

An area had been fenced off, the land within the boundary looked big and desolate. They found the gate but there was no sign of Lynch's Audi. They guessed he had already gone through. They followed a road that sloped down towards what Noelie believed to be sheds. Maybe there had been a factory at the location at one time; he wasn't sure. But there were no lights on anywhere.

He borrowed the night vision glasses. Before them lay about a hundred strange but uniform shapes. For a moment he wondered if he was hallucinating, the objects seemed so alien, but as they moved closer, he realised what he was seeing: an army of cherry pickers, with their extended arms stretched upwards, salute-style, into the night sky; scores of mini-diggers carefully parked in a line; cement mixers – big and small; scissor lifts; building site toilets; mini rollers; and trailers, too. All in all, about two football fields' worth of building gear, and that didn't include a series of open sheds filled with scaffolding.

'I read about this,' whispered Black Gary. 'Gear being collected since the crash and sold to the continent. All going at knock-down prices. There's a mini-boom in the East apparently.'

'Lynch had said they were going to ship Meabh to Romania,' Noelie reminded them. 'Maybe this is how they were going to do it – hide her amongst all of this. That means she probably is here, somewhere.'

'You mean you weren't sure we'd find her here?' asked Black Gary. 'What the hell, Noelie?'

'Well, I don't know what to think any more,' he replied irritably. 'An hour ago I was getting a lecture in politics from that fucker Lynch. Did I ever think I'd be listening to him telling me the facts of life? No, I did not.'

'Where is he I wonder?' asked Katrina. Her hair was matted, and water was dripping from her eyebrows.

They continued on slowly. It occurred to Noelie they could come upon anyone at any time in the present conditions. He could only see something clearly when he was almost upon it. He asked Colin if he could see anything with his night-sights.

'Fuck all. There's a couple of buildings up ahead is all.'

'We should split up,' suggested Katrina. 'He could be armed and then we'd be in the shit.'

Noelie and Katrina went one way while Black Gary and Colin Dalton held back. They would follow on behind but stay out of view in case anyone challenged Noelie and Katrina.

The building silhouettes became more pronounced. The rain appeared to ease but then came down even heavier again. They were soaked through. Noelie saw a dim light – a phone light? – up ahead, but it vanished again. He warned Katrina and they moved forward very slowly towards a line of Portakabins. These had been closed up and were empty inside; a window in one had been smashed in.

Noelie noticed tyre tracks in the dark muck. He sensed Lynch was close and warned Katrina. Ahead on their right there were mounds of stone – gravel and large aggregate. They passed along the side of it.

Katrina took Noelie's arm and pointed. 'Over there.'

Noelie saw the Audi parked between two lorry containers. They moved nearer. As they did, Lynch emerged from one of the containers. He left the door open behind him but Noelie couldn't see what was inside – if there even was anything. Where were those night glasses when he needed them?

They crouched down and stayed as still as possible.

'Should we confront him?' asked Katrina.

'Are the others close?'

They watched Lynch. He was just a shadow moving around. The rain was unrelenting and rivers of water ran alongside them.

'We should confront him together in case he's armed,' said Katrina. 'If he thinks you're on your own he could do anything.'

Noelie didn't understand what she meant. Was she saying Lynch was less likely to shoot two of them at the one time? Was he losing his mind? He watched Lynch. Why was he moving around so much? Then he worked it out: Lynch was having reception problems. He was either trying to receive or call someone but he wasn't picking up signal.

By now he had moved quite a bit away from his car and the containers.

'I could go in,' whispered Katrina. 'In case Meabh is in there.'

Noelie saw what she meant. 'Go for it. I'll be ready to intercept him if he comes back.'

Katrina left. Noelie moved closer to Lynch. From his new vantage point he could see the remnants of some type of big machine – a rock crusher of some sort? It was an eerie-looking hulk of a thing. The skeletons of various conveyor belts used with the crushers lay around it. The entire area and the crusher itself – if that was what it was – hadn't seen action for a long time. Near it was a hill of crushed stone.

Noelie heard Katrina whisper behind him. The emotion in her voice was unmistakable. 'I have her. She's here. She's safe.'

Noelie couldn't believe it. When they drew close he saw a very tired and dishevelled Meabh appear. Her hair was untied and wild and she looked a bit disorientated. He was overjoyed to see her.

He wondered if they could get away without Lynch knowing. The problem was the others. Where were they? Suddenly, like there was some telepathic connection between them, Noelie heard Colin Dalton. He had circled right around behind Lynch, who was now trapped between them.

'There now, piggy,' Colin taunted Lynch. 'There now.'

'Oh, for fuck's sake,' spat Noelie.

Lynch retreated, coming towards Noelie. In his haste, he slipped badly and fell in the mud. When he stood again, he saw Noelie standing in front of him. Lynch was soaked through. He was still holding his phone.

'Looks like I won't have to deal with the devil after all.'

'Do you think so?' said Lynch, not sounding a bit worried. 'I'm not so sure myself. Look.'

They all turned to look. Coming towards them at speed were two vehicles, maybe more – their headlights were blinding.

Colin lunged at Lynch. The older man slipped away and Colin ran after him. He was within an arm's length of catching him when the ex-cop leapt on to a level gangway that ran alongside the stones and scree. Colin followed, but the moment he stood on the gangway it collapsed sending the two of them spilling on to the mound.

What happened next was at first strange then frightening. Noelie thought he was hearing a million micro-sized crackers going off at once. But it was nothing so artificial. Instead the slope of stones began to move towards them all.

Lynch saw the danger first and attempted to get to his feet and jump to safety. But a depression formed where he stood and, instead, he began to sink. An avalanche of stones moved over him and he was covered. Noelie just managed to get a hold of Colin's ankle. Black Gary helped him yank their friend to safety.

The cars were close now.

'We'll have to find another way back,' said Katrina pointing towards a totally dark area at the back of the site.

Noelie hesitated. He watched the area where Lynch was buried for some sign of movement but there was nothing. He should try to do something – Lynch could still be alive. But it would be very dangerous.

Colin Dalton pulled him away. 'Don't even think about it.'

They skirted the wreck of the crushing facility and ran.

26

They hid for hours then slowly made their way along the edge of the site, heading for the area where they had parked. Colin had an excellent sense of direction, and he worked with Katrina to guide them to safety. The rain was unrelenting. When they neared the cars, they stayed out of view and waited some more. They arrived at Hannah's in the early hours of the morning.

Black Gary approached the apartment block on his own, then summoned the others to follow. Noelie was deflated. He had briefly seen the perfect outcome, only to have it snatched away from them again in an instant. If they had escaped with Meabh without letting Lynch know that they had found her, they could have passed Nora's video footage to Byrne then watched safely from the sidelines. Now, instead, anything was possible. Not only did they have a retired cop's death on their conscience, but Noelie's communications with Lynch were also written all over the city's mobile phone network. He was in serious trouble; they all were.

Whoever had arrived in the vehicles as they rescued Meabh must have known what was going on. Noelie guessed that they had been Branch or their associates. The only positive was that it would not be immediately obvious where Lynch was or what had happened to him. He was buried under a hefty pile of stones. That gave them a small window of opportunity, but they would still have to move swiftly.

Meabh hadn't been mistreated. She hadn't seen who had taken her at Llanes – they had restrained her from behind, covering her face and mouth to stop her shouting for help.

She'd been drugged and had no memory of the journey to the building site. She'd woken up in the same container they had rescued her from. She'd told them that it had been completely dark when she'd come to, and for an awful moment she'd panicked thinking that she was back in Albert's under-garden cavern. Eventually she'd worked out that she was in a metal box and, when her captors had brought her food, she saw that she'd been imprisoned in a transport container. There was a camp bed, a sleeping bag and a chair. She'd made as much noise as she could, banging and shouting, but the only people who came were the two men who brought her food.

The first time they'd opened the door, she'd lunged at one of them, but he'd pushed her away with ease; he hadn't even reacted. They'd said nothing to her about why she had been kidnapped or what was going to be done with her. In fact, they hadn't spoken to her at all and had worn balaclavas so she had no idea what they even looked like.

Noelie told her what Lynch had said about Romania. 'You nearly got your wish, Meabh.'

'I'm not afraid,' she replied defiantly. 'I've had time to think about everything and it's clear to me now that either he will die or we will. It's one or the other.'

'Well, this time we were the ones who came out on top,' Black Gary reminded them. 'We got our Meabh back alive.' Then he clapped Noelie on the back and said in his best Cockney accent, 'You did well, my son.'

'How did you find me?' Meabh asked then in a quiet voice.

Noelie brought her up to speed on everything she had missed. How finding footage of the argument on Douglas Street had really been key. He explained what he had learned about Shane's final moments.

Meabh was shocked and upset. She took Noelie's hand and held it tightly.

Lynch had been badly wrong-footed at their meeting.

Thinking about it now, Noelie felt sure Lynch would have tried to have double-cross them later – probably at the planned handover at the Shaky Bridge. Noelie knew that all in all it could have gone a lot better for them but he realised that it could've gone a lot worse too.

Meabh was allowed the honour of showering first. Noelie loaned Colin some clothes and warned him not to make any smart remarks.

He just couldn't be angry with the younger man though. Colin had just reason to despise Lynch. He was probably not the best person to have had roaming around in the dark looking for the retired cop. Noelie knew Colin would've liked to have given Lynch a clout or two, but the lad couldn't have foreseen what had happened.

Later, as Katrina showered, and Colin and Black Gary busied themselves in the kitchen making tea, Noelie sat with Meabh. He was so relieved that she was safe again. He nearly couldn't believe it.

He smiled at her a few times but she didn't smile back. He felt he understood why – she would've been terrified out there on her own and that kind of terror wouldn't go away easily. Fear like that had a way of working itself into the bones. He wondered if she – if any of them – would ever be the same again.

Vengeance Will Be Mine

27

From 6 a.m., Noelie scanned the Internet and listened to every news bulletin on local and national radio, but there were no reports on Lynch or the trouble near Buttevant. Shane's inquest, however, was garnering attention. One report on an online news site carried the headline 'Questions Raised About Youth's Drowning'. It outlined the errors in the mobile phone trail and Canning's recent post-mortem findings. An *Irish Examiner* report speculated that the garda investigation into the teenager's death could be reopened.

Everyone agreed that Noelie should talk to Byrne as soon as possible to give her a copy of Nora's video footage. There was less certainty over what they should do about Lynch and the events at Buttevant. Noelie suggested that Meabh could present herself to the gardaí and report that she had been kidnapped and had subsequently escaped. This might precipitate an investigation of the site at Buttevant and gain them some advantage ahead of the discovery of Lynch's body – which Noelie believed to be inevitable. He worried that, if the site near Buttevant became a crime scene, they could end up facing a murder charge. Lynch might be retired but he was still a cop. No effort was going to be spared. Inserting Meabh's kidnap into the equation was their best hope.

Meabh gave the idea a point-blank no. She suggested going back to the yard at a later stage and breaking into the Portakabin to see if they could find any records on her container's proposed destination. Noelie felt she wasn't grasping the seriousness of the situation they were now facing, but he didn't press it. Nobody else wanted to take up her suggestion either.

They had until Lynch's body was discovered. If it hadn't been found the previous night – which seemed to be the case – then matters could drag on until his family inevitably raised the alarm. With Lynch's car at the yard, however, it wouldn't really take too long once resources were deployed into the search. But what happened over the next hours and days would be interesting for other reasons too. Those who took Meabh had been outwitted. They would also know that the cover-up surrounding Shane's murder was about to be revealed. They too were up against the clock.

Katrina wanted to return to the library to continue working on the database of River Lee drownings and Black Gary was keen to go with her. Meabh, on the other hand, decided to stay put, which was understandable. Noelie would attempt to meet Byrne and then return as soon as possible.

The three of them set off together. The entire city felt damp. Rain puddles were everywhere. It was still overcast, and the temperature had dropped. Something else that Noelie liked about Amsterdam was its generally clear skies. At times around Cork it felt as if the greyness never lifted.

Along the way, he called Oakes. He had had another idea and it involved keeping the pressure on the other side.

Clearly Oakes had Noelie's number in his address book. 'Noel?'

'Yes. How is everything? Are you still in Cork?'

'In Limerick. We're setting up here. The Glen case is on hold. It might remain that way for some time now.'

'Any plans to come back here any time soon?'

'Not exactly.'

'It's just, remember the trade we did? Me owing you that half a favour? Well, I'd like to settle up.'

'I respect a man who repays his debts.'

'It's information about Copley and Spitere. Well, it's more a theory actually. It occurred to me before but, how shall I put it, I didn't want to tell you then as I felt you might laugh at me, or worse, think I was wasting your time. But other information has come to light that makes me think it may not be so far-fetched after all. It's information on a place, actually, one that is not so far from where you were searching that time we met, as the crow flies.'

There was silence. They had reached the entrance to the library so Black Gary and Katrina went on in, leaving him with a wave. Noelie looked around the bleak, empty Parade area.

'Look I'm interested, of course. I could be there in the afternoon. Would that do?'

'Perfect.'

'I'll text you when I'm leaving here. Be an hour and a bit from then. Where?'

'We'll meet at the Commons Bar car park – it's as you come into Cork – then go on from there. The place I'm talking about is only a few miles away.'

Noelie called Byrne next. He told her he had information on Shane's death and offered to call to see her at Anglesea Street. She suggested that they meet somewhere other than the station. They agreed on Idaho Cafe.

Noelie got there ahead of her. It was a pleasant oasis, on the upmarket end as cafes went, which probably explained why it was weathering the difficult economic climate in the city. While he waited, Noelie observed normal life happening around him. He had almost forgotten what that looked like. Between being unemployed and becoming embroiled in the ugly business of Albert Donnelly's life, he had lost perspective on what everyday life involved. How many people really walked around sleepy Cork constantly looking over their shoulder to see if they were being followed? When was the last time he sat with a coffee and read the sport's page? He wondered if he would ever get back to normality.

Byrne looked harried when she arrived, but when he asked her about it, she said it was just work – he didn't really know if he believed her. He thought about the tip-off Ciarán had given him, about her role during the Corrib Gas protests in Mayo. He decided not to make anything of it. He'd have to trust that she'd just been doing her job.

Right now he needed her good offices. If for any reason she didn't come through for him, or for Shane, then he would know better for the future. But he didn't doubt her actually. What he was about to tell her would help her too.

After ordering an Americano, she said, 'So?'

He went back, not as far as the beginning, but to when his suspicions about Shane's death had been raised. 'From the very first, I didn't want to be associated in any way with my nephew's death. At the time, with what had happened to me over the Dalton matter, I was flailing around not knowing what was really going on. I knew I had stepped into something dangerous and that I was out of my depth. When I learned that Special Branch could have links to Jim Dalton's disappearance, I knew I was heading into trouble. I was actually relieved in June when the mobile data trail suggested Turner's Cross and not somewhere near my house.'

He told her how the phone data upset at the inquest had forced him to reconsider everything, including the possibility that Shane had gone to his flat the afternoon he vanished.

'On that drive back from Kinsale, you told me you were certain that the documentation you had looked at, from the very earliest stage, had specified Turner's Cross. I became certain then that the Dream data had been deliberately altered. That led me to motive.'

'You'll be one of us yet,' said Byrne with a smile.

'Needs must I guess. Anyway, I became more convinced that maybe Shane's death could be linked to this matter of the mole, Brian Boru. But why? The only thing I could come up with was that he must have seen something the afternoon he went missing. That would explain why the search was diverted to a different area of town, to Turner's Cross.' Noelie paused. 'You had the same thought, didn't you? A source told me that you were around recently asking about Shane, if anyone had seen him on Douglas Street.'

'I was thinking along those lines but I didn't come up with anything.'

'The factor that I underestimated was that of Brian Boru and how important he was. I shouldn't have, I mean I'd been warned enough times, but I did. The night we confronted Tommy Keogh at Church Bay and he admitted to being Brian Boru, he pointed out that Special Branch had actually taken renewed interest in his role. He was angry at that. He had deluded himself into thinking that he might be able to retire on a state pension one day, but Branch had other ideas. They were breaking down his door again asking him what was going on inside Sinn Féin. Branch feared that the economic crash might launch them into power.'

Noelie shook his head, then continued, 'The Troubles may be over but that small matter of who eats most of the cake on the table still has to be managed. So, Special Branch didn't want any attention focused on Brian Boru. They certainly didn't want to lose him. However, if Shane's disappearance had got mixed up in some way with the Brian Boru project, it could have badly complicated matters for them. The death of a teenager is not easily brushed under any carpet.'

Noelie explained to Byrne that with time he had come to understand that Albert and his sidekick, Andrew Teland, had been behind the break in to his flat.

'I've never found out how Albert heard so quickly about me and my discovery of a part of the whistle-blower file on Brian Boru. But within a few hours of me being in Anglesea Street Station with Inspector Lynch, Albert was over in my place rifling through my stuff, searching for that film of his.'

Noelie thought briefly about Lynch's denial that he had tipped Albert off. Did he believe him? He didn't know. 'So, Albert was there with this guy Teland and I think they were waiting on Douglas Street for me to come back. They were hanging around. Maybe they had been into the apartment by then. What I now believe is that Shane surprised them. It was just bad luck. I think he went there and maybe the door was ajar, and he walked in on them. Maybe they panicked or maybe he did, who knows, but Shane's fate was sealed right then. Albert wasn't going to let the boy get away, and that left Branch with a mess to clean up. All Branch were thinking about was protecting Brian Boru.'

Byrne nodded. 'It's damning, Noelie, I'll give you that. I regret to say that it is plausible too. How do you know any of this actually happened though?'

Noelie produced the memory stick. 'On this drive is a video of a stupid disagreement over a parking space. Albert Donnelly and Andrew Teland got into a bust up with my former neighbour Sheila Carroll. It got right out of hand. Sheila's sister was there too and recorded some of what happened.'

Noelie handed Byrne a set of photos extracted from the video. They were copies of the one he had showed to Lynch.

When Byrne got to the last one, Noelie said, 'Take a close look at that one. In the movie it's far less ambiguous. But he's clearly identifiable in that.'

'Jesus,' said Byrne looking at Noelie, 'It's Lynch.'

Noelie was glad to see a look of genuine surprise on Byrne's face – in as much as he could read her expressions anyway. He dearly wanted the detective to come through for them on this; he definitely didn't want to discover that she was working for any third parties. For a split second he thought about how nice it would have been to tell her to call out to Lynch's house and arrest him. What a fuck-up having Lynch die like that. He had kicked Noelie in the balls one last time. But at least she hadn't mentioned anything about Lynch being missing, so it looked to Noelie that his body hadn't been found yet.

'Lynch's been involved in this matter from way back. You'll see for yourself in the video, but I think Lynch was in on the cover-up from the beginning.'

'Yes, why else would he be there? Do you think he could be in on this abuse?' asked Byrne.

Noelie felt he was on unsteady ground. He had learned quite a lot the previous evening when he confronted Lynch, and he needed to be careful about revealing what he knew.

'I'm veering more towards no,' he answered carefully. 'I think Lynch was acting on behalf of Branch. He didn't want Albert Donnelly fucking things up for Brian Boru. The problem is, Shane didn't drown in Douglas Street. He was taken from my flat to Llanes. Did Lynch know the kid was still alive when this video was recorded? If he did and he did nothing to stop the crime he knew was inevitable, then what does that make him?'

Byrne looked quite unhappy. She looked at the photos again.

'What is it?' he asked her.

'If the wrong people get a whiff of what's on this stick, they'll be all over this. It'll be taken out of my hands anyway. I have to think about what to do about it.' Hesitantly she added, 'I assume you have other copies of this video put safely to one side.'

Noelie nodded. 'A few.'

'Is Shane anywhere in the video?'

Noelie shook his head. 'No, and Sheila, the woman who was in the dispute with Albert, is currently in hospital. Her house burned down the weekend before the inquest, which is why this all took so long to come to light. My guess is that Lynch and Branch were behind the house fire too. I wonder did he have my sister's phone, or her solicitor's phone, tapped. I think my sister already knew that Taylor had found something in the Dream data before the inquest began. They may have talked about it perhaps? Lynch could have read the writing on the wall right then. Sheila was badly injured in the fire. She's in a coma but she will be taken back out of it soon and you might be able to interview her at that stage. I don't know if she saw Shane that day, but Lynch seems to have been worried that she did. He didn't actually know Nora's video existed or maybe he would have done something about that too. See, when Nora arrived the fracas between Albert and her sister was well underway. She had the sense to record the argument, but she never let on what she was doing.'

'Smart woman.'

Byrne looked at the photos once more. 'Okay. I guess I'll be talking to you again soon.'

'I guess.'

Byrne insisted on paying for the coffees. As they were leaving, she told Noelie that consideration was already being given to reopening the case into Shane's death. 'This info you've just given me seals it, I think.'

28

There was no sign of Oakes at the Commons Bar. Noelie pulled into a space in the car park and waited. Ted Toner and Colin Dalton were with him and he was glad of the company, even if Colin hadn't actually grasped the reality of their situation. Before picking up Ted, Noelie had discussed Lynch's death with Colin, pointing out the implications. They could be pursued on a murder charge and it might mean the remainder of their lives in jail.

'And, Colin,' Noelie added, 'you're a good bit younger than me … So work it out. Think about what we're going to say.'

Colin seemed oblivious. 'Bring it on,' he retorted, 'I want to tell the world what that fucker did to my father.' In the end Noelie decided to drop the matter entirely.

Ted Toner was a calming presence. Noelie only decided at the last minute to ask the historian to come along and Toner was pleased to see him. He had been busy and he had good news – he'd located a woman who had worked at the Donnelly farm in the late sixties.

'It was just seasonal work. She was a teenager at the time, and I think she got the position through an aunt who lived near Whitechurch, a little bit beyond Ballyvolane. The aunt is the connection I knew of, though she'd be long dead by now. The girl, well she's not a girl now, might remember something.'

'Worth a try.'

Oakes arrived finally and Noelie was relieved to see that he was in an unmarked car. He left Toner and Colin where they were and strode quickly across the car park. Oakes rolled down his window. He looked more relaxed than when Noelie had last seen him.

'Thanks for making the journey.'

Oakes frowned. 'I think I should be thanking you.'

'Is your new project suiting you any better?' Noelie asked.

'Something even more unsavoury.'

'The mind boggles.'

He told Oakes that they were going to the old Donnelly farm. 'It's about two kilometres from the slope in Glen Park that you were searching the day we met. We'll lead the way and you follow.'

Back in the car, Colin Dalton looked askance at Noelie. 'That's a cop car. Is he a cop?'

'Calm down,' said Noelie, then added, 'I was like you once. Tarred them all with the one brush. He's fine … I think.'

Colin shook his head, looking out the window in disgust.

Out past Conway's Cross, they parked inside the old estate gates, in a damp clearing. It was threatening rain again. Oakes came over and Noelie introduced him to Colin and Toner, who were going to remain in the car.

'They your bodyguards?' Oakes asked him as they headed across the field.

'I have become quite cautious.'

'I've got someone looking for that file on those remains found in the Glen. If what you're going to show me turns into something, I'll work on it all some more.'

'And if that file doesn't turn up?'

Oakes was hesitant. 'We could still go the long way around. I could find out who handled the case back then, as I did with Old Donnelly's death. I'm sure someone around remembers or will know something about it. We'd be relying on hearsay and memory but if that's all there is, then we might just have to go with that.'

Noelie wondered about telling Oakes about Youghal Boy

and what they suspected about his fate but they had all agreed that it was important to first talk to his sister. They would need to tell her about the abuse at the Old Donnelly farm and the nature of the film he'd been in. It would be difficult and Noelie was not looking forward to it.

They reached the woods. Noelie pointed to the fenced-off area farther in. 'So that in there is the ground on which the old Donnelly house was located. It was demolished in late 1970, we think, in some haste, for reasons we don't fully understand.'

Noelie produced the picture of the house that Toner had given him and then the touched-up copy of the shot discovered in Llanes. Showing the copies to Oakes, he pointed out the dark areas in the shot of the demolished house.

'These look like basements to me.'

They went closer and reached the gate. As they were out of the heavy shade, Oakes was able to get a better look at the photos. He agreed with Noelie's assessment.

'There's a heap of stone inside that I need a sample of,' Noelie told him. 'I hope you don't mind me breaking the law in your presence.'

'Go right ahead.'

Oakes helped Noelie to get up and over the gate then followed close behind, managing the climb easily. Noelie was impressed by the older man's agility but didn't remark on it. They walked towards the middle of the fenced-off area. There was wild vegetation almost everywhere – grass, nettles and thistles – but there were patches of concrete visible in a few places.

'I think Copley and Spitere could be buried here,' said Noelie.

'Why?'

'Because I think Albert's troubles, his real problems, began when those remains were discovered up at the Glen building site. A boy connected to Danesfort had gone missing and it was suspected he may have been abused at the Donnelly farm. Suddenly, with the discovery of these bones on the building site, all eyes were looking at Albert. Had he something to do with it? Albert denied it of course, but he realised he had made a major mistake too – he had left the remains in a place where they could eventually be discovered. My thinking is that, ever since, he's been careful not to get caught out like that again.'

Oakes walked around, and stomped on the ground here and there. Noelie fleetingly thought about the ground giving way and where they might end up.

'You have an idea who those remains found on the building site belong to, don't you?'

'In the film we saw there are a number of boys at this place. We think at least one of them was killed – it could've been accidently of course.' Noelie paused. 'I don't know why Albert had this place knocked down, but its demolition coincides with when we think Spitere and Copley were killed. As the place was being sealed up, perhaps Albert decided to put the two bodies in there. I mean, they could be covered in concrete under there for all I know. The reason Egan, the third blackmailer, was found elsewhere might be because he was killed later than the first two. At least two months afterwards, I think. By then, this place might have been done with.'

Oakes was silent, so Noelie went on. 'It might also explain why Albert has held on to this part of the house. There are probably hollows under here. There was always the risk that someone would go poking unless he kept it protected and off limits.'

'I think it is worth looking into,' said Oakes. 'There's new equipment around now that would allow us to take a peek under here without having to dig the place up, or commit vast resources. I'd need to get a warrant for that, though, so I might hold off for now. Better first, I'm thinking, to find out as much as I can about those building-site remains and why there doesn't seem to have been a full investigation. At the very least I'd like a bit more time to try and locate that missing file – that way I'll have more of a sense about who and what I'm dealing with before I tip my hand. One of my old bosses used to say, "Never rush headlong over a hilltop until you know what's on the other side".'

'Sensible.'

'There are a lot of sensible people in the gardaí, Noelie. You seem to have missed them somewhere in your travels.'

'I certainly have. I'm more familiar with the "brute force and ignorance" brigade …'

Noelie went across to where there was a rough mossy mound. He pulled away lots of sticky-back weed and selected a rock.

'You collect stones too?'

Noelie smiled at Oakes, 'Present for a friend.'

At Llanes, when he'd seen the photo of the outdoor swimming pool, he'd realised something immediately: Albert's under-garden cavern was much smaller. Clearly then, a lot of the original pool had been filled in and covered over, and Noelie wondered if the builders had used some of the rubble from the old Donnelly home. The sample he collected might be useful to Canning.

At the library, Katrina and Black Gary had spread out over the two tables in the local history section. Stacks of newspaper folios were waiting to be checked. Black Gary saw Noelie lingering by the door and came over; Katrina only nodded at him. She reminded Noelie of Hannah that way – Hannah would never stop what she was working on until she was good and ready. Occasionally Noelie would have had to wait ten or fifteen minutes by her desk while she typed like a maniac.

Black Gary suggested that they stand out in the hall as they could close the door for privacy, and because the librarian had already chastised them for making too much noise. The hall area was an airless space with a room off to one side where the microfiche viewers were located; one was in use.

Black Gary's news was good or disturbing, depending on how you wished to view it. 'We focused on drownings between St Vincent's footbridge and Wellington Bridge.'

'Thomas Davis Bridge now.'

'Except everyone still calls it Wellington Bridge, Noelie. Anyway, we found just under an average of one drowning a year in that stretch of the river.' Black Gary looked at his notes. 'So ten in the seventies; nine in the eighties; six in the nineties; and eleven in the noughties.'

Noelie nodded.

'We began looking at all of these but then realised that age is a decisive factor. See, we are looking at things in relation to Danesfort and the Old Donnelly farm during a specific six-year period, 1958 to 1964, with boys who were, at that time, aged between six and ten. I won't go into the exact calculation, but Katrina worked it all out – a guide based on the age bracket and the decade we're examining. That's allowed us to cut the number of cases we need to examine significantly. So, for the seventies we have four individuals who match our criteria. We were able to rule out two by examining what was reported in the newspaper. We have a question mark over one but the other we think is definitely one of ours.'

Black Gary went back inside and returned with another notebook. 'So, 1973. Sean Dale, aged eighteen. Body found near Irish Distillers, close to where Shane was discovered, I believe. Dale had recently returned to Ireland from London. At the time of his death he was living in St Vincent's Hostel for men. Inquest verdict: accidental drowning.'

Noelie nodded. 'So born in 1955. Aged seven in 1962.'

Katrina came out to join them, catching the end of the

conversation. 'Dale's a possibility. All in all, we've identified six similar cases. Seven if we include the case Canning gave us. Each one of these individuals would have been aged between seven and nine between 1961 and 1963.'

Noelie thought about this. 'Seven is probably a number Canning could handle. But I bet the elaborate testing for what was under a victim's fingernails is a relatively recent innovation. There may not be anything in the records for cases drowned before 1990.'

'That's where my partial register of industrial school survivors could come in handy,' said Black Gary. As I said before, it has gaps in it but we might see a name or two. We have to work this list of potential cases and find out everything we can about each person.' He added. 'I'll need to go down to Sherkin, but Meabh said she'd like to come along. We could go later.'

'As long as there are two of you,' Noelie reminded him.

'We might join you tomorrow. I'm beat from this anyway,' said Katrina.

'Me too.'

After leaving the library, Noelie called Ellen and said that he needed to talk to her. He suggested somewhere outside, where they could walk together, and then proposed the Marina – a recreational area downriver of Cork's old factory quarter and the docks. Clearly Ellen had worked out that he had something important to tell her because she agreed immediately. To his surprise he learned that she had already heard from Byrne. The detective wanted to let her know that there had been further developments in Shane's case and that she could expect a significant announcement soon. Byrne had also told her that it was unlikely she would be leading this new examination. That bit of news worried Noelie.

He began carefully, telling Ellen as they walked, that he and the others had been the source of this crucial new information. Without going into the details of his confrontation with Lynch, he explained that they had found effective confirmation that Shane had inadvertently walked in on two people – Albert and Teland – at his flat and that this was probably why he had been killed.

'It was essentially to do with the mole, Brian Boru. His handlers were prepared to do anything to hold on to him. They looked the other way when Shane ran into trouble.'

In the summer, around the time of Shane's disappearance, Noelie and Ellen had argued bitterly about Noelie's behaviour at that time – he had briefly gone into hiding as Shane disappeared. Noelie's subsequent inability to properly account for where he had been had done him no favours with Shane's dad, Arthur, who had then accused Noelie of putting Shane in danger.

'So it turns out Arthur was right after all.'

Noelie didn't know how his sister would react and he was not optimistic. He knew he had to tell her everything but it was nightmarish really. All he felt that he could do was tell her, and hope that in some way that would prepare for the other revelations that were ahead.

He had been cavalier back in June. After he'd found his punk record collection, he'd gone to Don Cronin's house – Cronin had had possession of the damning whistle-blower file for years and done nothing with it – and demanded an explanation. Of course, he wasn't to know what he was getting himself involved in, and he couldn't be responsible for how others – Albert, Teland and Lynch – had acted, but he felt his own foolhardiness coming back to bite him.

Ellen hadn't spoken. A few joggers passed them as they walked while, out on the river, a line of rowers headed in perfect synchronicity towards Blackrock Castle.

'I'm very, very sorry, Ellen. I had hoped right up until the end that I wouldn't have had any hand in Shane's death. But I have to face it now, I did. I never meant to but ...'

After a silence Ellen asked, 'Are these the same people that killed Hannah?'

Noelie nodded. 'Yes. Teland and Albert were there the night we found Hannah's body.'

There was a seat ahead, facing the river. Noelie suggested they sit down and Ellen reluctantly agreed. He turned a little to look at her. She had dried her eyes and he saw an expression on her face that he knew well – she was trying her best to put on a brave face, in spite of everything. He put his arm around her and pulled her close.

29

As he reached the turn for the hill leading up to Canning's house, Noelie stopped the car, turned around and drove back towards the city. At Passage West, he changed his mind again, turned the car once more and headed back to Monkstown. Once there, he parked outside her house and fetched the Ballyvolane rock from the boot.

He knocked on her door and a different daughter answered this time. She frowned when she saw what Noelie was holding and then called her mother.

'You're making a habit of this.' Canning said drily.

'Not pleased to see me?'

Canning looked exasperated. 'This isn't a good time.'

Noelie left the rock down outside the door. 'That isn't your actual thank-you present Andrea. I'll bring that another day. But I thought it might be useful. Do you have a few minutes?'

Canning hesitated and then came out, pulling the door half-closed behind her. 'Let's chat down there,' she said, nodding to a sitting area in the lower garden.

They walked down a snaking path, which led to steps, another short path and more steps. The seat was in a pergola, smartly cocooned by hedging on two sides. Noelie sat down. Canning remained standing. She folded her arms.

'There's been a breakthrough in Shane's case,' he said, 'separate entirely from what has happened at the inquest. Byrne's on it now. I won't say any more so as not to compromise your evidence, but if you do want to find out more, she's the one to talk to. We think we know the place where Shane drowned – this "non-river" location, I mean.'

Canning shook her head. 'I'm so sorry, Noelie. I've been fearing the worst, I have to say, but that's terrible.'

'It's looking like the worst thing that could have happened probably did happen. Anyway, that stone up there, it may be useful to you. I don't know. Maybe it will be a match to the grit under Shane's fingernails.'

She nodded.

'There's something else, Andrea …'

'I was afraid of that.'

He looked at her. 'My life has changed. I've been through a very difficult time, I'll freely admit that. But–'

She finally sat down. 'Can I interrupt?'

'Do you have to?'

She nodded. 'You need to stop. I sense where this could be going.'

He looked at her for a long time and she looked back at him.

'I can take a hint.'

She smiled. 'Good, right now my life is very complicated. In a while things might be different but not right now. Do you understand?'

He waited and she didn't move. 'I could say something about the garden, how beautiful it is?'

'No,' she smiled, 'you don't need to.' She watched him. 'I'm so sorry about Shane, Noelie. I'm usually very removed from cases. I don't know those involved and that's as it should be. Are you okay?'

'Just going day to day really, but I can do that, for another while anyway. I'm trying not to think about a lot of things.'

'That won't work long term.'

'I know.'

She smiled again.

'It's very nice here.'

'Thank you. But, look, I have to go back.'

They walked back to the house together. There was another

car in the driveway, Noelie noticed, apart from Canning's and the L-plated hatchback, which was parked further along.

'I'll be in touch,' she said.

'I'll hold you to that.'

'Good.'

30

The next day, Noelie and Katrina took the long road to Baltimore, crossing the Cork–Kerry mountains and arriving at the Old Kenmare Cemetery by Kilgarvan and the bridge at Sheen Falls. Hannah's gravestone wasn't in place yet. Instead, an oval-shaped woodcutting with her name on it occupied the space. They removed a bunch of withered flowers and placed their own on the mound of earth. It was quiet apart from occasional birdsong. Noelie found a perch on the edge of the adjacent grave while Katrina knelt on the dry grass. As cemeteries went it was pretty, overlooking the river estuary with the Kerry mountains in the distance.

Noelie had probably been to his parents' graves a few times over the years. It was a duty call for him for the most part. He realised more and more that he hadn't had a strong relationship with either one. Hannah's grave was different. The moment he was close to it, his mind filled with memories of her. He could almost touch the place in himself that was missing because she was. He had tried to define it at one point, perhaps to better protect himself from the loneliness he felt when he thought about her, but he hadn't been able to get at the essence of it. What he did know for sure was that a part of him had died with her.

Now there was Martin too. Less than two weeks ago he had been with them – he'd been there to greet them on arrival in Sherkin. His hopes and plans were now all gone too.

He watched Katrina. Her strength was something he was coming to value more and more. He didn't know her well enough to know where or what it came from but it was definitely there. She hadn't flinched during what they had been through. Meabh's disappearance had affected her, but that was as it should be. Katrina, like Noelie, believed that Meabh had been murdered almost as soon as she'd been taken. They'd both admitted later that Hannah's death haunted them.

'What are you thinking?' he asked.

'Only that I miss her and I wish she hadn't died.'

A big family group was also in the cemetery. They were having difficulty walking along the narrow graveyard paths.

'Are you glad you stayed to help?'

She looked at Noelie and nodded. 'Oh yes.' She sat down opposite him, perched on one of the other graves. 'Meeting that woman in Ardmore, Mary Corrigan, has bothered me a lot. I've thought about her a good few times since. I'll tell you sometime, I don't think I can talk about it right now. But if there are others like Paul Corrigan, as it seems there are, I'd like to get their stories out into the open finally. I feel we owe it now to Hannah and to Martin to do that.'

Noelie nodded.

The drive over the mountains to Bantry and then on from Skibbereen to Baltimore was easy and quiet. They didn't talk about the investigation. Instead Katrina asked Noelie about his time working in the chemical industry and he gave her the nuts and bolts account. 'I'm nearly at the point that I'm getting nostalgic for it now.'

'Then it's true that every cloud has a silver lining.'

'Well, that is certainly what's said, but I don't know any more. Some of the clouds I've seen this last while ...'

'Tell me about it. So do you think you'll ever go back to that line of work?'

'You know there's a lot of pleasure in just working with

people on very ordinary tasks. I do miss that. How about you? Are you missing work, your real work, I mean?'

'A bit. This has all been so intense I haven't had much time to think about it. I miss Eva and I miss my home there. If I was rich, I'd get Eva to come over here.'

Noelie asked how they had met.

'Through a few Irish people I know in Melbourne, of course, exiles as well. Eva's Greek– Australian. They all hiked together and I fell in with that naturally. Victoria State is coming down with wonderful national parks. She's a lawyer. Very sweet. I'm much closer to her than I realised.'

At Baltimore they parked in the harbour car park and went up to Bushes Bar to have a pint. Noelie was looking forward to getting out on to the island. He knew he would feel safer there.

Black Gary called to say that he could get the boat and not to take the ferry. He'd be another while though and would text to let them know when he was on his way. He told Noelie that his neighbours, the husband and wife pool-playing team, had cleared out of the house beside him.

'I guess that answers that,' said Noelie. 'How's Meabh?'

'She's good,' said Black Gary, then added quickly, 'Correction. She said to tell you she's doing better than that.'

'Didn't take long.'

'Well, it was helped along by other news. We checked my mini Danesfort register and three of the seven Lee drownings we were researching involved individuals who were at the industrial school.'

'Fuck,' said Noelie.

'Exactly,' agreed Black Gary. 'The news has Meabh all fired up now. That's what I mean about her being better.'

Noelie might have smiled but for what he had heard. True, it was satisfying to have another piece of the jigsaw move into position, but it was heartbreaking too. At some point, Albert had got a taste for killing and somewhere along the line, he'd found a way to satisfy that craving while making amends to the men he served. A slew of voices had been silenced before they'd even had a chance to speak.

When the call ended, he told Katrina.

After a while she said, 'Can Albert really have been doing this on his own all this time? Who was helping him before Teland arrived?'

'I don't think we've got to the bottom of this yet.'

Katrina said nothing for a while. They watched the activity in the busy village. It was good not to be dwelling on the ugly side of life for a change.

Eventually though she said, 'Two is too many to lose, Noelie. I want to uncover those secrets but I want us to make it to the end of this alive. Promise me that will happen.'

'I wish I could.'

When Black Gary texted them an hour or so later, they finished their drinks and walked down to the inner harbour to wait at the small slipway Black Gary had used the last time. The smell of the sea and harbour was refreshing. They still had some time, so Noelie decided to take a walk over to the main pier. Katrina was happy to stay put, and sat down beside their bags.

A ferry had docked. Noelie watched the passengers as they disembarked. Two young men with trim beards came up the steps. Noelie didn't recognise either of them, but one seemed to be staring right at him.

He looked back at Katrina, to check she was okay – she was right where he'd left her. However a garda car had pulled in nearby. Noelie watched it and then went over to the other side of the pier, where he'd be able to see Sherkin and the bay. There was a stiff wind and no sign of Black Gary. Quite a few sailboats were out.

Three guards had got out of the squad car. A black car had

pulled up alongside it and two men got out. To be on the safe side, Noelie decided to go back to Katrina. He walked down the pier, but to get to her he would have to pass the guards. He waved at her but she didn't see him.

At that moment he heard an explosion – dull, heavy and loud. One of those bizarre moments of total silence followed and then people began running towards him and past him. A few climbed on to the wall nearby and Noelie followed them. He saw flames and black smoke rising into the sky from the direction of the pier at Sherkin. Noelie turned cold.

The gardaí near the squad car were clearly panicked too. One ran along the pier past Noelie. Another was on his phone and gesturing at people to remain calm. However the two detectives were walking towards Noelie, one a short distance ahead of the other. The older of the two was bald and Noelie recognised him. He had been with Lynch at Leslie Walsh's month's mind back in July. At the time Noelie had nicknamed him Kojak because of his resemblance to the TV detective. He hadn't known for sure he was a cop, but he knew now.

'Mr Noel Sullivan?' he called.

'Yes.'

The detective held out his badge as he drew closer. 'Detective Sergeant Gill. Mr Sullivan, I'm arresting you on suspicion of the murder of Denis Lynch. You have … '

A uniformed guard took Noelie by the arm and handcuffed him. Other people on the pier couldn't decide whether to watch Noelie's arrest or the inferno across the harbour.

Katrina arrived with her phone held to her ear. Noelie watched her closely as he was led away. She shook her head.

Acknowledgements

I am immensely grateful to Blackstaff Press for publishing this book. Huge thanks in particular to my editor, Michelle Griffin, for her skilled and tireless commitment to the novel. Thanks also to Jacky Hawkes and my continuing gratitude to Patsy Horton for her belief in the series.

Solidarity Books is mentioned a number of times in *A River Of Bodies*. A bookshop, a meeting place, a home for those fighting austerity – it was all of that and more. To those who made it happen, my sincere thanks for allowing me to dream.

Finally, Mary, Reidín and Saoirse, I reserve my deepest appreciation for you – for your love and continued support.